I0768430

The
FALLOUT

S. EVEREST

THE VEIL
SERIES

The Fallout Copyright © 2023 by S. Everest
ISBN: 979-8-9884753-0-9

Cover Design by Paul Allen (paulallendesigns.com)

All rights reserved. No part of this book may be used or reproduced in any manner whatsoever without written permission except in the case of brief quotations embodied in critical articles or reviews.

This book is a work of fiction. Names, characters, businesses, places, and incidents are either the product of the author's imagination or are used fictitiously. Any resemblance to actual persons, living or dead, events, or locales is entirely coincidental.

All brand names and product names used in this book are trademarks, registered trademarks, or trade names of their respective holders. The author is not associated with any product or vendor in this book.

Printed in the United States of America.

THE FALLOUT

THE VEIL SERIES • BOOK ONE

PLAYLIST

I Can Hear the Heart Breaking As One
Ricky Eat Acid

Sea Of Voices
Porter Robinson

No One's Gonna Love You
Band of Horses

A Way To Say Goodbye (Puppet Remix)
Seven Lions, Sombear, Puppet

Everything
Pacifier

Rush Over Me
Seven Lions, Illenium, Said The Sky, Haliene

THE DEATH OF PEACE OF MIND
Bad Omens

Blood Runs Cold
Rain City Drive

Pieces
Red

Fallout
Masked Wolf, Bring Me The Horizon

Distraction
Sleep Token

Burial Plot
Dayseeker

This book does *not* have a Happily Ever After.

This book contains sensitive subjects, such as alcohol abuse, drunk driving, drug and tobacco use, adult language, explicit sexual scenes, and extreme violence with gore.

Other triggers are considered spoilers and will not be listed here but will *always* be available in full on my website.
If you'd like to see the full list, please visit
severestbooks.com/triggers

This book is only intended for those 18 and older.

To my sun and my moon.

PART ONE

THOMAS

I leaned forward in my chair, resting my elbows on my knees, the beer bottle chilled in my hands. The night was colder than usual, the breeze dropping the temperature down a few degrees, the dark green leaves rustling against the wind. It was quiet, peaceful, and the only place I could unwind after a long day.

That's exactly what I was doing when I saw her.

A girl walking on the side of the road. Black jeans, a black sweatshirt with the hood pulled up, and a small messenger bag with the strap crossed over her chest. Strands of her strawberry blonde hair peeked out from the sides of her hood. Although I had a perfect view of her from my balcony, I found myself leaning forward, straining to get a better look at her face. As I studied her stride, I tried to pinpoint the very essence of her that had me oddly curious for more. Who was she? Why was she here? My vision could only catch small flickers of her since she didn't take a single glance up in my direction. Her walk was brisk as she passed under an orange-tinted streetlight, her hair briefly shifting colors with the luminous glow. I leaned back, tearing my captivated eyes away from her for just a second, craning my neck to see inside my apartment. I looked at the bright blue numbers on the microwave.

1:14 am.

What was she doing out here this late?

As soon as I glanced back, I noticed a silver car coming up the road behind her. It was gaining speed, getting faster by the second, its tires skidding against the pavement. Swerving a few feet to the right and then to the left, the car had no signs of slowing down or moving away from the side of the road. As the car got closer, the girl turned and looked over her shoulder, her feet never breaking stride. She squinted as the car flashed its high beams, blinding her. I watched as she attempted to shield the light with both arms, bringing them up to her forehead. A knot formed in my gut as I opened my mouth, trying to yell to the girl, to the car, to anyone. But my voice was instantly frozen.

That's when I saw it all happen.

The girl's spine, bending backward, folding herself onto the hood.

The car, never trying to stop the collision, without a single tap on the brakes.

The smack of her face and the bounce of her skull on the pavement as the car drove away.

The crunch of, what I believed to be, bones under the tires.

Oh, *fuck*.

Without hesitation, I jolted up from my seat and ran out of the apartment, flinging the door wide open. Running down two flights of stairs, two steps at a time, I made it out to the street in record time. We were too far out from civilization for anyone else to hear or witness what just happened. I looked down the road; the taillights of the car that hit her were long gone. She was face down, with her arms raised and legs bent at awkward angles.

What the hell? No one *ever* drives down this secluded back road, especially not in the middle of the night. And sure as fuck, no one ever takes a leisurely walk over here, either. It wasn't adding up, but I had no time to even spare a millisecond to think about it.

I kneeled next to her, gravel sliding under me as I turned her over to see the damage. Not even a minute had passed, yet her entire face was already covered in fresh, bright blood. I pressed my fingers to the side of her neck, checking for a pulse. It was slow, it was faint, but it was there, thank God.

I frantically looked around me, searching for something big and heavy. I found a large rock a few feet away, my body stretching and reaching to grab it. Once it was in my palm, I flipped it around, getting a feel for its weight, and then launched it toward the building. It hit exactly where I wanted it to, right at the sliding glass doors on the first floor. It left a giant, diagonal crack through half the glass. Fuck it, I'll fix it sometime this week.

"Mrs. Reeves!" I shouted, yelling from the depths of my voice. This was my only idea, with only a minute to act on it.

"Mrs. Reeves!" I tried again, louder. She was my one chance at this since there wasn't another soul around.

I was mentally kicking myself for leaving my phone in the apartment. Maybe if I went now and ran fast enough, I could get it, but I didn't have it in me to leave this poor girl bleeding out on the road. Maybe I could carry her to my truck and get her to a hospital myself, but that would require picking her up and moving her, which I didn't want to do, in case that would make things worse. And it also required my keys, which were up in my apartment.

Dammit.

I heard rustling from the apartment building as the cracked glass door slid open.

"Thomas?" The tired, unsteady voice came from Mrs. Reeves, the woman who owned the apartment building and lived on the first floor. "What's going on?"

"Call an ambulance." My voice was loud, stern, and straight to the point. Thank God I was always nice to the old woman. She had no reason to doubt me or ask any questions. With her steps light, she quickly vanished into her apartment.

Turning back to the girl, I began looking her over. My hands found their way under her head, lifting her off the pavement and supporting her neck. A big, open wound lined the top of her forehead, with small rocks stuck to her skin as blood poured over her eyelids, cascading down her soft cheekbones. My eyes moved down her body to check for more injuries. It was hard to see with the heavy sweatshirt, so, with caution, I slowly lifted it up to look at her stomach. The skin along her ribs was a gruesome purple, a color I've never seen in skin before. I could see where her bones were shattered into pieces, disconnected in pure disarray. What should have been a perfect ripple of bones, mountains and valleys in perfect unison, were broken by someone's complete carelessness. And the fuckers just kept driving as if she were only roadkill.

The purple in her side was beginning to darken by the second. Internal bleeding.

Fuck.

My eyes moved down the rest of her body, scanning for more. Thankfully, from the waist down, all I could see were jeans with fresh rips along the seams and some minor surface scrapes on her legs. Besides the gush from the cut on her head, there wasn't as much blood as I thought there would be. The sound of her body connecting with the car painted a different picture in my mind.

God, that's a sound I'll never get out of my head.

I moved back up to her face, studying her, my hand still cradling her. Blood dripped from her lengthy, black eyelashes, a red drop in a crimson ocean. Through it all, underneath the closed, red-layered eyelids, a part of me wondered what color her eyes were. As I was taking her in, my eyes trailing down to her lips, I watched as she took her final breath. Her life escaped her as her shallow breathing stopped and her skin stilled.

No. *No.*

Gently rocking her head back and forth, I whispered, "Come on, stay here." My voice was quiet but demanding, speaking through clenched teeth. "They're coming soon."

My fingertips moved back to her throat, trying to find her pulse again.

Nothing.

I knew it was now or never before the ambulance came.

"Thomas?" Mrs. Reeves appeared back on her patio. "Thomas, I called them. Is she all right?" The old woman's cotton nightgown fluttered in the wind. There was a set of slippers on her delicate feet and curlers placed in her short, peppered hair. A black and white cat appeared behind her, snaking around her legs, purring. Ever since her husband, Jerry, died, the cat and I have been her primary source of companionship.

"Wait for them out front, Mrs. Reeves."

Without saying another word, Mrs. Reeves nodded and retreated back inside, sliding the door shut behind her.

I lifted the girl up slightly and propped her up on my thighs, my hand still supporting the back of her head. With caution, I pushed her hood down. Strands of her hair were pasted to her bloody face, and I used my fingertips to push them away gently. My thumb wiped scarlet blood from her slightly parted lips. They were soft and pink, as if she had just applied lip balm a few minutes ago. Freckles lined the bridge of her nose in a perfectly painted pattern. In this moment, I couldn't help but notice how beautiful she was. With her limp hand draped over the side of my leg, and with every part of me pulsing with adrenaline, I took in a deep breath.

Now.

I leaned down, and with my entire soul, with my entire mind and body, all of my focus solely on her, I closed my eyes and pressed my lips to hers.

I *kissed* her.

Goosebumps lined my forearms and worked their way up to my shoulders, sending a quick chill down my spine. A few moments passed, feeling like hours, before I pulled away. I stared down at her eyes, which were still closed.

The streets were quiet.

The night was only illuminated by the orange streetlight a few feet over and the silver moon above.

A minute passed. Then another minute, and another. I watched, unblinking, never taking my eyes off of her.

Where the hell is the ambulance?

Then, with a quick, small jolt, so subtle that I barely noticed it, her eyes began to open. A slow blink, and then another. Her chest started rising and falling with every slow breath she took.

She was breathing.

Sirens went off in the distance.

She's breathing.

She looked around with her eyes, not moving her head, blinking to focus. Her soft cheeks began to regain color, and although masked by the blood, I could see her skin flush. I placed her gently back down, her back flat on the pavement, with my heart beating out of my chest. There was a moment when our eyes locked, her stare filling every empty space in the depths of my soul.

Green.

Her eyes are green.

A beautiful, breathtaking, emerald green.

Blood began to sputter from her lips, a cough coming up from deep in her lungs. The sirens were getting louder, coming closer. And that's when it hit me. It worked.

She's alive.

THOMAS

"Sir, I'm going to need you to step aside." A paramedic walked in between me and the girl. I took a step back, wiping my mouth with the inside of my wrist.

I looked down and saw blood. Her blood.

Quickly grabbing the bottom of my shirt, I used the hem to wipe my mouth clean. If anybody sees any blood, I'll just claim I was trying CPR. It's believable.

With the paramedic by her side, she was still lying on the ground, her forehead relentlessly bleeding and her eyes wide open. Her expression was unreadable.

"Where—" Her voice came out in a rasp.

The paramedic cut her off. "Ma'am, please relax, stay calm. We are taking you to the hospital."

I couldn't believe it. One second, she was dead. Completely lifeless. No breathing, no pulse. The next, she's awake, trying to talk, putting puzzle pieces together in her mind.

I couldn't *fucking* believe it.

The paramedics lifted and placed her on a stretcher. A stretcher that could've had a body bag on it if it wasn't for me. I expected her to scream in pain as they handled her, but she didn't. She was alert and cooperative, a fragile calmness washing over her as she listened to a paramedic speak. Watching her, I could see right through her act of forced serenity. Her shoulders were tight, her posture held firm, and her eyebrows dipped in confusion for a fraction of a second.

She looked moments away from losing all control.

Then again, how could anyone expect her to stay composed when her ribs were crushed to pieces?

A police car pulled up next to the ambulance, the blue and red colored lights bouncing off the scene. A tall, older man stepped out and began talking to the paramedics, regularly glancing in my direction. Of course. I stood there, waiting for the inevitable conversation with sweat beading on my forehead, the summer air running slick on my skin.

Every bit of me was glad the girl was okay, but a wave of deep anger was brewing inside me. What kind of person hits someone—no, runs them the *fuck* over—then leaves them for dead? I wanted this person found and handed to me so I could *personally* beat the shit out of them, then leave them for dead so they know how it feels.

But here I was, staring at the doors of the ambulance, watching the girl get carted inside. Her consciousness was the only thing keeping me from going out and finding the driver myself.

The *kiss* was keeping my feet planted on the ground, with my gaze locked on her.

Usually, kisses are heart-stopping, breath-taking, and soul-sucking. Not this one.

This was the opposite in every sense.

Obviously, I couldn't tell the officer the truth without him thinking I was batshit crazy. And I had no desire to.

Good thing lying has always come easy to me.

The officer turned his shoulders away, speaking into the radio strapped to his shirt before heading in my direction.

"I'm Officer Anthony Harper." He extended his hand in greeting. I shook it, eyeing him, recognizing a hint of familiarity in his face. I knew him from somewhere but couldn't place my finger on it. Brushing it off,

I let go of his hand, silently hoping to not smear any blood on him. Officer Harper was an older man, possibly in his late fifties. His height matched mine, his hair in a dark buzz cut that landed right to the scalp. "Can I get your name, son?"

"Thomas Diesel."

"Ah, you're Jackson's boy?"

I gave a single nod, still not remembering how I knew him.

"Well, it's nice to meet you, Thomas. Do you mind telling me what happened here?" Officer Harper asked as he took a pen and small notepad from his shirt pocket and flipped it open.

"Sure," I said as I slid both hands into my front pockets. "Uh, I was up on my balcony, I saw her walking, and a car came up and…" my voice trailed off.

"Hit her?" He tried to help me finish my sentence.

More than that. They ran her over.

"Yeah."

"And what did you do when you saw that happen?"

"I got up and ran down here. Tried to help her."

"Did anyone else see it happen?"

"I don't think so." I looked over my shoulder at the building I lived in. It was tucked away in a quiet location, a few hundred feet away from any road besides the one that snakes behind the apartments. No stores for over a mile, no gas station until you're almost to the highway. There's no good reason for people to explore this side of the small town. "If they did, they didn't come to help," I added with a hint of sarcasm in my tone, since I knew damn well I was the only one to see it.

The officer nodded, then thrust his chin in the direction of the ambulance. "Do you know her?"

"No."

He jotted down more notes. "A female called 911. Do you know who that was?" He asked without looking back up.

I glanced at the first floor of the apartment building and pointed to her sliding glass door, which was now broken. "Yeah, Mrs. Reeves. She lives in that apartment, there."

"Okay." He looked up at me. "Do you happen to know who was driving? Who struck this woman with their car?"

I shook my head, the fire rising in my chest. "No, sir."

"Did you see the make or model of the car?"

I closed my eyes, the lids suddenly feeling heavy. "It was silver. A car, not an SUV or truck. It looked older, maybe mid-2000s. But I didn't see the model."

My jaw ticked as I silently cursed myself for not getting a plate number. I was too focused on helping the girl that I didn't have a chance to see it. So, now we're left with only a generic silver car. How fucking specific. I'd have better luck finding Amelia Earhart.

The officer scribbled some more words in his notebook, asked for my phone number, then closed it shut. "Thank you, Thomas. If I have more questions, I'll contact you."

I nodded, letting a polite smile flash as he gave me a pat on my back, the expression disappearing as he walked away. With a quick inhale, I stole another glance back to the ambulance. The back doors were closing, and I eyed the girl sitting up on the stretcher inside. Her face was wiped clean, although some small streaks of blood were still dripping from her forehead. Her sweatshirt was off, showing her tanned shoulders that were smooth and spotted with freckles, a grey sports bra acting as her only coverage. My eyes dropped to her breasts, her nipples hard under the fabric, and I could feel my mouth curl up in the corners. The medic wrapped a cuff around her upper arm, taking her blood pressure. Her eyes met with mine, our gazes locked, with neither one of us able to look away. I could feel my breathing stop in that instant, my mind thrashing with one main thought.

There was no way, no way in all holy hell, that my lips, my *kiss*, could revive her.

Right?

ANNA

AUGUST 23, 2021

The sun cast an orange and purple glow across the horizon as I pushed open the glass doors in front of me.

It was already dawn?

How long was I in there?

Even though everything seemed to take forever, I didn't expect to see the sunrise when they discharged me. Stepping down to the sidewalk, the fresh air hit me like a tidal wave of relief. I closed my eyes, feeling the slight wind brush against my skin like velvet. The morning breeze was exactly what I needed.

And maybe some Advil.

I've only been living in Kittanning for two months, and I've already made myself known to the hospital and police. This town is so small, everyone knows everybody, so when last night happened, they immediately knew I wasn't from here. Even though that was true, they still treated me as one of their own. The nurses, doctors, and police officers made me feel welcome, gave me the care I needed, and ensured I was mentally and physically stable before leaving the hospital. And in the days and weeks prior to all this, I grew to love this little town, with the small corner grocery store that always stocked my favorite cinnamon almonds, the car wash that had free vacuums, and the town park that had a beautiful fountain right in the middle. It was exactly the place I wanted to be after spending my first twenty-two years in a big city.

I glanced down at the plastic bag in my hand. Inside was my messenger bag, my jeans that had ripped so badly they were deemed unsalvageable, forcing me to wear an extra pair of scrub pants, and another small, white paper bag with a small tube of ointment. I grabbed my messenger bag and pulled out my phone. Along with a fresh, new crack in the corner of the screen, there was only ten percent battery life, but that was enough life for me to get an Uber. Once it was scheduled with a wait time of twenty minutes, I put my phone back in my bag and leaned against the hospital building.

For the past few hours, the doctors and nurses have been constantly examining me, poking and prodding, never leaving me to dwell in my thoughts. I had lost a lot of blood, some of it still dried and crusted to the sides of my face. Adding that to my minor concussion, my sprained wrist, and twelve attractive stitches in a line across my forehead, I felt like I was in a daze. My mind was foggy, my head was pounding, and even though the last few hours were a distraction, all I wanted to do was lay in my own bed.

But once the doctors and nurses let me go, with my signature scribbled along the bottom of discharge papers I didn't bother to read, my mind could only focus on one thing.

Him.

The man who saved my life.

I took in a deep breath, replaying everything I could remember in my head. First, before anything, I remember his touch. One hand gripping the base of my skull, cradling me, the other pressed upon the side of my face. His skin was so soft, feeling like silk on mine. It was the first comfort I felt while slipping into a moment of consciousness, ripping through me like an arrow.

The next thing I remembered was his scent. As soon as I took in a breath, I could smell him, a swirling aroma of woods and musk mixed into one. It sent me into a spiral, intoxicating me and almost slipping me back into darkness.

Then, I opened my eyes, slowly blinking away any blur in my vision. The cloudless night sky was painted above me with bright stars glistening and flickering. I looked to my right, a forest of trees swallowing blackness with no end in sight. I looked to my left, and that's when I saw him. His short, brown hair, tousled and messy, his eyebrows cinched in worry, and his eyes the brightest, clearest blue.

He looked to me, and I to him.

Neither one of us could speak, yet it felt like a thousand words were spoken between us.

My heart felt like it was struggling to keep up with the rest of my body.

My mind was thinking of all the ways to pull myself up, but he backed away before I could move, leaving me on the bloodied pavement.

Once the ambulance came, I was whisked away by a paramedic and he was pulled away to talk to the police. Before I knew it, I was being bombarded with questions, my nerves ramping up at the severity of it all. That's when I realized I had no idea where I was or what had happened to me. Everything caught up to me at once, the alluring haze surrounding the guy who saved me was suddenly pushed away, and the fact that I was sitting in the back of an ambulance had me in a tailspin. I looked down at my hands, the ends of my hair, and my hoodie that I ended up ripping off, realizing everything was damp with fresh blood.

And the scary thing was, I couldn't remember why or how.

The last thing I do remember is leaving my apartment to take a walk. I made it about thirty feet before blinking and waking up in a stranger's warm arms.

His arms.

Heat rushed through me as I closed my eyes, remembering the feeling of it. Out of everything that happened, that was the one thing I kept coming back to. It was what my mind and body wanted to remember most. An ache bloomed in my chest at the fact that I didn't manage to ask his name, or even simply tell him thank you. But I did manage to steal a look before the doors of the ambulance closed, only to find his eyes already piercing through me.

And that said everything.

Thankfully, my keys to my apartment were still in my bag from the hospital. I opened the door and walked in, the keys rattling as I threw them on a small console table. Living alone definitely had its perks: no one was hounding me with millions of questions about where I'd been, why my wrist was wrapped, or why I had a giant gash on my face. The silence was more than welcome.

My apartment was small, with only one bedroom, one bathroom, a kitchen, and a living room, but it was just enough for me. A ceiling fan spun slowly above me as I entered the kitchen, giving just enough of a breeze to keep the air circulating, a strand of hair brushing across my cheek. I grabbed a glass of water and two Advil, hoping to alleviate the pounding headache, and downed it all in seconds. Sunlight warmed the side of my face as the morning rays flooded the apartment with a white glow, streaming in from a few windows that overlooked the small town. It wasn't an incredible view, but all I really cared about was letting natural light into the space.

With an exhale, I let my shoulders drop and relax.

I walked through the living room and back to my bedroom to plug in my phone, setting it down on the nightstand. I sat on the edge of my bed and paused for a minute, letting the phone turn on by itself, only to discover six missed text messages. The first five were from my friend, Olivia.

Olivia: Anna?
Olivia: Annnnnnnnaaaaa
Olivia: Where are you?
Olivia: You're missing extension day!

Olivia: Text me later so I know you're okay!

A wave of frustration came over me as I pressed my palm to my head, careful not to touch my wound.

After everything that happened last night, school was the last thing on my mind.

Extension day. It was one of the most critical days in cosmetology school. Someone comes in from Pittsburgh to teach the class how to correctly put in hair extensions. If I learn to do it correctly, I get a certificate at the end of the course, allowing me to add it to my list of qualifications. I acquire more clients, and in turn, more money.

And here I was, sitting on my bed, missing it.

I groaned at the thought of having to make this class up.

My fingers began typing in the chat box.

Me: I'm fine. Stomach bug. I'll be back tomorrow.

A rumble ran through my torso at the mention of my stomach. I was starving. After pressing send, I checked the other message, wincing at the name. It was from someone I used to hook up with, a guy named Evan.

Evan: Can we talk?

Rolling my eyes, I almost had to laugh at the idea. The last time we spoke was over a month ago when he tried to drive to Kittanning for a quick hookup. I instantly denied him, not wanting to go back to our old ways that consisted of one-night flings with no relationship in between. Now that I've settled here in Kittanning, I felt like I was finally in a good headspace, and I didn't want to let Evan mess that up.

Clicking on his contact, I blocked his number and put the phone down. An order of takeout and a long, hot shower was calling my name. I needed to refuel, get out of these scrub pants, and wash last night off my skin.

By the time I was done showering and eating, I could barely keep my eyes open. All the adrenaline that kept me awake through the night was gone. My headache still lingered around my skull, the throbbing dwindling down to a dull pang. I ended up falling asleep, and when I opened my eyes, it was clear from the change in sunlight and the shift of shadows along the wall that several hours had passed.

Climbing out of bed, my body began to feel the pain and soreness that was to be expected. My shoulders ached as I pulled a dark blue sweater over my head, and my leg muscles cramped up when slipping on my jeans. The reality of it sunk in. I was hit by a car in a hit-and-run accident.

Before leaving the hospital, I was told to visit the police station to finish filing a report within the next day or so. All I wanted to do was get it over with, so I decided to go that night. Once I got there, things felt like they would never end. The station smelled of old paperwork and mildew, and the room they put me in, some sort of interviewing room, couldn't be any more bland. The walls were an off-white color, with no pictures, no windows, not even a pattern on the floor or table for my eye to catch. Two and a half hours with stale coffee in an uncomfortable plastic chair was agonizing. The police officer that reported my accident, Officer Harper, was dealing with another issue, but the secretary made me stay knowing I had to fill in some gaps for the report. Alone in the room, I let my mind wander, but it never strayed far from the man who saved me. His broad shoulders, his thick arms wrapped around me, his hands and his touch. I closed my eyes, trying to get a clearer picture. There was a pull to him, something I've never felt before, and no matter how hard I tried to get him off my mind, it didn't work.

When Officer Harper finally managed to find me and sit across from me, giving me his undivided attention, I couldn't help but notice the bags under his eyes. He looked like he got about as much sleep as I did in the past twenty-four hours. He asked me a series of questions, and although there wasn't much he didn't already know, I managed to fill him in on my visit to the hospital and my injuries.

"I'm really sorry you have to deal with this." He closed the folder that held my paperwork, a clear sign that he was done asking questions. "Some people can be heartless."

"Does that mean you don't know who hit me?"

"I'm afraid we don't."

I looked down at my hands. Part of me didn't want to know the truth of who did it, because I refused to believe there was someone who would do such a thing. But of course, the other part of me needed to see the person's face. To show them what they did to me. To look the person in the eye and force them to face the consequences.

"There was a security camera on the side of the apartment building, but it hasn't been working in years."

Of course it hasn't.

"One last question, and then we can be done for today."

Keeping my eyes on the table, I noted the caution in his pause.

"Is there anyone you can call? Or be with? Your family, your parents?"

I shook my head. "My dad is dead, and I don't really talk to my mom."

Officer Harper leaned back in his chair, not wanting to press any further. "I'm sorry, Anna. We will do our absolute best to find the person who did this."

Forcing myself to give a small smile, I stood to leave. I knew it was his job to say that, just like I knew it was his job to make me believe they would find the person who hit me. In reality, my folder would be added to the rest of the cases that would turn cold. There were thousands of silver cars, and the one that hit me was probably long gone by now. Maybe they had a dented front bumper or a broken headlight, but those are both easy fixes that might have already been done.

I could feel an ache in my chest as I accepted the fact that they would never be caught.

The fresh air felt good on my face as I left the police station. The summer sun was slowly setting along the horizon, taking the warmth with it. Even though it was the end of August and still technically summer, the air that wasn't touched by the sun felt bitter and chilled. I pulled my sweater closer to my body as I walked to my car.

Lucky, fortunate, blessed; whatever word fit, it's what I felt. I was alive. My heart was beating, my lungs were breathing, I could walk, talk, think, speak. But it wasn't until that moment, sitting in my silent car, with the keys dangling in the ignition but the engine still off, that I started sobbing. Tears stained with mascara fell from my eyes like water from a tap, dripping off my face and falling onto my legs.

I began to filter through my memories, picking out the ones that shined the brightest in my mind.

The red dress I wore on my first day of kindergarten.

Hitting the jackpot on the Cyclone game at the arcade, winning five thousand tickets.

My first kiss on my sixteenth birthday with a boy named Gavin.

My dad, holding my hand as he lay in the hospital, telling me he loves me.

All of those memories, suddenly adding up to nothing as my brush with death would've taken them all. I began to feel alone, with no one to turn to, no one to help me pick up the pieces that were beginning to break off of me. My tears were not close to stopping as gasps of air filled my throat, my chest heaving.

There was an intense feeling of death looming over my shoulder, breathing on me, waiting for me.

And there was nothing I could do to push it away.

After what felt like hours, the crying had slowed. My eyes were red and swollen, my sleeves were damp from wiping the tears away, and my cheeks were spotted and blotchy, but I forced myself to shake the emotion out of me. I reminded myself that I was alive.

Alive.

I was here, sitting in my car, ready and able to move forward. I turned on the ignition and drove out of the parking lot.

THOMAS

A loud bang at the front door rumbled the house, pulling me right out of my sleep. A familiar voice shouted; muffled yelling lost in the thick wood of the walls. I groaned, peeked one eye open, and looked over at the clock. 11:48 PM. The banging and shouting at the front door continued.

"D! Open the door!"

I knew that voice. I knew it. It took me a minute to gain clarity in my mind before realizing who the voice belonged to. It was Parker Moore, one of my best—and loudest—friends.

"Come on, D. Don't make me break the door!"

Sliding my legs off the side of the bed, I rubbed my eyes with the backs of my hands, keeping them from watering as I yawned. I doubted Parker wanted to see me in just my underwear, so I pulled on a pair of grey gym shorts, along with a white t-shirt, and headed downstairs. As the steps creaked under me, there was no need for me to stay quiet since Parker's fist wasn't easing up the pounding. If his hand wasn't bloody by now, I'd be surprised. Normally, I would hope that my dad wouldn't hear Parker or me, but if this didn't get his attention, he clearly wasn't home. Knowing him, he was probably passed out drunk somewhere, next to some chick he's calling by the wrong name. Ever since my mom died two years ago, he spent almost every night drunk into oblivion, not giving two shits about me or anything I'm up to. Most nights, I didn't mind. It gave me the freedom teenagers dream of.

Finally, I opened the door to Parker's mischievous smile, thankful the loud pounding had stopped.

"You ready for this?"

"Ready for what?" I asked, rubbing a hand through my hair, making it stick up in all different directions.

"Oh, come on. Your birthday. It's in exactly… eleven minutes," he said, checking the time on his phone.

I scratched the back of my head, my mind still groggy. "So?"

Parker let himself inside, wrapping his arm around my shoulders and giving them a squeeze as we walked towards the kitchen.

"So… you're about to be eighteen. You know what we do when we turn eighteen."

Of course I knew. It was the town tradition.

But that didn't mean I wanted to.

Leaning my side against the center island, I stayed in the kitchen and watched as Parker made himself comfortable in my living room, grabbing the remote and flicking on the tv. I was right, my dad wasn't home, considering he wasn't sleeping on the couch and there was still no response to Parker's yelling.

"It's your turn, D. Time to go get ready." He waved me off with his hand. "And hurry, the guys are probably already there."

I rubbed both eyes with my index fingers, causing the room to spin as blackness swallowed my vision. I really wasn't in the mood for this. I had a calculus test tomorrow, and if I didn't get my shit together, I could fail the class.

"Can't we do this tomorrow? When it's my actual birthday? Or this weekend?"

"No way. Don't play dumb, D. We've been talking about this for weeks. You know its tradition to do it when the clock strikes midnight." He yelled over his shoulder without looking at me.

As annoying as it was to be woken up only an hour after going to bed, I knew he was right. In the ever-so-great small town of Kittanning, Pennsylvania, it was tradition for every guy to go out on the eve of his eighteenth birthday. My dad did it, my grandfather did it, every guy I know has done it. How it started, I have no idea. All I know is that I would be the talk of the town if I *didn't* go out. And as much as I hated the idea of following some stupid, outdated tradition, I hated being the center of attention even more. I was the second to last one in my group of friends to turn eighteen, with Jason Walter being the youngest and the only one not invited out tonight. As every birthday approached for the next friend, I heard them all talk about their plans. Of course, I wasn't eighteen yet, so I was excluded.

Until now.

I walked upstairs and took a quick shower. Parker was going to be pissed that I was taking so long, but I didn't care. I pulled on a pair of faded jeans and a dark grey, long-sleeved shirt. Since my birthday was in November, the air was nowhere near warm, so I slid on a dark green jacket and a beanie over my damp, brown hair. Jogging down the stairs, Parker was standing at the door, waiting for me with his shoulder leaning against the doorframe.

"There's my guy," he cheered as I came up next to him, his hand pressing a paper bag to my chest. I looked down to see a glass bottle of whiskey. The smile on Parker's face was so big, it almost looked painted on.

The clock on our phones read 12:07 AM. It was now November fifth.

"Happy birthday. We're officially seven minutes late. Let's go!"

The blue pickup truck rustled its way into the crowded parking lot of Stoney's. Parker chose a spot closest to the edge of the row, placed it in park, and we both opened our doors and jumped out. Traditions die hard, but now that I was here, I was happy to be part of something with my friends. I could hear the heavy bass bleeding through the walls of the building, clear music breaking through when the entrance door was opened. A bouncer sat on a stool right next to the door, eyeing us as we approached.

"IDs?"

Parker pulled his card out of his wallet, flashing his million-dollar smile as he handed it over. I did the same, but without the ass-eating grin. The bouncer handed them back after checking the birthdates.

"Go ahead."

Once inside, Parker leaned over to my ear and shouted over the music. "What a dick. He could've at least wished you a happy birthday."

Ignoring the comment, I looked around at the place. As soon as you step over the threshold, there was a bar to the left, with two bartenders serving drinks. There were tables scattered throughout the open room, with groups of men sitting at each of them. A handful of waitresses cruised around wearing all black- the color of dark seduction. They dressed in tank tops that plunged low in the front, the shortest shorts I've ever seen, and knee-high boots with heels. I watched as one waitress passed in front of me, and I couldn't help but stare as she crossed my path, letting my eyes linger a second too long. Music blared from the speakers placed in all corners of the floor, up on the beams in the ceiling, and along the catwalk that was right in the center of the room. There were red lights everywhere- some were placed high in the ceiling, there were string lights hung from high beams, and there were even flashing strobes planted in the floor, covered by frosted glass. Some bulbs would move and scan the room, placing a demonic glow on the guests seated at the tables. It wasn't a high-end place, and most men didn't care about the lights, the paint that was chipping on the ceiling, or the high price of their beers. They cared about the dancing. The show. The women.

It was a strip club.

"D!" A loud roar came from a table ahead of me, causing the entire place to turn and look at us. There were three guys facing the stage, Caleb Rittner on the left. He came to the club on his birthday with his older brother, Logan, and the next day no one could get him to shut the fuck up about it. Greg Snyder sat in the middle. Even though he was older, had already graduated, was attending community college, and was better friends with Logan than any of us, he never passed up an opportunity to come here. His birthday lands on Christmas Day, and Logan wouldn't take no for an answer when trying to get him to go to the club. He picked him up at his church right as Christmas Eve service was ending and had him back home in time to get an hour of sleep before opening gifts in the morning. Marcus Kennedy sat on the right, the most recent one to turn eighteen. He hesitated when coming here for his birthday, and his girlfriend, Jenny, cried when she found out about it. Marcus groveled the entirety of the next day.

Caleb stood up, rushing to us and engulfing me in a bear hug. "Happy birthday, man! Welcome to the beautiful land of adulthood!" He opened his arms wide in display of the stage.

As if on cue, a dancer came out from behind the stage curtains. Her black stilettos clicked with each slow, sultry step, her legs long and slim, leading my eyes from her ankles up to her thighs. Her red thong hiked up over her curved hips, the lace fabric leaving little to the imagination. She was completely naked from the waist up, with only her long, red hair draped over her breasts. She made her way to the pole, located at the foot of the catwalk, and hooked her leg around. With the crook of her knee holding her weight as she spun, she closed her eyes and tilted her head back, soaking in the stares from everyone around her.

It all looked effortless. She was captivating.

Caleb interrupted my gaze. "This is for you." He slapped a fifty-dollar bill on my chest. "Well, not really for you. For her."

I couldn't hide the roll of my eyes. *Nice.* His family has always been well off, never short on money, and if he asks his parents for some, they always oblige. No questions asked.

All I wanted to do was sit and watch her perform, but I knew the guys would give me shit if I didn't do this. My stare found her again as she knelt down, the pole hugged into her arms and in between her bare breasts. With her head tilted up and her eyes still closed, the cold steel caressed her soft jawline as her body gently slid down the length of the beam, causing my mind to go to forbidden places.

Quickly closing my eyes, I forced the thoughts away and tried to control my dick from growing.

Taking a step forward, I glanced at the men sitting at the foot of the stage, all of their eyes glued to every exposed piece of her. Single dollar bills were scattered all around the floor, an offering to a goddess, all for her.

As I approached the stage, my chest began to feel heavy with need. My steps carried me to her, but in her presence, I felt like I was floating. When I got close enough, I held out my hand with the bill folded in half, crisp in my fingers. The dancer glanced at me from the corners of her eyes, a slight smirk forming on her red, glossy lips.

It was obvious why I was here. The dancers all knew about the town tradition, too.

Leaning down into a crawl, she moved her face close to me, her nose almost brushing against mine. The smell of her vanilla perfume filled the air around me, her breasts close enough to send a surge in my jeans. With one hand, she went to grab the money, and with the other, she pressed a finger under my chin, lifting my eyes to hers.

Thank you.

Her mouth formed the words, her wet, pink tongue sliding out past her white teeth in emphasis, but she didn't bother to try to speak over the music. My focus bounced all over the place, from her touch under my chin to the fullness of her lips, to the nakedness of her skin only inches away from me. My cheeks flushed involuntarily as she sent me a wink and continued with her routine.

Holy *fuck*. That was hot.

"Atta boy!" Parker patted my back as I returned to the table. When I took one last look at the dancer, I noticed that she never took the smile off her lips, or her eyes off me.

ANNA

"Hey, Anna! Are you feeling—" Olivia's words caught in her throat the second she turned and looked in my direction. "Anna, what the *hell?*"

The door to the salon hadn't even closed behind me before the question poured from her mouth.

Her voice became louder, causing other students to turn and look my way. "*What. The. Hell?*"

"Hey, Olivia." I walked over to my station and put my bag down on the floor by my feet. "It looks a lot worse than it is," I said as I scanned the room. While most of the students were looking at me, their eyes lingering on my forehead while trying their best to hide their whispers, the others ignored Olivia's booming tone and paid no attention to us.

I lowered my voice. "Let's go to the back room, okay?"

Olivia followed me, closing the door behind us once we were alone. She stood across from me, her height towering over me. She was the girl everyone loved to look at, with long, slender legs, chestnut-colored hair falling just past her shoulders, and twinkling brown eyes to match. She even had bangs that rested right below her eyebrows, and with just one look at her, she had you wishing you had bangs, too.

"You have about…" she checked her smartwatch. "…fourteen minutes before class starts. Fill me in, please."

A deep breath filled my lungs, and I explained all the events from the last thirty-six hours.

The walk, the accident, the hospital, the police, the guy.

By the time I was finished, Olivia's eyes were wide with shock.

"Anna, holy *shit*. How are you alive? Most people would *not* have survived that accident, let alone walk around as if nothing happened. I mean, you're not even sore?" It was posed as a question as her expression cinched in bewilderment.

I could feel the smirk rise on my face. "Well, my wrist hurts if I move it the wrong way."

Olivia raised her eyebrows. "And now you're cracking jokes about it all?"

I shrugged. Even though I cried about it last night in my car, I wasn't about to wallow in fear and misery about what *could've* happened to me. It *could've* been worse. One inch to the left and I *could've* died. But that's not what happened, and I wasn't going to dwell on it.

Olivia changed the subject. "Tell me more about this guy. The one that helped you."

The mention of him thrust me right back to the road, into his arms, cradling me. With his eyes gazing down to me, he kept me conscious while waiting for the ambulance to come.

"I don't know who he is. I didn't get to talk to him."

Olivia paused. "What did he look like?"

"I… don't know."

It was partially the truth. I remember his eyes, the shape of his face, his arms. But waking up in a daze made my memory soft around the edges. I had faith that I would recognize him if I saw him, but my mind couldn't picture him in complete clarity. And after answering questions for the doctors, the police, and now Olivia, all the unknowns coming out of my mouth were beginning to unsettle me.

Olivia must've picked up on it because she sighed and pulled me in for a hug. "I'm sorry all that happened. It had to be so scary."

She pulled away from the hug, linked her arm through mine, and guided me back into the classroom.

"If you need me, I'm only a text away, okay?"

I nodded, thankful for our friendship.

AUGUST 30, 2021

As I pulled onto the back road, I noticed the streetlights along the side were either dim or completely burnt out. The neglect was clear, and the isolation was evident. This hidden area was only a twenty-minute walk from my apartment, but it was in a direction I never typically took. There was no sidewalk, only a section of grass a few feet wide before a forest of trees began on the left. I couldn't see past the trees, but the leftover glow from the sunset peeked through the top of the leaves, leaving a purple streak in its escape. Traffic was on the main road a few streets over, with no signs of any travel on this back road. It was a beautiful, quiet area with solitude and privacy.

I pulled my car onto the grass, placed it in park but left it running, and stepped out. The headlights illuminated the street ahead of me, casting my shadow on the pavement, and my feet carried me along the road with the sound of loose gravel under my shoes.

This is the road I walked exactly one week ago.

I paced forward, scanning the ground below me, looking for any signs of myself. A minute later, I came upon a spot in the road, a dark red circle close to the edge of the pavement.

This is where it happened. This is where I was hit.

This is my blood.

Right then, a voice called out to me.

"Hey."

My eyes darted up to the building on the other side of the road, my mind trying to focus on the voice. There was a man standing on a third-story balcony, his forearms resting on the railing as he held a beer bottle, a lounge chair placed behind him. The light was on inside the apartment, making him backlit, hindering my ability to see his face. But I could see the outline of the jeans that scaled his legs and the ripple of his t-shirt in the breeze as it hung from his torso.

"Hi," I managed to squeak out as a small smile curved up from the corner of my mouth. The headlights from my car shined on the side of my face as I turned the rest of my body in his direction. The wind picked up, the leaves rustling behind me, my sweater fluttering in the air as I pulled my arms close to my chest.

"Wait there." His voice was deep, covered with a grit that came naturally, creating flutters in my chest. He stood straight, took a swig of his drink, and walked back inside. I watched his apartment through the glass door, only able to see the ceiling from where I was standing. The light flicked off, sending my heart into a gallop, unease flowing through my body.

A minute passed as I studied the dried blood once again. In the seven days that passed since the accident, there has been no rain to wash away the dark, tacky remnants. It was surreal to see me, or rather, the blood from my body that keeps me alive, plastered in a dry puddle on the road. Anyone could walk by and see it and not think much of it, even though the story behind it was traumatic.

A door at the bottom of the apartment building opened, the squeak of the hinges forcing my head to turn and look. The man came walking out, my eyes catching a glimpse of a stairwell behind him. He jogged over to the same side of the road I was standing on, but he stood on the other side of the blood, facing me. My body was blocking the headlights from shining in his eyes, but I could still see his face as he put his hands in his front jean pockets.

My heart dropped from my ribs to the bottom of my stomach, my breath slipped from my lungs, and my stomach did a somersault, all at the same time.

It was him.

I looked at him and saw the way he looked down at me the week before.

I watched his mouth and remembered hearing him yelling to someone.

My gaze trailed down his arms, tanned and corded in veins and muscle. They were the same ones that held me up as the ambulance came for me.

He was tall, and even though he was standing a few feet away from me, I still had to look up to see his bright blue eyes. His hair was a shade lighter than brown, a bit shaggy but neatly cut above his ears. Freckles brushed his face so lightly that you would only notice them if you were specifically looking for them. His jawline was sharp, his shoulders were broad, and his chest looked firm. His eyes were fixated on mine, and for a moment I was embarrassed that he caught me exploring his body, but his stare was so intense that everything in that moment vanished except for me and him. The thought of him looking straight at me made my cheeks turn bright red and my knees weaken.

He cleared his throat, causing both of us to break our focus. "So, you're the one that…" His voice trailed off as if he was dancing around the right words to use for the fragile subject.

"Yeah. How'd you know?"

He pointed to his forehead in reference to mine.

"Oh. Yeah. Pretty, isn't it?" I let out a sigh, trying and failing to make it sound like a laugh.

"What did—"

"You're the one that helped me, aren't you?" My eyes narrowed and my eyebrows furrowed. My eagerness made my words sound more accusing than I intended. With hesitation, he glanced around, looking anywhere except at me, all while my eyes stayed locked on his face.

He arched an eyebrow. "I didn't do anything."

I shook my head before he could say more. "No, no. If you weren't there, things would be a lot different."

My words were ignored as they rolled off his shoulders. He jutted his chin in my direction as his eyes looked for more injuries. "What did the doctors tell you?"

"Well, as you've already noticed, I got twelve stitches…."

I gestured to my forehead.

"…I'm sure it will leave a lovely scar. I also sprained my wrist…"

I held up my left arm to show him the cloth bandage.

"…And I got a concussion."

I tapped my temple three times with my index finger.

We both paused, waiting for one another to speak. When he realized I was done, that those were the only injuries I ended up with, he blinked, his face blank and unreadable. His lack of emotion caught me off guard because if I were him, I would be surprised. From all the information from the police report and his statement, it seemed to be a pretty bad hit.

I took a deep breath. "I'm lucky. It could have been a lot worse."

He didn't try to be discreet as he scanned the length of my body. My legs, stomach, and chest all felt the heat from his stare, then his eyes moved back up to my face, making me self-conscious for a moment. I swear I saw the corners of his lips turn up into a smirk, lasting only a fraction of a second. "Yeah. It could have."

Warmth spread to my lower stomach and down my legs. I might have been reading into this more than I should've, but I couldn't help it. When a guy this attractive saves your life, you can't help but feel some sort of way for him.

There was another pause, then his deep voice brought me back to the conversation.

"Do you remember it?"

My mind instantly flashed back to last week, looking up at him as the stars shined above him like a halo, the stubble settled on the line of his jaw. I didn't feel any pain, at least not in that moment. All I felt was his touch, his comfort, and his safety.

A few seconds felt like hours as his eyes remained locked onto mine, waiting for an answer, the outer glow from the streetlight illuminating the space between us. My hands became clammy, and my heart started beating faster as I struggled to get my voice over a whisper.

"No. Only you."

It was an admission I wasn't sure I wanted to reveal, but it was the truth. It was the same thing I told the police when I filed the report. I don't remember anything except him before I was taken away in an ambulance. Normally, I would have fear in the fact that I was alone, waking up to a complete stranger with injuries I couldn't remember getting, but there was something about him that brought me peace. Waking up to him, in my opinion, was the best-case scenario.

His eyes dropped down to my lips, his tongue briefly licking his own. I swallowed as blood rushed to my cheeks, turning them a bright red.

"I owe you."

His response was quick. "You don't owe me anything."

A smile spread across my face as I shook my head in disbelief. I turned around and walked back to my car, still feeling the heat of his eyes pressed onto me. Pausing behind the driver-side door, with one foot in the car, I looked at him again. "Will you be here tomorrow?"

He remained in the same spot and nodded. "After six."

"Good." I climbed into my car and shut the door. It wasn't until I was back onto the main road that I realized I never got his name.

THOMAS

It wasn't until I saw Caleb walking back to our table that I realized what he had just done.

"That chick is fucking *stunning*. Enjoy yourself, birthday boy." He clapped his hand on my shoulder while the other guys cheered. The bouncer standing at the back hallway looked over at me with a giant wad of cash in his hand and motioned for me to follow him. I stood, took off my jacket and hat, and followed. He led me down a red-lit hallway with old wooden doors on both sides, each with a gold number ranging from one to ten. There were two doors at the end of the hallway, and judging by the "employees only" sign, I assumed those were the dressing rooms for the dancers. We stopped at room six, the bouncer pushing past dangling beads and opening the door.

"She'll be right in."

I nodded and he closed the door behind me, shutting me in a small, dark room. Black lace accented the walls, extending from floor to ceiling, with only enough space to fit a black couch and an end table. The bass of the music from the main room could still be felt through the floor, but it was oddly quiet once the door was closed. My ears began to ring from the adjustment. Matching the atmosphere from the rest of the building, the room held dim, deep red lighting. A few candles were scattered around the room, all burning a vanilla-scented wax. The end table had a black vase holding a dozen black roses. I walked over to it, pressing a velvet pedal between my fingers, feeling the softness against my calloused skin.

Right then, the door opened.

I turned to see the dancer from earlier, wrapped in a red silk robe. Her red hair was twisted up in a clip, and her black heels clicked with each step. She closed the door and leaned her back against it.

"Hi."

I cleared my throat. "Hi."

She motioned for me to sit on the couch. I obeyed.

"Thomas?" My name escaped her mouth with a breath.

I could feel my pulse skip as I nodded. Caleb must have told the bouncer my name.

Her smile spread slowly across her glossy lips as I studied her skin. Her rosy cheeks were so smooth, making her look like a porcelain doll. Shadows ran down the left side of her, away from the lights and candles, kissing every crevice it filled. With the lift of one leg, she placed the heel of her stiletto on a boom box, a square button caving under her force. Sultry, instrumental music began to play, and either the volume was too low, or my senses were too focused on her to hear it. She dropped her leg back down, pushing them together, both long, with no blemish or scar residing on either of them.

She took one step towards me.

Then another.

She looked down at me, into my eyes, as I tilted my chin up.

"Is today your birthday, Thomas?"

Caleb must have mentioned that, too.

I nodded again, saying nothing. Her words flowed from her lips like liquid, her voice resembling the feeling of the rose petal between my fingers moments ago.

The smile never left her lips as she turned her back to me. She reached up to the clip in her hair and pulled it out, the loose curls cascading to the middle of her back as her hands effortlessly tousled the waves apart. She glanced over her shoulder, her long, dark eyelashes fluttering against her cheeks as she looked down. With a swift movement, she untied her robe, letting it fall to the floor.

I felt myself inhale sharply as I took in the sight. The only thing she was wearing was a seamless black thong to accompany her heels. The skin on her back matched the skin on the rest of her body- perfect, smooth, almost airbrushed. She brought her shoulder up to her chin in a playful gesture. The curves of her hips rounded down like the lows of a valley, her ass tight and firm.

She was the definition of perfect.

In the past, I've been with girls from my school, losing my virginity at fifteen and fucking other girls since then. And like all guys, I use the computer and my hand as a girlfriend some nights.

But *this*.

This was a *real* fucking woman.

She finally turned to face me, her arms above her head, her hips swaying slowly to the music. My eyes immediately went to her breasts. Her nipples hardened from the lack of covering.

God, could she get any more perfect?

I could feel a tightness rise in my jeans as I tried to mentally push it back down. I didn't want her attention on me or the fact that my dick doesn't know how to control itself, even though that's the whole reason why she's here.

She took another step towards me, making herself only a foot away.

Everything in me tried so hard to keep my eyes locked on hers instead of trailing down her chest. I shifted, my legs bending uncomfortably, the leather of the couch grumbling beneath me. She could tell that I was hard as a fucking rock, and that made her move closer. She placed both arms on either side of me, leaning down so my face was almost touching hers.

"I have something for you, Thomas."

She could say my name a million times and I would never get tired of it.

My eyes flickered between her blue ones. Even in the dark, I could see how bright they were, my vision discovering a hint of silver shining through the irises. She leaned in so close to me that the tip of her nose brushed against mine. I watched her as she closed her eyes, her breath warm on my lips.

In that moment, a wave of euphoria washed through me.

The pit of my stomach knotted.

My hands rested on my knees, sweat clamming my palms.

Her breasts dangled inches away from my chest.

Her soft lips tenderly connected with mine.

She kissed me.

And I kissed her back.

Reluctantly, my eyes closed as well, but I wanted to keep them open to make sure this was really happening. With the touch of our lips fitting together like puzzle pieces, a darkness washed over me, darker than the view behind my eyelids. This was a picture, a room of shadows, like I was on the outside of a window trying to look in.

Everything paused, time and space and life and sound and the spin of the Earth.

Stopped.

My body froze with my lips still planted on hers. Then, with everything on mute, my eyes sealed shut, a figure appeared in the upper corner of my eye. This version of me, whether I was dreaming or hallucinating or dying, looked up, trying to get a better view. It was a woman, turned away from me so I couldn't see her face. She was sitting on the moon, the crescent shape acting as a cradle, with her arm draped over the side, letting it dangle. As I approached, my steps in a glide, she turned her head to look over her shoulder, only to have an empty hole as a face. There was nothing to her, only a blankness where she should be. I struggled to breathe, the air around me unmoving and thick. My gaze was set on her as she ran her other hand along the inside curve of the moon, the edge slicing her fingertips open, bright red blood dripping down the sides. There was nothing I could do but watch. Then, she held out her hand to me, the blood falling in droplets, and I reached out and grabbed her hand. As soon as I touched her, a sudden shock ran through my entire body, launching me back to reality. A surge ran down to the heels of my feet, buzzing through every pore in my skin, all the way back up to the base of my neck. The hair all over my arms and legs stood on end, with pinpricks filtering through my entire nervous system. Pain throbbed in my lips as I pulled away from her, the feeling of a knife slicing me from one corner of my mouth to the other.

"*Fuck*, did you bite me?"

My eyes shot open as my lungs were finally beginning to operate.

What the fuck just happened? What felt like an hour was really only a few seconds.

Waiting for a response, she exhaled with a smile. Her soft laugh would have annoyed me if it didn't sound so seductive. She shook her head and straightened her body, towering over me as I remained sitting on the couch. Even if I tried, I don't think my legs would let me stand. My knees felt like Jell-O. I no longer heard the quiet music, felt the bass in the floor, or smelled the vanilla candles. I moved my fingers to my bottom lip, rubbing it, soreness spreading through the skin slowly. There was no trace of blood or any bite marks.

The last time I checked, this wasn't something strippers normally did.

"A gift, Thomas."

"What?"

"A gift of life." She turned around and bent over to pick up her robe, shoving her ass in my face in the process, a final treat for me before ending her routine. She slid her arms into the sleeves and tied the belt, covering herself.

"I don't—"

"One person. You can save one person. If they die, you can bring them back."

"What... the hell?" My words filtered out in a laugh. My mind could make no sense of what she was saying. "Did my friends put you up to this?"

Her gaze never strayed from mine. "I've given you the gift of life."

"Would you please stop saying that?" Growing annoyed at her evasiveness, I couldn't stop my voice from turning bitter.

There was a moment of silence as she took a deep breath. "If someone dies, you have the choice to bring that person back. If you don't want to, leave them. Let them go. If you want to save them, you now have that ability."

There was a deafening silence between us as I processed what she was saying. "So, you're telling me," I pinched the bridge of my nose as I squeezed my eyes shut. "I can bring someone back… from the *dead*?"

She smirked as she nodded. I couldn't help but tilt my head back and laugh again.

"This is great. This is… this… Why would I ever believe this?"

"You saw it, right, Thomas? You felt it, too?"

A tap of pressure appeared in my jeans when she said my name.

"Felt… the kiss? Yeah, you bit me."

"Thomas, listen to me. This is an extraordinary gift. Now, you have a choice. You can pretend as if this never happened, ignore me, and let the gift linger inside of you until you die, or you can give someone another chance to live."

The candles surrounding us continued to flicker. Looking at her, really, deeply looking, I could see the honesty in her eyes. There was something glowing, a shimmer of truth that was pouring out of her. It was the most absurd thing I've ever heard, and part of me was screaming to not entertain the idea at all. But there was another part of me, sitting in front of the most beautiful woman I've ever seen, the buzzing feeling of her lips still sending me into a shock, that wanted to believe her. Maybe I was drunk on the belief that someone like her would have any interest in someone like me. That thought took over and convinced every other part of me to trust her, but I didn't want her to know, and I didn't want to show it.

"Yeah…I think I'm going to go…" I began to stand up from the couch, but before I could steady myself on my feet, she pushed me back down with her stiletto on my chest.

"Be patient. Let me explain."

She took her foot off me and began to pace back and forth. I waited for her to continue.

"You can only save one person. Not two, not ten. One."

I nodded.

"They must be dead. No breathing, no heartbeat, no pulse. Dead. But you can't save someone who has been dead longer than four minutes. Once four minutes have gone by, it won't work."

I looked down at the floor. Memories from two years ago came to the forefront of my mind. My mom lying in a hospital bed. Flowers surrounding her. My hand holding hers as she took her last breath. If I had this when she died, I could have saved her. I would have done anything to bring her back. My life was broken without her.

I pushed away the memory and looked back up at the dancer.

Her heels clicked loudly on the hard floor. "You can't save yourself."

I frowned, then shrugged it off.

"And lastly…" she turned to face me, placing herself between my knees. Leaning down, she pressed a finger under my chin, lifting my face to hers. "…in order to save them, you have to kiss them."

The fuck?

"Kiss them? Kiss a dead person?" I asked in confirmation, my eyebrows raised.

Her voice was stern, her eyes matching her tone. "Save a dead person."

The thought of kissing a dead person made me wince. Call me crazy, but death isn't much of a turn-on in my book.

She slowly straightened her body, her legs still between mine, and smirked. I tilted my head, looking up at her face. There was a sense of power she held that was unlike anything I'd ever experienced, and it was shown in the way she carried herself. But there was also something I couldn't place, something missing from the equation of her and I, and it felt crucial for me to find out.

"Who are you?" I asked as I narrowed my eyes.

A pause. "Eve."

I sighed. Simple question, simple answer. I was hoping for a bit more, but I'll take whatever I can get.

"Okay, Eve, why am *I* the one that has to do this?"

She let out a spark of a laugh. "Well, you're not *the* one. You're one of 'the ones.' There are about a hundred people out there that have the same ability you do, but you'd never know it. Those people you hear about in the news- 'Man saves boy from drowning!' 'Woman saves life during transatlantic flight!'" Her voices and gestures were exaggerated for dramatic effect.

"Those are people like you. Sometimes, there's more to a story than what's told."

All kinds of thoughts bombarded me as I tried to think straight, but trying to dissect her words was more complicated than I could've imagined. My disbelief was etched on my face as it openly expressed my confusion. Just as I lifted my eyes to ask her something, I caught her heading for the door, and my heart sank. I felt like I had a million more questions, but nothing was coming to the surface. Every bone in my body didn't want her to go, at least not yet. Her presence held answers, and in turn, comfort in knowledge.

If she was telling the truth, then she just dropped the biggest bomb on my life. Someone's life could be in *my* hands. I wasn't sure if I was ready to take that on just yet.

I watched her body sway with each step she took as she reached for the door handle.

"Wait, that's it? What if I need to find you? What if I have more questions?"

"You won't."

Her answer left me dissatisfied. I got the courage to ask one last question.

"Why me?" My voice hovered just above a whisper.

Her blue eyes locked onto mine, and both of our gazes intertwined. For a second, I thought I saw a look of excitement flash over her face, like she was aroused at the sight of me in this state, but the look was gone before I could catch it.

"Because I chose you."

The door clicked shut behind her as I leaned forward, my elbows on my knees, my head in my hands.

ANNA

AUGUST 31, 2021

Before leaving the parking lot, I checked the clock on my phone for the hundredth time. It was 6:04 pm. The passenger seat held a six-pack of Guinness, sitting perfectly in the folds of the cushion. Moments ago, the liquor store cashier, who looked to be easily over fifty years old, asked for my ID. I pulled it out of my wallet and handed it to him, the hologram overlay shimmering under the light as he verified that I was twenty-two years old. Then, with his eyes studying the picture on the card before moving to me, he caught sight of my forehead. Judging by his wide eyes, he was too afraid to say anything about it.

So, this is going to be a thing, isn't it? People staring at me, whispering about me, but too scared to ask me about it. For a second, I thought maybe I should get bangs like Olivia, to cover up the wound, at least until it fully heals. But then I thought better of it. It was proof that I was alive, that I survived, a reminder that I cheated death. No matter how many people were going to stare at me, it wouldn't change that fact.

I paid for the drinks and the cashier handed me the receipt, his eyes failing to meet mine as I left.

Now, here I am, fumbling with the steering wheel as I sit in my car, the engine idling in the deserted parking lot.

Tapping the screen on my phone, I checked the time again.

6:05 pm.

Before I could second guess myself any more than I already have, I put the car in reverse, pulled out of the parking lot, and drove out onto the main road.

There were two rows of parking spots as I pulled in, not a single car in the lot. I looked around, confused. Was I at the right place? Regular work hours are over, so there should be at least one or two more cars here, if not more. I glanced back up at the apartments. The building wasn't too small; it was three stories high with large windows on both sides and an open staircase running down the middle, splitting the rentals in half. Since the accident happened on the opposite side of the building, I never had a chance to see the front, but I was sure this was it.

But why wasn't anyone here?

I pulled into a spot in the corner of the lot, turned off the car, and waited. Checking the time, it was only 6:17, so I told myself to give it at least ten more minutes. He said *after* six, so technically, he wasn't late. Or lying.

As the engine ticked down, the silence growing louder, I rested my hands on the top of the steering wheel. I don't know what to look for. I don't know what kind of car he drives. I don't even know his name.

After a few minutes, a rusted, red car pulled into the lot, driving at an extremely slow speed. As it parked in front of the stairwell, I leaned back, pushing my body into the seat as hard as I could, trying to not be too obvious that I was watching. An older woman stepped out with a green, reusable grocery bag gripped tight in one hand and a set of keys in her other, not sparing me a single glance. I watched as she fumbled around, trying to find the right key, and I knew this could be my one and only opportunity to find my way in. I grabbed the beer and stepped out of my car, shutting the door behind me. A brisk walk brought me to the old woman, standing outside apartment two in just a matter of seconds.

"Can I help you with that?" My hand extended out for her bag, a smile spread wide on my lips.

She looked at me and returned the grin. "Oh, thank you, dear." She handed me the unexpectedly heavy bag of groceries as she searched for, and then found, the correct key for her apartment door. It unlocked with a single click. Her eyes scanned the parking lot, then looked back at me as she pushed the door open.

"Are you here about the ad?" she asked.

My head cocked to the side. "Ad?"

"To rent an apartment?"

"Oh, no. I'm here to see…" Before I could finish my sentence, a truck rolled into the lot, the engine roaring as it turned. A man, hidden by the sun's reflection in the windshield, parked in the spot located right next to the old woman's car. He turned the ignition off and swung the door open, the tight muscles in his arms pulsing as he gripped the doorframe. I could feel his eyes pressing into me, sending waves of heat to the back of my neck and down the length of my spine.

"Thomas!" The old woman exclaimed, her dainty smile running from ear to ear. "How was your day?"

Thomas.

Finally, I have a name to put to the face.

After a minute of waiting, or what felt to me like a long, drawn-out minute, he finally approached us. Small streaks of sweat caused by the August air beaded down his temples, dotting his slick skin. There was a blank look on his face, essentially unreadable, and once he was done staring in my direction, he ran his hand through his flattened hair, giving it an ounce of life.

"My day was fine, Mrs. Reeves. How was yours?"

That *voice.*

The voice pulled all the feeling out from my knees and tripled my heart rate.

I had to bite my bottom lip to stop myself from making any sort of noise.

As the old woman, Mrs. Reeves, if I heard correctly, rambled on about her day and things she needed done, all I could see was him, his jeans ripped and dirty, his arms tanned, his hands slipping his truck keys into his pocket, his gaze locked on mine. My ears stopped listening, my tongue felt swollen with words I couldn't speak, and my heart leaped into my throat. I could feel my pulse beating in the cut on my forehead. Before my mind could catch up with my heartbeat, there was only a foot of space between us, and he finally turned his head toward Mrs. Reeves to acknowledge he was listening.

"Yes, I can fix the drip in your faucet. I'll swing by on Sunday. I'll be here all day."

I tucked that sentence away into the back of my head.

Sunday. Here. All day. *Noted.*

"Oh, thank you, Thomas." Mrs. Reeves took the grocery bag out of my jelly arms before I even noticed it was gone. "This is…"

"Anna Sunfield." I finished her introduction, and the corner of his mouth tilted up into a smile at the mention of my name, sending me up into the air, floating in the sky.

"Thomas Diesel. My friends call me Diesel."

I wasn't sure if he was telling me that as an invitation to call him Diesel, or as a warning that I didn't know him well enough to call him that.

He offered his hand, bridging the gap between us. Looking at it for a moment, I placed my hand in his and shook it, fire coursing through me from his touch. It took everything in me to keep a blank expression, considering this was the first time we touched since the accident.

"Thomas Diesel, as in, the toy trains?" Biting back a chuckle, I let go of his hand, immediately missing his warmth in my palm. His response was a subtle eye roll, and I suddenly wished I could shove the words back in my mouth and swallow them.

He leaned his shoulder closer to me, a whiff of a wooden scent filling my lungs, matching the same scent I inhaled the night of the accident. I tried to keep my composure, but the blissful aroma was short-circuiting me. His eyes never left mine as he spoke softly. "Yeah, my parents didn't really think that one through."

I felt myself relax, his ease putting me right with him.

"She's here to look at an apartment," Mrs. Reeves interjected. For a minute, I forgot she was even here, even though she was standing right beside us. As I glanced at her, I noticed there was something innocent about her, something delicate, being a woman relying on her younger neighbor to help with things around her place. And throughout this whole time with her, she never once brought up the gash on my forehead.

I'm not sure she even looked at it.

Thomas looked unamused. "Let me show you around, then." He took the six-pack off my hands and motioned to the stairwell. As Mrs. Reeves closed herself in her apartment, I waved goodbye and began side-stepping up the concrete stairs, my body turned towards Thomas in an attempt to explain myself.

"I'm not actually here to look at an apartment, she just assumed I—"

"No, I know. She does that a lot."

"Does what? Puts ads out for this place?"

"No. Assumes."

I nodded.

"Do you do this often?" he asked, raising the six-pack. "Bring strangers beer?"

I felt a wave of nerves float through my legs, wondering if this was a mistake. "Only the ones that save my life."

As we rounded the corner of the second flight of stairs, he shook his head.

"You're not going to let this go, are you? I didn't do anything," he said as he stared straight ahead. His tone was brisk, and his demeanor was callous. His words would've stung if I didn't try to see through them, to look past whatever façade he was putting on.

We reached the top of the stairs. The third floor held only two apartments, one on the right and one on the left. Judging by the location of his balcony, I knew his apartment was on the right. Apartment six. His keys clinked together as he pulled them out of his jean pockets and found the correct one.

Right before he was about to open his door, I stopped him, placing a gentle hand on his elbow, feeling small traces of dirt under my fingers. He looked down at my hand, which lingered a beat too long before I dropped it, then he moved his stare up to my eyes.

"Hey, Diesel, I'm not trying to impose,"

There was a pause in my voice as I waited for him to correct me on his name, but he said nothing.

"I, um, just wanted to bring that by…"

I pointed to the drinks as a reference.

"…for you. As a thank you."

Once again, I was trapped in the blue ocean waves of his irises as he stared at me, with my lungs trying to keep up but feeling as if they were drowning. I tried to force out a goodbye, but cement plastered my throat, and no sound made way. I turned on my heel to leave, but the sound of his voice stopped me from spinning all the way around.

"You're not going to make me drink alone, are you?" he asked, the sound of a swallow slipping through the cracks.

My knees instantly buckled at his question. Even if it was for just one drink, he was inviting me to stay with him. The echo of his voice was husky as I turned back around, noticing a tinge of need to his words.

"Unless you have other plans."

I took one step toward him. "I'd be happy to join."

Twisting the key in the door, he unlocked and opened it.

THOMAS

I could feel the blood draining from my face as I walked back to the table. The guys were watching the dancers while still conversing with each other, their voices drowned out by the music. I sat back down in my chair, and their attention returned to me.

"He's back!" Parker yelled as he and Greg both grabbed my shoulders and shook me.

"Did you have a good time, birthday boy?" Caleb yelled to me from across the table. I forced myself to smile, to act normal, to pretend like my life didn't just change in a matter of ten minutes.

Eve's voice played back in my head.

You can pretend as if this never happened.

Now that I was back with my friends, laughing and having a good time, I came to my senses. This had to be a joke. There was no way a stripper could give me some sort of unexplainable, unnatural power. She had to be messing with me or playing some sort of joke. Maybe she was even high on some kind of drug. But on the other hand, I've seen Caleb do some shit in the bathroom—coke, pills, whatever. I've seen how he acted after it kicked in, and Eve was not in that state of mind. And if she was, she sure hid it well. Her voice was clear, her body language was unmistakable, and her presence was bleeding with honesty.

The problem with the situation was all on my end.

I'm the one that refuses to believe it.

I'm the one that thinks it's a joke.

I'm ignoring the pictures in my head of a woman on the moon, and the pain in my lips from a harmless, soft kiss.

I rubbed my chin with my hand and nudged Caleb with my elbow. "Hey, what did you tell the bouncer when you paid him?"

He wrinkled his nose. "What? Why?"

"Just answer."

"I said, 'My friend wants a lap dance.'" He took a drink of his coke, his eyes suddenly growing wide. "Why? Did you get more?" An obnoxious smile beamed as my lack of an answer made him jump to conclusions. "Did you hook up with a stripper?"

I ignored his question. "Did you give him my name?"

He shook his head, his face turning to a frown.

"Did you tell him it was my birthday?"

He shook his head again.

Fuck.

This was real.

I can save one person.

My head began to spin as I pulled on my coat and hat, standing to leave. "I have to go. My dad wants me home." I looked at Parker, who couldn't care less that I was going. "I'll get an Uber."

The guys didn't try to fight me on staying. As long as they were there, watching the show, they didn't care about celebrating or not. At the very least, they wished me a final happy birthday as I left the table. Heading to the exit, I scanned the entire room one last time, hoping to catch a glimpse of red hair.

No luck.

I pushed open the door and walked out into the bitter cold night.

Getting home, I saw my dad's car in the driveway. He must've come home while I was gone. I walked up to the front door and pushed it open, not surprised that it was left unlocked.

We have this unspoken rule that we always leave the front door unlocked when we know the other one of us is out late. Most of the time, it's me leaving the deadbolt open, hearing his footsteps enter the house well after midnight. But tonight, I was the one sneaking in, trying to step in all the right places to keep the floor from creaking under me. After shutting the door, I only managed to take a few steps towards the staircase before I heard my name shouted through the house.

"Tommy D! My boy."

Jackson Diesel, ladies and gentlemen.

"Well, you're not such a boy anymore, are you?" His slur over the word "such" gave me everything I needed to know.

He was wasted.

I walked into the living room where he lay sprawled across the couch. The tv was on, but the volume was so low there was no way he was paying attention. I looked at the arm that was dangling off the couch, almost touching the floor, and saw the bottle of whiskey Parker had given me earlier.

"Dad, what are you doing?"

"Celebrating. It's your birthday, right?" He swung his legs down to the floor, steadying himself and attempting to stand, but the brief look of queasiness kept him sitting. "I didn't forget."

His hair hung over his forehead, casting a shadow over the deep purple rings around his eyes. Moments like these reminded me how glad I was that I looked nothing like my dad and only took after my mom. His hair was dark and wavy, mine was light brown and straight. His skin had an olive tint, while mine was fair. We were complete opposites in every sense.

"Where've you been?" he asked.

I sighed deeply. "Stoney's."

He raised his eyebrows, the realization hitting him. "The tradition. Oh, God." The slur was becoming more profound with each sentence. "How was it? Did you become a man?"

He spoke with his eyes barely open, exhaustion printed out all over his face.

Ignoring him, I took a step in his direction. "You should go to bed."

"No, you should go to bed," he snapped. "I'm the parent, remember?"

I stared at him blankly. Ever since my mom died, his drinking has gotten heavier. In the first few months, he would sneak it, try to keep it to a buzz, and stay away from me. His attempts to hide it from me failed. I could smell the alcohol lingering from room to room. Sometimes, I could hear him crying outside my door when I pretended to be asleep, his efforts failing in trying to keep that quiet, too. But as time went on, he started to care less. He would bring a six-pack home after work and stick it in the fridge as if it was a gallon of milk. His drink of choice at dinner was Miller Light, and bottlecaps began to litter our kitchen. Over time, one drink wasn't enough, so he moved to two. Then three. Then it wasn't uncommon for him to drink an entire six-pack in one night.

Now, I'm not entirely innocent; I also had my fair share of drinking nights. Friday nights after the football games, when everyone was gone and our team was packing to leave, we would stay and hang out under the bleachers and drink whatever we could get our hands on. The coaches always turned a blind eye. Saturday night house parties were always stocked with free booze. But in there lies a rule to myself- only drink on weekends. I hated the way I felt at school after a night of drinking. Once I was done with school or football on Fridays, I could let myself go. And unlike my father, I didn't hide it. He knew some of his drinks would go missing, and he didn't care enough to say anything to me or to put an end to it. Like a good parent would've.

His head fell between his shoulders as he ran his hand through his hair, resting it on the back of his neck. "Sorry." The word came out in a mumble, barely audible.

A quiet huff escaped me as I turned to go. He was right, he was an adult, the parent, whatever, and he could decide where he wanted to sleep and what he wanted to do with his time. I had other things on my mind and wasn't in the mood to start arguing with him.

After climbing the staircase two steps at a time, I came to my bedroom, the second door on the left. My bed was still half made, untouched from earlier when Parker woke me. I took my shirt off, climbed in, and looked up at the ceiling.

My eyes refused to shut, snapping back open like rubber bands every time I tried to sleep.

Looking up at the fan, I watched as it spun, the blades creating a light breeze around me.

And at that moment, lying alone in my bed, my life felt like it was cut.

Split in two.

It was a simple before, with the kiss from Eve marked as the point my after began.

ANNA

AUGUST 31, 2021

The door to Diesel's apartment closed behind me as my steps followed close to his. The living room, on the left as soon as you entered, was bigger than it looked from the road below.

Heat rose up my neck and to my cheeks at the thought of picturing the inside of his apartment after only meeting him one time.

Khaki-colored paint lined the walls and a wooden ceiling fan spun slowly above. The kitchen was small, located to the right of the front door, with a few cabinets floating above a decent amount of counter space and an island planted in the middle. Past the kitchen were three doors, one I assumed was a bathroom, and the other two spaced far enough apart that they were probably bedrooms. All the walls had perfect white trim that ran along the floor, which was a beautiful, old-fashioned hardwood.

"Wow, this is a really nice apartment."

"It is." His back was to me as he placed the beer on the kitchen counter. He opened the fridge and began putting the individual bottles inside.

"How long have you lived here?" I asked as I looked around, my eyes floating over to the glass door that housed the balcony.

"About five years. It's close to my work. It's a hole in the wall in this town. No one ever drives by, so no one knows about it."

I snorted. "Well, I wouldn't say that no one ever drives by…" The words, accompanied by a quiet laugh, escaped me before I could stop them. I couldn't help it, it's my coping mechanism. I like to make light of my situations. The last thing I want is for people to tiptoe around me for the rest of my life.

I turned to face him as he shut the fridge and remained at the counter, his back still to me, without a single response.

Okay, awkward.

"I'm kidding," I said, trying to cover my tracks.

With no response, he ignored that, too.

I turned back to look at the living room, casually walking along the wall, my fingers tracing the edge of the tv stand next to me. I brushed off my poor joke and tried again.

"So, Mrs. Reeves wants to rent out the apartments? I imagine it won't take long for someone to move in since they're so nice inside."

Diesel turned, watching me speak as he walked to his couch and sat down, beginning to untie his work boots. "No one's moving in." Spoken as a matter of fact.

I stopped. "What?"

"There is no ad." He slid off his left boot.

"But she said—"

"I know what she said. She asked me to put an ad out for this place. She doesn't know how to work all the new renting apps, or anything on the internet, really. I told her I would, but I didn't. They're not ready."

"What do you mean?"

He slid off his other boot, then leaned forward and rested his elbows on his knees. "The apartments aren't up to code. Not yet, at least. She walks in and sees fresh paint and new trim and thinks everything's ready, but she doesn't see all the electrical issues and the leak in the pipes that I still have to fix."

I narrowed my eyes. "Is this what you do for a living?"

"Not here, no."

"Then why do *you* have to fix it?" I realized I was pestering him with a lot of questions, but I didn't care. It puzzled me, but I also liked getting to know the mystery behind him.

"Ever since her husband died, I've been doing all the maintenance work. Fixing the place up. All the odds and ends. Whatever's needed."

"No, I mean, why don't you guys hire someone to do all that?"

His shoulders straightened as his spine went rigid. "It's complicated," he bit out, and that was that.

I picked up on his abrupt answer and moved along. "So, it's just you two? In this whole building?" I asked, trying to keep a small distance from him, even though there was a magnetic pull bringing me closer. I stepped toward him without even realizing it.

"You know, you ask a lot of questions." He stood and walked to the kitchen, grabbing a beer out of the fridge from the set I brought. With a quick, fluid motion, his hand slammed the top of the bottle on the corner of the kitchen island, sending the bottlecap spinning. It was a trick I'd seen done dozens of times, but the ease of his ways sent a shiver through my chest. Part of me wanted to call him out and tell him that he would end up leaving scratches in the countertop, but I'm sure he'd just tell me he would fix it himself.

He turned to hand the bottle to me, my fingertips grazing his as I took it. He opened another bottle for himself. "But yes, it's just us until everything's ready. But for now, I enjoy the quiet. I don't want to deal with other people's shit when I come home from work."

"Like mine?" I joked.

"Like yours." A hint of a smile graced his lips but vanished as quickly as it appeared.

I took a sip of my drink and sat on the couch, the brown cushions comfortably caving under my legs as I tucked them beneath me. "So, what do you actually do then? Why do you come home covered in so much dirt?" I asked as I pointed to his grey t-shirt.

He looked down at the streak of black across his chest, just now noticing the dirt. "I own a construction company."

"Wow." I raised my eyebrows. "That's a huge accomplishment."

Looking past all the dirt, to the lines etched into his face and the creases in his forehead, I would guess he was in his mid-twenties, and owning a business that young was an enormous feat. But with the slow nod of his head and his drifting eyes, it seemed to be another subject he didn't want to explore. And with this being one of our first real conversations, his disposition cold enough as is, I wasn't going to push the topic.

I stood to my feet, taking another quick sip of the beer before setting it down. His gaze watched me, studied me, as I padded to the balcony doors. I looked over my shoulder at him, grabbing the handle of the door.

"May I?"

He gave a single nod, and I slid the door open. Summer air rushed against my skin and my lungs instantly inhaled as a breeze covered me. I stepped over the threshold, walked to the railing, and rested my palms on the cool metal. The trees swayed, the leaves danced, and everything around me was quiet and soft. I could see what he meant, why he likes it here.

As much as I like to joke around about the accident, I found myself short of breath on the balcony. Everything was different up here. The air was softer, the views were clearer, and the comfort of the apartment behind me acted as a safety net. Up here, I felt serene, away from the memory of the chaos below me. It also helped that the small amount of alcohol that was simmering inside me gave me the courage to look down, to see the road from what would have been Diesel's vantage point. I blinked, and for a second, I saw myself lying there, helpless, alone, bleeding, but when I blinked again, the road was empty.

A sudden onset of heat coated my back, and I knew Diesel was standing behind me. My chest began to heave in fragments, my body trying to catch its breath in an attempt to keep me alive. Just the feeling of his presence was enough to send me into a tailspin.

He stayed behind me for what felt like an hour, but was probably closer to a minute before I couldn't take it anymore.

It was just me and him now, face to face in my vulnerability.

"Was it bad?" I asked through a whisper, turning around completely to face him, my back against the railing, my hair catching in the wind.

"Do you really want to know?" he asked, a crease forming in his eyebrows.

I nodded, even though I suddenly wasn't sure that was true. I was fine with never knowing the details, with the cut on my forehead being enough of a reminder. But I also wanted to know what it was like for him, to dive deeper than what was written on the police report. I wanted to know how he felt, what he did in each moment, and what I looked like to him.

I wanted his truth.

He put both hands on either side of me, caging me in, leaning close to my ear. The smell of wood and musk overtook me, my senses tingling, aching for more.

"I took care of it."

His breath was warm on my skin, sending chills down my neck, and my eyes closed at the sound of his harsh voice so close to me. He hovered over me for a minute, our bodies so close that the breeze couldn't fit between us. Adrenaline kicked in, pumping through my veins as I stood between him and the road below, suddenly hyperaware of the spot where I almost died. I tipped my head back, just a fraction of an inch, indulging in the rise of my heartbeat, replaying his words over in my head.

He took care of it.

He took care of it.

He took care of *me*.

He wasn't playing coy anymore and he wasn't being modest. He was finally admitting that he had a role in saving me. And now, I caught the sense that there was more to it than what he said. But his words, soft yet firm, felt like they were meant for only me, a secret never to leave the space between us. His sentence was so simple, but I could hear the need in his voice, the way his phrase lingered on the tip of his tongue, leading me to believe there was a deeper meaning, something he wasn't telling me.

He took care of it.

I opened my eyes to see him standing straight, keeping one arm on the railing. The other arm reached up, his fingertips grazing my forehead, his electric touch lining my stitches. It was a good feeling, like warming your cold hands by a fireplace, or stretching when you wake up in the morning. The movement sent heat down to the pit of my stomach and between my legs.

Bending my knee, I went to take a step forward, moving in closer to him. With a swift motion, as if I was on fire, he dropped his hand and turned slightly to the side, opening a path back to the inside of the apartment. Just as my body was beginning to warm up, something in him snapped, forcing us both out of the intensity we were sharing, the feeling fleeting.

I must've misread the room because the look in his eyes led me in a completely different direction.

He cleared his throat, ignoring the embarrassment written across my face. "If you ever feel like taking a walk, or can't sleep, let me know. Chances are, I'll be up."

Snaking his arm behind me, he pulled my phone out of my back pocket, his eyes moving down to my lips, which parted slightly at his forwardness. He unlocked my phone, typed his number in as a new contact, and placed the phone back in my pocket.

I stared at him, utterly confused. What was this game he was playing? Why were his eyes saying something different from his body? I knew he felt what I was feeling, I could see it. But why wasn't he seizing the opportunity? Maybe it was too soon, maybe things were going too fast, but I've never known a guy to stop something before it started because it was moving too quickly.

Whatever it was, whatever was going on in his head, it was giving me emotional whiplash.

I took the hint, his body still standing off to the side, and walked past him back into the apartment, straight to the front door. I didn't want things to end on a bad note, especially since I had no idea what he was thinking, so I turned to face him as I opened the door.

"Thanks, Diesel."

For what, I wasn't sure. Saving me? I had already thanked him a handful of times. Inviting me in for a drink? Maybe. But after the words left my mouth, I tried to read him, to see if there was any emotion he was willing to give me, but his face stayed blank with no response. I went to close the door, and there was a small glimmer of hope deep inside me that wished he would stop me from leaving, or even follow me out of the apartment.

He didn't.

THOMAS

"Dad! I made some bacon!" I yelled from the bottom of the stairs up toward the second story. There was no answer, no sound except the sizzle of the bacon in the kitchen.

"Dad?"

Heading back to the stove, I double-checked the clock on the microwave. 7:28 am. I knew there were only a few places he could be.

One, he would be sleeping upstairs or on the living room couch. My memory had no picture of him sleeping on the couch this morning, but I checked anyway.

He wasn't there.

My call upstairs was left unanswered, and I didn't hear him come in during the night, but I headed up to the bedroom anyway. He wasn't there either. The bed was still made, pillows untouched, meaning he didn't sleep there at all last night.

Two, he could be at work early, but I could count the number of times he's done that on one hand. If he wakes up with the sun up his ass and feels like putting in some sort of effort, he sends me a text or leaves a note. I checked my phone- no text, and I looked around the kitchen- no note.

Three, he was with another woman, and I'd put my money on that guess. He started dating again about six months after my mom passed, which surprised me, being so soon. But then again, we barely talked anymore, and I had no idea if he was ready to move on or not. One day, he went out after work with the guys, met someone, brought her home and tried to sneak her upstairs. But the loud stumbling of his drunken steps and the thumping of his headboard were doing a shitty job of keeping it hidden.

The last girl he brought here walked into the kitchen the morning after their fun, asking me for a cup of coffee, only for me to turn around and see it was a girl I graduated high school with, sending me to the darkest depths of mental hell. Since then, he never brought another woman home, but instead went to their place. When he would come home in the morning, if he made it here at all, the smell of faded perfume trailing behind him and the smudged lipstick on his neck told me more than I wanted to know.

As I flipped the bacon, I tried to file my brain, recalling the last time I talked to him.

Yesterday afternoon, we were both leaving the warehouse, his smile as bright as the sky.

"Hey, I'm going to meet up with some of the guys down the road." His arms rested on the hood of the dark blue Honda Accord as I stood at the front of my truck. I assumed he meant he was going to The 87, a locally-owned pub just down the street from the warehouse. It had the best burger in Kittanning, and it was so hidden that only the people that lived here knew about it. Everyone here would do anything to keep it that way.

"I'll probably be home late and catch you in the morning."

I nodded, trying to force a smile out, knowing what his true plans probably are.

"You alright?" he asked, the sun shining on his face causing him to squint one eye shut.

"Yeah, Dad. I'm fine," I replied without looking, the driver's door squealing as I opened it and climbed in. The truth was, I was tired of my dad always going out and drinking. I don't care if he has a beer or two, I don't care who he's fucking, but the constant hangovers combined with picking up his slack at work made my days heavier. My dad was the boss, but as of late, I was the one who was present at work, who was answering everyone's questions, and who was calling the shots. It was a job for someone with more experience, not a kid whose twentieth birthday is in six hours.

"I'll see you tomorrow."

My truck turned on with a roar. I checked around me before reversing and peeling out of the parking lot. The sun was hot, feeling as if it was searing into me through the windows, my dad's eyes feeling the same as he watched me over his shoulder.

I pulled my phone out of my pocket again, the screen lighting up with no new messages. With a quick tap on the screen, I called my dad's phone. It went straight to voicemail. Sitting down at the kitchen table, I grabbed a piece of bacon and bit into the crunch, annoyed that this was another day I would have to take his workload until he could find the strength to stroll in at lunchtime and hide away in his office. All he would have to do is flash his million-dollar smile or rub elbows with the guys to make up for it. The guys at work never felt an issue with my dad not showing up, because if he wasn't there, the responsibility fell to me. I carried the weight of the business without the pay or title to back it up.

But the thing is, as aggravating as he can be, he's a good boss when he's intentionally productive. Our business never struggled, the company makes good money, and we always have projects. That's because of Jackson Diesel and what used to be his incredible push. The houses we build are fucking *flawless*. People hire us year-round, even when we have to dig through three feet of snow every morning, all because they want the nicest house on the block. The buildings we renovate are always top-notch. It's not long before word spreads between businesses and we get calls from other places to do the same thing. Since we have a good reputation, our employees are always working their asses off, which in turn makes them good money. No one ever complains.

Right in the middle of my third piece of bacon, my phone rang, and a jumble of numbers appeared on my screen. The number looked unfamiliar, but it was local, so I accepted the call and pressed the phone to my ear. Before I could even speak, an automated voice came through.

I pushed my head back on my chair and closed my eyes.

You've got to be fucking kidding me.

ANNA

"I don't know, Olivia. It was weird. He seemed to be..." I struggled to find the right word. He was confusing. One minute he was giving me short, clipped answers, the next, he was whispering in my ear, his body heat covering me. I wasn't sure if his actions were because of me, because of the accident, or because of something else entirely. I had spent the past three nights thinking about it, dissecting everything I could remember, tossing and turning at the thought of him.

His eyes, his hands, his arms, his lips, everything, sending heat through every part of me.

I had wanted to kiss him, and for a moment, I thought he wanted that too.

But when he backed away from me, I couldn't help but feel like I misjudged the moment.

I sat in the client chair at my beauty station, with Olivia seated at the station to the right of mine. After learning more about the specialty of men's haircuts, all while powering through another headache, the class was finally done for the day. All the other students had left, giving myself and Olivia the space to talk freely about whatever we wanted. Our teacher didn't mind if we stayed after class as long as we left before she did. Considering the fact that she was in the back of the room doing paperwork, we seemed to have plenty of time.

I slid my back down the chair as the bottoms of my shoes pressed against the edge of the countertop, the chair swiveling slowly as a rhythmic comfort.

And I told her everything about that night.

Olivia crossed her arms over her chest, facing me while leaning back in her chair, her brown-eyed glare more piercing than ever. "Anna, I want you to stop and think about this. Really hard." She crossed her long legs at the knee, not a single crease in her light-wash jeans. She had legs that gave every supermodel a run for their money.

"I have. Trust me, I have."

"You think things were moving 'too fast' for him when there are other guys out there who would fuck you after knowing you for ten minutes?"

I rolled my eyes, letting my head roll with them. "Not all guys are like that, Olivia."

"No, you're right. But you guys have this weird connection, right?"

I stayed quiet, digesting her question.

"You felt something with him? And you saw the look in his eyes that said the same?"

My mind reeled back to his balcony. When he came up to me, his arms close to me, his lips close to my ear.

I took care of it.

My body shivered, wishing I could be back in that moment again.

I snapped out of the memory, my eyes flicking to the hair tools scattered on the counter. Cutting shears, curling irons, blow dryers, and a round brush, all waiting to be packed away where they belong. I shrugged instead of replying, my mind toying with the idea of uncertainty and apprehension, and that maybe my expectations of Diesel were too high. Olivia sighed, and I knew there was a library of lectures stored away in her brain, waiting to be used the second I expressed any insecurity in myself or my life. It was nice to hear someone care enough about me to give me that kind of pep talk, but right now, I liked her calmness more.

"Listen, I'm not saying you need to fuck him right away," Olivia snipped, gathering her things and placing them in her bag. "But you should at least text him."

I paused and looked at her. "I think he has better things to do on a Friday night."

She got up and turned on her heel to leave. "Fine. If you don't want to take that chance, that's up to you. But do me a favor and find out if he has a brother."

I couldn't help but laugh, resting my head on the back of the chair.

"Or a sister." She lifted her shoulder to her chin, a devious smile spread upon her face as she stepped out of the building, her floral perfume like a cloud following her.

I sighed, my smile fading as I looked back to my workstation, trying to find some energy to clean up and leave. Olivia was right, we have a connection, something I've never felt before and something that couldn't be explained. I saw it when I looked at him and I felt it in his energy. Rejected kiss and hurt pride aside, I knew I wanted to text him and talk to him again. It was all a matter of getting the courage to do it.

I rubbed the color out of my eyes, my fingertips squeezing them back into my head, my vision turning into a starry shade of black for a few seconds. I organized my area, packed up my bag, and left.

It was Sunday night before I became brave enough to text Diesel. My mind replayed the conversation with Mrs. Reeves and his mention of Sunday being his day off, and I figured my chances would be higher to catch him at a time when he wasn't busy.

As I sat on the side of my bed, I pulled out my phone and opened a blank text box with his name, staring at the blinking line for longer than I should've. There were so many things I wanted to say to him, to ask him and talk to him about. I decided to give it another chance. I owed myself that much.

Me: Up for a walk?

I pressed send and placed the phone in my lap, unable to look at what I'd just done. My heart was racing. What if I scared him off with the way I acted before? What if he thinks I'm crazy? I bit the tip of my thumb with anticipation, and only thirty seconds passed before I felt my phone vibrate.

Diesel: Give me your address. I can be ready in 15.

A smile beamed across my face as I felt my nose scrunch in delight. Maybe I didn't scare him off completely. I typed in my address and hit send. I slid on black leggings and pulled a black sweater over my head. Even though it was the end of August, and the sun had another hour or so before it would fully dip under the horizon, the Pennsylvania nights could get chilly. I tried to smooth my hair, bringing it to the right side of my neck and letting it drape over my shoulder, my hand forcing some strands to cover the stitches on my forehead. Then, I did my best to fix my makeup, adding a thin layer of mascara and blush to my cheeks. I headed for the door, slipping into my sneakers and locking the deadbolt behind me.

The cement stairs descending from the main door of my apartment complex were a perfect place to wait for Diesel. His apartment was only a mile from mine, so his drive over shouldn't take long.

The stairs led out to a side street sprinkled with streetlights. It wasn't busy unless you were cutting through to Main Street or driving to someone who lived here. It was the perfect balance of hidden and exposed.

I sat on the second step down from the top, rubbing my hands on my legs as I waited.

After a few minutes, an old, grey pickup truck drove down the road, pulling to the curb and stopping at the base of the steps. Stepping out of the truck, he walked around the front and opened up the passenger door.

"Get in." He motioned with a tilt of his head, his eyes trailing me up and down. A quick flash of something unreadable crossed his face but he pushed it away without thought.

After a moment of hesitation on my end, he sighed and continued. "I want to show you something."

I stood up, brushed debris off my leggings, walked down to the truck, and climbed inside. He was wearing a dark grey hoodie and dark-wash blue jeans with boots. I noticed the hem of a white shirt poking out of his collar, contrasting the skin of his defined throat. His short, light brown hair was gently mussed, looking soft, like it was just washed. He closed the door for me once I was fully inside with my legs tucked in.

The truck was clean and nicely kept, even for an older model, and the seats were surprisingly comfortable. The black leather was smooth under my touch, with no tears or rips, and even though the padding was worn in with age, it cradled me nicely. I buckled the seatbelt and turned to look at him, only to see that he was already sitting inside, watching me.

"What?" A flash of insecurity surrounded me, my cheeks growing warm.

"You know," he said, one hand gripping the steering wheel while the other had a hold on the shifter. "If you're going to go out for walks, you probably shouldn't dress in all black."

I looked down at my clothes, black on black, and with a smirk, I realized he was right. On the night of the accident, I wasn't thinking twice about what I was wearing. Tonight, I wanted to be comfortable but still look somewhat cute, never considering the fact that we would be out at night. But when Diesel pulled out into the road and I turned to tell him he was right, I realized he was in the same boat.

"You're wearing dark clothes too."

He stole a glance at me, then looked back to the road. "I never planned on taking a walk."

My skin flushed, and the beat of my heart quickened, unsure of what he had planned.

Turning to look out my side window, I watched unfamiliar small storefronts pass us by.

"Where are we going?"

I could tell he sensed a bit of confusion from me because he asked, "You're not from here, are you?"

"Kittanning? No. I moved here a few months ago. Born and raised in Pittsburgh."

Even though I've grown comfortable here in Kittanning, my heart gave a small squeeze at the thought of my hometown. Growing up in Pittsburgh was fun; there was always something to do and somewhere to go, even in the middle of winter. The baseball, football, and hockey games, the rolling hills with amazing views, the incline, the restaurants, the life of the people, it was all extraordinary. The city will always be rooted in me, a place I call home, with the tall skyline, the busy streets, and the three rivers gliding right through the heart of it all.

The streetlights illuminated the inside of the truck with a warm yellow hue as we continued driving. We reached the town bridge and drove across, taking us over the Alleghany River. It was a river I knew very well, its body beginning up in Northern Pennsylvania and ending in Pittsburgh, my summer nights spent on friends' boats coasting in its drift.

It's strange to think that this river could have connected me to Diesel all this time. I think back to every moment I've brushed my hand through the river, the water falling through my fingers, wondering if he could've been feeling it too.

Once we were on the other side of the bridge, Diesel took the first right and drove into a subdivision, his truck taking the winding roads with ease. The roads led us up a hill to the back lots, home to a series of unfinished houses sitting in a perfect row before us, only the wooden framework standing tall. The houses were huge, almost like miniature versions of the mansions I've seen on the hillsides of Pittsburgh. Diesel pulled the truck up into the dirt next to one of the houses and placed his car in park, the headlights shining on a forest of trees ahead.

"Wow," I said, craning my neck to look up at the top of the houses through the windshield. "This is incredible. Are we allowed to be back here?"

Diesel nodded. "My company is building these houses." He leaned back, allowing me to see past him, and pointed to his left to a sign down the road.

Diesel Construction Co.

A slight laugh escaped me, and my eyebrows raised in disbelief. "Diesel, this is amazing. You build mansions for a living?"

"They're not mansions. They're close, but this is still a suburb. A lot of these houses are just cut-and-paste blueprints. Cookie-cutter houses. Nothing too crazy."

"They must cost a fortune when they're done."

He smirked. "Small fortune."

After I studied the houses for a minute, I leaned back into the seat and asked, "So, why did you bring me here?"

A slight grin flashed on Diesel's face. "Come with me."

Following his lead, I climbed out of the truck and trailed behind him, his steps taking us into the heavily wooded area behind the houses. There was a dirt path, one that was small but easy to follow, taking us through the trees. The sun had officially faded, setting into darkness, only the moon giving any source of light. I watched Diesel's silhouette as a guide, his broad shoulders acting as my compass, his arms pushing and holding branches out of the way. We came upon a clearing as the trees came to an end, and Diesel took one last step up onto a large landing. He turned and reached back for me, grabbing my elbow and helping me climb up. His touch, even from something so small and gentle, gave me goosebumps.

Once I had my feet planted, I looked at the view surrounding me. The river was streaming down below us slowly, the movement of the water so balanced and graceful, the lapping of waves creating a calming tune. The town across the river was quiet as I watched a few cars drive down the roads slowly. There were shops and small buildings with their lights on, glowing streetlights that lit the roads and sidewalks, and traffic lights that switched colors in rotation. All the lights gave the town a captivating warmth, but as I lifted my chin, I noticed they didn't touch the sky.

Suddenly, my breath caught in my throat at the sight.

The stars flooded the cloudless night sky, some dim, some bright, some small, some large. The moon lay next to the hundreds of constellations, gleaming brighter than I ever could've pictured. I smiled to myself, whispering wonders under my breath as the stars swirled together flawlessly.

It was a picture so pure.

It took me a while to pull myself out of the sky and back down to Earth, but when I did, I turned to see Diesel sitting on a large boulder, his hands in his pockets and his legs stretched out.

"Don't get views like this in Pittsburgh, do you?"

I smiled and walked over to the rock, taking a seat next to him. "Well, Pittsburgh has some nice hills. But usually, all the lights from the city drown out the stars." We both sat in stillness and watched the stars as they flickered, creating perfect harmony with one another.

"How did you find this?"

"We had to survey the land to build the houses. There's a good two acres here, just on this one lot, and when I was walking the perimeter, I found this."

"So, whoever buys the house you parked next to will get this, too?"

He nodded, his eyes still watching the sky.

"Wow. That's a big selling point," I said as I pulled my feet up onto the rock, my legs close to my chest, a pause between us. I leaned toward him, so slightly that it was barely noticeable and said, "You should buy it."

He didn't look away from the stars as he said, "There's better out there."

"Better?" I gasped. "Than this view?"

He nodded. "You'd be surprised, Anna."

His voice was filled with secret promises I was itching to know. I kept my face to him, my eyes glimpsing at his full lips as he finally turned to look at me. I caught myself and looked back up to the stars, my cheeks flushed, the tip of my nose also turning red.

Nothing was more annoying to me than my own skin deceiving me, showing someone my true feelings even when I tried to hide them.

I changed the subject. "So, you said your only days off are Sundays? Why do you work so much?"

"Well, technically, I never said I had Sundays off. I just said I'll be home. Sundays are the days I work from home."

"You work *seven* days a week? That sounds like a nightmare."

He exhaled with a smile. "It's not so bad once you get the hang of it."

I squinted my eyes, testing him. "When's the last time you took a day off? And being sick doesn't count."

He paused. "I don't remember."

Okay, his tough exterior was acting as a challenge to me. I knew I had to crack him, to find something human about him.

All work, no play? No way.

"Don't you have anything you like to do in your spare time?"

He shook his head. "No spare time."

"When's the last time you had a nice home-cooked meal?"

"The 87 has incredible burgers if that's what you mean."

I sighed, rolling my eyes. "That's *not* what I mean. But I'm sure they're delicious."

It took less than a second for him to look at me. "You've never had The 87?"

I shook my head.

"Holy shit. Trust me, it's the best burger you'll ever have."

I nudged him with my elbow, noticing how firm his body was. "Don't change the subject. Answer me."

"Last home-cooked meal?" He pondered, looking to the stars as if they held the answer. "Long before the company."

"Diesel," my heart throbbed at his statement, the sympathy cutting through my voice like butter. I felt for him as I lowered my voice. "You can't live like that. That sounds miserable."

He didn't have to look at me for me to know it was true. You don't have to know a person for long to see when a job is weighing them down. It's spelled out in the way they carry themselves. Diesel had a good head on his shoulders, I could tell, but I could see right through his endless lifestyle.

He quickly rubbed a spot above his eye and cleared his throat. "So, how long are you here for?"

"Well, I'm done with beauty school in June. After that, I'm not sure what I'm going to do."

He shot a confused look, as if I was speaking another language. "Beauty school?"

"Yeah, you know, to become a hairdresser."

He didn't respond, and I figured he probably didn't care, but I continued on anyway. "I've always liked it. I always obsessed over my hair in high school, I would dye my friends' hair, and I even gave my dad haircuts when he was in the hospital. It ended up becoming a passion of mine."

I could feel Diesel straighten next to me at the mention of my dad, his body language doing the talking, and I surprised myself at how well I could already understand him.

"My dad died last year. Kidney disease."

"Fuck," Diesel said through an exhale, his body relaxing. "I'm sorry."

I shook my head, shook the thought away, shook the heartache that lingered inside me at all times. It was a pain that was still fresh and taking time to heal.

He must've noticed my evasion to continue on about my dad since I overexplained everything else we've talked about, because he took a deep breath, his brows furrowing as he rubbed the same spot above his eye from before, a simple nervous tic I picked up on.

"I know what it's like. My mom died when I was sixteen. Cancer."

I blinked.

There he was, his defenses lowering, his olive branch extending to me as an act of solidarity and unity. An array of emotions shuffled inside me. Sorrow for the sixteen-year-old boy in Diesel that lost his mom, understanding for the constantly healing version of Diesel that has to live with only one parent, and longing to reach over and hug the current Diesel that was overworked and shut out from the rest of the world.

"Diesel, I…"

I opened my mouth to try to find the right words, but my tongue stumbled with jumbled thoughts. Maybe this is why I felt like we were so connected. We both lost a parent. We felt what it was like to have a lopsided family, to think of the future without them, all the important events they would miss, to feel like time stood still in a life after them. Maybe he felt it in me, the longing for something you could never get back, something you could never replace.

"When you said you were from Pittsburgh," he said, shifting slightly. "It reminded me of her. She used to take me to baseball games when I was younger. My favorite memories are there, in the stadium that overlooks the skyline."

I smiled at the visual of my hometown, knowing exactly what he was referring to. "It's beautiful, isn't it?"

Maybe I missed Pittsburgh more than I realized. My heart tugged.

He didn't answer, his throat moving with a choked swallow, and I knew that was the end of the topic. With his tough exterior, I knew that was more than he was planning on telling me, so I stayed quiet, not pushing, not prying, just sitting with him in silence.

I took a deep breath, my lungs filling with the fresh air I so badly loved, and rested my head on top of my knees that were still pulled up to my chest.

"So, any reason for wanting to go out tonight?" he asked, his face turned up to the sky.

My words felt stuck in me as I wanted to tell him the real reason. I wanted to spend time with him, I wanted to figure him out, and I wanted more of whatever happened on the balcony. I wanted to see if he felt the same spark I did. There was something there, I *felt* it in my bones, like an electric current running through me.

But I wasn't sure if he felt it too.

My mind liked to play games when I was alone, talking myself out of this feeling I get when I'm around him. But when I'm here, standing in front of him, there's no denying the way my breath picks up, my skin tingling at his closeness, everything in me telling me this is true.

I shrugged, it being the best answer I could give him.

I felt him turn and look at me. He wasn't just looking at my face, my skin, or my hair. I could feel him *really* looking at me. Studying me. Reading me.

I swallowed, forcing myself to stay where I was, keeping my body and face straight. He didn't turn away from me as his gaze remained glued to my skin, soon traveling up to my forehead.

"How are you feeling?" he asked, his words slightly above a whisper even though we were completely alone. The velvet in his voice made my knees shake.

"I'm okay. I'm still getting headaches, but they're manageable."

His hand moved to the back of his neck with a shake of his head. "Unbelievable."

"What?"

"You. Surviving."

I shot him a confused look. "I don't think it was *that* bad."

But my mind went back to the conversation with Olivia, who said the same thing. I somehow managed to scrape by with minor injuries, fortunate that it wasn't worse.

I thought of Diesel and the look on his face every time he sees me for the first second, a dash of awe breaking through his mask.

At this point, his whole body turned to face me, his posture straightening, the mood sobering.

"Anna…"

My name in his mouth took all gravity away from me, sending me up to the sky.

His eyes moved back to mine, whisps of my hair sweeping across my face, his hand reaching out and tucking a strand behind my ear, away from my stitches. In that moment, I knew it was something I didn't have to hide from him.

And I knew that this, whatever this was, wasn't one-sided.

I reached up and placed my hand over his as it rested along the side of my face. His ocean blue eyes, vibrant from the moonlight, cut into mine, wide and unblinking in their stare. A shiver ran through my body, my spine holding me as I jolted, whether it was from the air or adrenaline, I wasn't sure. But just in the last few minutes, the temperature had dropped a few degrees, the warmth of his hand in mine reminding me that I didn't dress warm enough for the breeze that was beginning to pick up around us.

He realized it too, because he took my hand, and then the other, and placed them both in his, lowering them to rest on his knee.

"You're freezing."

"I'm okay. Really. We can stay." But the chatter in my teeth contradicted my pleading.

He shook his head at my stubbornness, standing and pulling me to my feet. "I should get you home." He dropped my hands, the sudden cool doing nothing to help, and began to lead me back to his truck.

Maybe he was right, maybe it was time to go, because once I realized I was cold, I couldn't stop thinking about it. But behind Diesel, listening to his footsteps take me through the dark, deserted forest, I grinned. I absolutely love this time of year, the end of summer switching to the beginning of fall, the tips of the leaves crisping and changing color, the earth under our feet turning cold. The days grew shorter but stayed long enough to enjoy, the air smelled of shifting winds and hot coffee, and my favorite sweaters moved to the front of my closet. All things I looked forward to every year.

Upon returning to the unfinished house we began at, we walked to his truck, climbed in from our own sides, and made our way back into town. Along the ride, the only words echoed in the truck were from me- "Your hands are soft for a construction worker," which resulted in him not responding vocally, but instead shooting me a wistful glance, his eyes bright. After a quiet but comfortable drive, we arrived back at the front steps of my apartment complex. Diesel pulled to the curb, placed the truck in park, and stepped out in unison with me. My heart pulsed against my chest, harder than I'd ever felt before. He walked with me up the steps, my feet purposely moving slowly to make this moment last longer. We reached the top and I eyed the door, the slab of steel only one move away from separating us.

Our bodies faced each other.

The beat of my heart never ran so fast.

Here I was, torn between feelings of doubt and pleasure. My mind jumped back to his balcony, where he stepped to the side when I thought he wanted to kiss me. But then I think of tonight, the heat of his palm resting along my face and his look of longing.

For *me*.

I needed to speak before he did, to keep my feet on the ground, stabilizing me.

"Thank you, Diesel. It was beautiful up there. But I don't want you to think I need you to drop everything whenever I text you."

He blinked, and his expression paused.

"I don't want you to feel like you have to, you know, check up on me or anything."

He continued to stare at me, his breathing steady, his lips opening slightly as he finally answered in a whisper.

"Is that what you think this is?"

I didn't know what to think anymore. I was being pulled in multiple directions, and all I wanted was clarity. But as his voice heated, his single step to me not going unnoticed, every shred of doubt I had was being pushed farther away into oblivion.

"You think I feel…obligated?"

I said nothing, looking off to the side before turning back to him, my answer waiting in the quiet, my body silently in panic mode.

He slid his hands into his pockets, his eyes piercing into mine, never faltering.

He took another step toward me, and that was the moment I stopped breathing.

He dipped his chin down and raised his eyebrows, the dark shadows caressing the side of his face like a half-moon.

"That's not why I came here."

My stomach twisted all the way down to my toes.

Our eyes never left each other as his words hung in the air like a vapor, circling me, keeping me still.

My breath sped up, my lungs matching my heart rate.

I matched his whisper. "Then why did you come here?"

I've never felt anything as intimate as our eye contact.

He drew in a sharp breath.

"I think you know why."

Everything around me ceased to exist. Right here, on the top step, it was only me and him. His words felt like an invitation, but I couldn't bring myself to move. It seemed like forever passed before either one of us looked away or said anything.

But then he said two words that ended the night, leaving nothing to explore.

"Goodnight, Anna."

I watched him as he turned and jogged down the steps to the truck, his shoulders tense and tight under his sweatshirt. He moved to the driver-side door, and as he pulled it open, he looked at me one more time, a coy smile playing on his lips.

THOMAS

NOVEMBER 5, 2015

I placed my phone, wallet, and keys into a grey bin and let it slide on the conveyor belt. Holding my breath as I walked through the security arch, the guard looked at me and told me I was good to go. I collected my things and walked to the front desk, sweat forming at the base of my neck. There was an employee just behind the counter, and when she saw me, she opened the glass window.

"Last name?"

Not sure if she meant mine or his, but I guess it didn't matter.

"Diesel."

"Do you have your ID on you?"

I fished the card out of my wallet and handed it to her. She placed it in a scanner, pressed a button, and returned to her computer. She read her screen for a few minutes before speaking again.

"You're here for… Jackson?"

"Yes, ma'am."

She handed my ID back and I placed it in my wallet.

"The guard will escort you back."

I nodded and thanked the woman as I turned to follow the guard. He led me through a wide set of steel doors and into a series of hallways.

It was the first time I'd ever stepped foot in a jail, and now I understand why people say it's depressing. The lighting was a dim yellow and the cement walls were blank and lifeless. What I assumed to be an attorney and her client, confined in handcuffs, walked briskly past me, not making eye contact. I looked at the guard as he brought me to an open room scattered with tables and chairs. He was the same six foot three inches as me, probably in his forties, greying hair cut short to the scalp, and looked to be bored out of his fucking mind.

The guard motioned for me to sit at the table closest to the entrance as he left, exiting through another door on the other side of the room. I leaned back in the hard, plastic chair, the air stifling and stale, and looked around. No one else was in the room, and the only noise was the rattle from the air conditioner on the far wall. After a few minutes of waiting, just as I was about to get up and rip out the air conditioner to make the sound stop, the door swung open. The guard entered with my dad walking next to him. I stood to my feet.

"You have twenty minutes," the guard said as he walked back out. We were alone, but judging by the cameras placed throughout the room, I'm sure people were watching us.

My dad, wearing a tan, short-sleeved jumpsuit, walked to my table, pulled the chair out and sat down, all without making eye contact with me.

"Dad, what the hell?"

He ran his hands over his face, still not saying anything. His eyes were lined with dark circles, his hair was a tangled mess, and he looked like he hadn't slept in days. There were a few cuts along his cheekbones and one on his bottom lip. He crossed his arms on the table.

"Dad, what is going on?" I asked as I finally sat down at the table with him and leaned forward. He looked up at me, and I finally knew why he's been avoiding eye contact. His eyes had a sharp glisten to them, as if he was using all his strength not to cry.

"They didn't tell you?" His voice cracked as he spoke.

"No. I got a call from an automated system telling me your name, inmate number, and visiting hours. I tried calling back for more information, but no one answered, so I came here."

My dad sniffled and cleared his throat, both tell-tale signs that he was trying not to cry. There was no mistaking it since I've heard it hundreds of times.

"What happened?"

There was a long pause, the rattle still running behind me, as he continued to look down at his fumbling hands. He finally took a deep breath before speaking.

"I was, I was driving down Main Street. I, um, had a little too much to drink, you know, with the guys."

In an instant, my hands tightened, knowing exactly where this story was going.

"This, uh, this car just, pulled out in front of me…" His voice trailed off as tears streamed down his face.

I looked down at my fists placed on my lap.

"I didn't stop. I couldn't stop. I tried to swerve, but I think that made it worse."

"God, Dad."

The tears were flowing more freely now as his weeping became louder. "I'm so sorry."

"Are they dead?"

He nodded, his shoulders shaking with his sobs.

I stood up, moved my hands to the top of my head, and began pacing back and forth. Fuck. All I wanted to do was to kick a chair, throw a table, rip that *damn* air conditioner and smash it to the ground, *something* to get this growing, burning rage out of me.

"Dammit. *Dammit!*"

"I'm sorry." He wiped his face again, his damp hands stopping to cover his mouth.

"I'm not the one you need to say sorry to." My voice came out strong, from the depths of my lungs.

A thought passed through my head, and for a moment, I shielded it away from me, out of mind. But I could feel the words clawing up my throat, into my mouth, and out into the open.

"What would Mom think? What would she say to you right now?" My words echoed in the empty room in a harsh rasp.

I could see whatever light was left in his eyes turn off. It was a low blow, as I intended it to be, but killing someone didn't warrant any sympathy in my book. None at all. His face turned sorrowful, even more than it had already been, the rims of his eyes flaring red. He hung his head low and ran a hand through his hair. His scabbed-over knuckles and bruises on his arms were evidence that his body was hurt, but he was healing, unlike the person whose life was taken hours ago.

A minute passed with his eyes still aimed at the floor, and he refused to answer me even though I was never really looking for a response.

I was mad, I was fucking angry. I've put up with so much of my dad's shit in the past few years, ever since my mom died. He had been hurt, so devastated by her death, that the rest of his world came crumbling apart. And in the rubble, in the remains of his broken world, he left me to pick up the pieces, even though that was supposed to be his job. I was broken, too. Losing my mom was the hardest fucking thing I've ever been through. I was sixteen, trying to navigate through high school and football games and graduation and whatever else without a mom to help guide me. I could've easily let it all fall apart. God, it was so *easy* to shut myself in my room, turn up my music, and drown every single thing out.

But I didn't.

I pushed on, knowing she would be heartbroken if I didn't try to keep going. But now, at twenty years old, I was here, sitting across from my dad who was now considered a murderer. I could barely recognize him, not because of his exhaustion or his busted lip, but because he turned into someone I didn't know.

Someone I didn't *want* to know.

I rubbed the stubble on my chin as I chose my words carefully. "How many people were in the car you hit?"

"Just one."

His voice sounded wounded, like a dog that was just scolded.

"Do you know who it was?"

He shook his head. "I saw the paramedics take him out of the car, but that's it. He was older."

"Did he die instantly?"

"I don't know." He sniffled again, and I could tell he was getting tired of all the questions. But if there was anyone he owed answers to, it was me.

I paused, then pressed my palms hard on the table, looking him in the eyes. "You killed someone, Dad. Someone is *gone* because of you."

His eyes began to well up with tears again, but only a single drop fell this time. "I know."

I squeezed my eyes shut and pinched the bridge of my nose. "What am I supposed to tell the guys at work?"

Not a moment of hesitation passed before he answered. "The truth."

Clearly, he's been thinking about this.

His demeanor changed like a switch, and he suddenly straightened his shoulders and voiced his authority, like the boss he had always claimed to be. "I don't want any bullshit stories spreading around. I don't deserve to be painted in a good light. Those guys deserve to know the truth, and they need to hear it from you. Not from the news, the internet, or someone else."

Oh, I get it now. Suddenly, my dad wants to man up and take the high road, to be honest and try to balance out the horrible thing he's done. Of course, it doesn't work that way, but this is one request I can get behind.

"You're right," I say, still leaning onto the table.

Keeping his stance, he lifted his chin and looked up at me. The door on the other side of the room swung open, the guard from earlier coming back. My dad didn't flinch, only stared at me. "There's something else I want to talk to you about."

I blinked, almost rolling my eyes, but the guard cut in before I could react.

"Time's up."

My dad ignored the guard and continued. "I already met with my attorney this morning. We all know how this is going to go in court, and I'm prepared to take the consequences for it. I'm pleading guilty. But there's one thing I need to take care of first."

The guard grabbed his arm, forcing him to stand, my dad stumbling with the chair screeching on the floor.

"I can't run the company from here. I need you to do it. I need you in charge, and I'm prepared to sign things over to you until I'm done here."

My muscles tensed from my feet all the way to the top of my neck as I watched this responsibility drop in front of me so casually, as if this conversation wasn't about to change the rest of my life.

"Me?" I pushed my own finger into my chest, my voice uncontrollably filled with uncertainty. "Me? Why me? Why not one of the guys who already put everything they have into their work? Jim? Darrell?" At this point, I was scrambling to say a name, *any* name of someone I knew that would do a better job with the company than I would.

His answer was simple, as if it was common sense, with no doubt in his mind.

"Your mother would come back to haunt me if I let this business out of the family."

The mention of my mom coming from my dad's mouth froze me, as if he knew her best and knew what she wanted given the situation. But as furious and heated as I was, he was right. She would've wanted to keep it close, keep the business in the grips of our palms, to not let any third party come and fuck it up.

And the fact that my dad was right was more aggravating than anything.

My shoes felt glued to the slick tiled floor as I was rooted to the spot. The guard was becoming impatient, his grip tightening on my dad's bicep, giving a small tug.

"You can do it. I'll take over again after I serve my time."

No response came from my mouth. No response *could.*

The guard led my dad to the door, scanning his ID card to unlock it, while my dad looked back with a hint of a smirk and a wink. "And happy birthday, T."

ANNA

I stared at the mannequin head in the mirror before me, the brown-haired wig draped over the plastic scalp. The haircut was horrendous; the length was uneven, the bangs were pointing out in multiple directions, and the style had no consistency. Squeezing the shears tight in my palm, I could feel the pinch of the curves indenting my skin. I needed to focus. My mind kept wandering up out of my skull, with my eyes refusing to sharpen back to normal vision as I thought about Diesel.

It's been three days since he took me to his construction site to look at the stars. And it's been three days of replaying the way his mouth moved as he said my name, the heat of his hand on mine, if only for a single moment.

A shiver ran through me instinctively.

"Your assignment is to fix the client's hair. Whether it be an incorrect haircut, a color correction, or a combination of both, it's up to you to make the client happy again."

The shears stayed in my hands, the crease pushing deeper as the students around me began working. A presence slid into the space beside me, making me jump out of my trance.

"Hello? Earth to Anna?"

I sighed, grabbing hold of the mannequin head in front of me. "Olivia. Hi."

"Hi? That's it?" She moved between my mannequin and the mirror, forcing me to look at her. "Are you okay? You've barely talked to me the past few days. And I texted you last night and you never answered."

"Sorry." I gave her an apologetic look and then turned back to the task in front of me. "I can explain after class."

She paused, her hands resting on her hips.

"It's him, isn't it?"

"What?"

"He's the one making you all…dazed and confused. It's cute."

I felt the heat rising up to my cheeks. Was it that obvious? "We'll talk later."

Olivia smiled, knowing she was right, and pranced back to her station. Deep breath. All I needed to do was get through class today and then I would allow myself to dwell on everything that happened. It was a habit of mine, to replay and dissect everything I could remember, just so I could relive it again and again. Even bad memories were on repeat in my head at times. It was a sick form of self-torture.

Once class was over, with my mannequin looking better than ever, I gathered all my belongings and packed up. Olivia finished alongside me and met me at the door, ready to leave. We walked out into the late summer heat together, the humidity sticking to my skin.

"Okay, I'm dying. What's going on?"

I laughed. The girl loved being in everyone's business. "Nothing, yet."

"Nothing?" Olivia almost sounded offended. "You made me wait all class to tell me *nothing*?"

Our walk outside was short. Our cars were only a block over from the beauty school, and we reached them before I could explain anything. And since there wasn't much to say yet, I figured everything could wait. But I knew she wouldn't leave me until I gave her a piece of something, any sliver of gossip that she could cling to.

"Okay, okay. I saw him on Sunday night. He was nice."

"And?"

"And that's it."

"Oh, God, Anna. You're killing me." I could practically hear her eye roll as she opened her car door and got inside. I walked to my car, parked directly behind her on the side of the street. She poked her head out the window to yell at me before leaving, her brown hair ruffled as she pushed her sunglasses onto her face. "Please get laid."

"Not with this nasty thing on me!" I pointed to the cut on my forehead. It's been over three weeks since the accident and the wound was healing up nicely. Besides the itching. I did my best to ignore it.

"You think that's going to stop a guy? They like that shit."

I laughed as I sat in the driver's seat and rolled down the window.

Olivia looked back and yelled at me once more. "Hey, whatever is going on, I hope it works out. But promise me you'll stop ignoring my texts."

"Okay! I promise." I shouted back, waved goodbye, and turned the key in the ignition, the engine grunting to life. Olivia pulled out in front of me, heading in the opposite direction I needed to go, with her turning left and myself turning right.

Leaving my window down, I enjoyed the warm air flowing through my hair, the smell of summer's end wrapping around my neck and filling my lungs. Although it was short, my drive home was my favorite part of the day. I passed by a few small shops, a corner cookie store, and a horse ranch, where a half dozen horses were enjoying the weather, too. The small-town feel gave me a warm sense of satisfaction, a sense of belonging, even though I was still mostly unknown to those who lived here. But there was an understanding of community within the town walls, with everyone so welcoming and refreshing.

Within minutes, I pulled into the parking lot of my apartment building, the spot I always park in still empty, waiting for my occupancy. I turned the car off and stepped out, my body freezing as soon as I took a step toward my apartment.

My feet were planted on the pavement, even though I felt as if I was floating.

My eyes were locked as they stared straight ahead, and my instant smile never had a single chance to hide.

There he was, sitting on the bottom step, a brown paper bag in between his feet.

Diesel.

Waiting for me.

"You hungry?"

He grabbed the paper bag and stood to his feet, my eyes catching his freckles that darkened in the piercing sun. I could smell it, the grease wafting through the air around us. It was heavenly. My stomach growled in response.

"Starving. What is it?"

"Burgers. And some fries."

"From the place down the road? The…"

"The 87." He nodded.

I grabbed the bag from his hand, my fingers brushing across his. "Say no more. Want to come up?"

I began to walk up the stairs to the door, only to turn around and see that he was still at the bottom. He shook his head. "I can't. I have so much work to do."

A pang of disappointment pushed into my chest. For a moment, I watched him, his body facing the cars as if he needed to leave, but his shoulders turned to me as if he wanted to stay. Sometimes, body language says more than actual words ever can.

"Enjoy it. Best burgers around."

"Diesel…" My voice rolled his name as I took one step down toward him, then another, and slowly another, until I was only a foot away, a smirk spreading across my face. I could see the breath catch in his lungs as I approached, his vision moving down to my lips, then quickly jumping back up to my eyes.

"You're not going to make me eat alone, are you?"

"Wow." It was the only word I could muster out with a mouthful of burger.

"Right?" Diesel echoed the same satisfaction. I had only taken one bite while he was already halfway through his burger. We sat on the floor of my living room, facing each other, the ground between us covered in scattered napkins. I took one, dabbing the grease from my lips, and went in for another bite, both of us leaning against the couch.

"This is incredible," I said with a hand covering my mouth, hiding my open mouth chewing.

Diesel licked his lips and popped the last piece of his burger in his mouth, the expression on his face wishing he had more. The room was quiet, but only because we were so content with the food and our mouths were busy chewing. Even though there wasn't much talking, this was the first time I could see a shift in him. It wasn't much, since he still had a rough exterior to him, but I could see it. He was beginning to let his guard down, and his facial features were softening. The redness in his cheeks grew the deeper he grinned.

The brown paper bag sat to the side, with grease spots bleeding through in decoration. Diesel picked up the bag and pulled out a small paper bowl of fries, offering them to me.

"The fries aren't as good as the burgers, but they're fries. Can't really screw them up."

I hummed in thought. "I think you're wrong there."

"Oh? How so?"

"Burnt fries. Cold, soggy fries. Sweet potato fries. Fries that have that really crispy outside but hardly any potato on the inside. All awful." I grabbed a fry and bit off a chunk from the top.

"Okay, you've got a point," he said while chewing, looking perfect even when he was eating greasy food.

"So," I began, sticking the rest of the fry in my mouth and swallowing. "a few questions for you, Thomas the Train Diesel."

"Please don't call me that."

"Fine." I scrunched my nose, trying not to laugh at his seriousness. I began again. "Diesel, how did you manage to fit this into your work schedule today? After all, it's only…"

I checked my phone for the time, my pinkie finger tapping the screen.

"…4:56 pm. Seems quite early for you to be done for the day."

He shrugged. "I left early."

My stomach gave no warning before it did a flip. After all that talk about him constantly working and now, he made time for me?

"Are you going to get into trouble with your boss?"

He let out a quiet laugh, those crinkles I love forming in the outer corners of his eyes.

"Next question." His smirk never faded as he ate another fry.

"How did you know I would be here?"

His cheeks flushed as his expression faded with embarrassment. I watched as he rubbed the spot under his eyebrow with his nongreasy hand.

"Lucky guess."

My eyebrows raised in suspicion. "Lucky guess? Are you stalking me, Diesel?"

There was that laugh again. "No, I'm not. If I was, how would I have beat you to your apartment?"

"Stalkers always find a way," I said easily as I took a sip of my pop, my eyes narrowing, still not convinced of his answer. He knows the town better than I do and may know a faster route here. The silence swirled around us. I waited to see if he would really answer the question.

He finally cleared his throat. "I called your school."

I blinked, catching my straw and biting down on the tip.

"The website didn't give the hours, so I called. They told me class ended at 4:30."

My stomach proceeded to somersault as my heart rate sped up. It seemed as if time had stopped as my brain hyper-focused on his answer. He could've easily texted me to find out when I'd be home, but instead, he wanted to surprise me. And not only did he make time for me in his busy schedule, but he *also* took time out of his day to figure out *my* schedule?

No way. No. Way.

This is really happening.

I can *feel* it.

I can feel myself falling.

Deeper and deeper, day by day.

There was an unspoken conversation happening between us, our eyes doing the communicating. He didn't look away, as I didn't either. It was my way of telling him I was grateful for the gesture, and I knew the underlying reason for it all. I *felt* it. He felt it too. I could see it.

Right as I was about to thank him for the food, his phone buzzed on the coffee table a few times. He glanced at the screen, then at me, and I gave him a nod.

"By all means." I motioned for him to answer the call as I placed my drink on the floor and tossed another fry into my mouth.

"Hey," Diesel answered with a calming voice to the person on the other side. I watched as he stood, taking slow steps around my living room, his free hand shoved in his pocket. His stance was powerful, the demeanor of a man in charge, and I couldn't help but notice how incredibly sexy it was. I tried to listen to what he was saying, but all I could pay attention to was something about supplies needed. Everything else was a jumbled mess lost in the room as I stared at his arms. The muscles were perfectly formed, the sleeves of his navy-blue t-shirt wrapping tightly around his biceps, the veins guiding my eyes in a trail to his hands. Wondering down to his stomach, I could only imagine how chiseled his muscles were under his shirt. My thoughts were cut short as he said goodbye and hung up the call, placing his phone in his pocket.

"I have to go. The guys need more supplies, and I have to go sign off on them now, so they'll be ready by morning." He took a few strides toward me, stopping directly in front of where I was sitting.

I wiped my hands on a napkin and nodded. "Okay. Thank you for this, Diesel. This was really sweet."

He continued to stand in front of me, looking down with a gaze I'd come to memorize. His stare was full of awe and wonder, as if I was a famous painting he was seeing for the first time. It was the kind of attention I've craved my whole life. He waited a beat, then extended his hand to me, an invitation to feel his touch.

My eyes dropped to the motion as he reached for me, his palm turned upward, and his fingers gently bent.

"Come with me."

The words took me off guard, the stutter in my voice a giveaway. "To… work?" I didn't wait for his answer before I grabbed his hand, using it to pull myself up off the floor.

He nodded.

My mind was racing. He was offering to extend our time together, something I wanted since the moment I saw him today. He was willing to let me into his world, the place where he spends almost all his time, the business that filled every day of his life.

I didn't need to be convinced.

"Let's go."

THOMAS

The same day I visited him, after he told me what had happened, I left the jail and went straight to work. He was right; the guys there deserved to know what happened, to hear it from me, rather than hearing it from the news or the internet.

No bullshit.

I arrived during their lunch break, their fluorescent yellow shirts shining brighter than the sun. I was slow to walk up to the construction site, my steps heavy, my eyes weary and tired. I stopped right at a yellow spray-painted line in the dirt, marking what would be the top of the driveway. My hand brushed against the stubble across my jaw while my other hand rested on the belt of my jeans. I wasn't sure how to go about this. I've never been in a position like this, where I had to break the news to someone. These people depended on me, had families to care for, and needed this job to survive. Of course, their jobs weren't in jeopardy, but it was a serious responsibility to watch over.

As soon as they noticed me, they stopped their jokes, quieted their laughter, and gave me their full attention. It wasn't uncommon for me to visit them as they worked, but the fact that I stood there without joining in on the work or banter had them at a standstill. After I told them what had happened, the atmosphere instantly changed, becoming more somber by the second. Letting them know that my dad was now considered a murderer wasn't something that simply rolled off the tongue. And for some of the guys, the ones who were with him last night, the news was weighing heavy on them. I could see it in their stance and their expressions, but it wasn't their fault, not in the slightest, and I made sure they knew that.

And even though telling them I was filling his position as the owner was uncomfortable, with most of the guys twenty years older than me, they simply accepted it, no questions asked. I respected them, all of them, from the supervisors down to the grunt workers, so their approval of me mattered. They asked a few questions, trying to get more detail as to what happened, wondering if my dad would ever come back after he was released. But in the end, they were supportive of me and the new role I was about to take on. I had been more hands-on in the last two years than my dad had been in the past four, which now played in my favor.

With the guys wishing me a happy birthday on my way out, I exhaled my relief as I walked back to my truck, thankful it was over. I climbed inside, started the engine, and looked back to the worksite. They were back to work, hauling up more wood for the framework, the weather unusually perfect for November in Pennsylvania.

At that moment, I knew this was where I would be for the rest of my life. I knew I had to take care of these employees by showing them the same compassion they showed me during this shitshow.

I drove back home, hoping to shower and temporarily hide from anyone who knew my dad. Which, in this painfully small town, was everyone. I had already told enough people the real story, and word travels fast around here, so I'm sure everyone will know within the next couple of days.

As I walked into the house, the walls were quiet and still. I closed the door behind me and leaned against it. My head tilted back, resting against the wood, as I rubbed my eyes with my hands.

Everything has changed.

I was barely out of high school, the cap and gown still in my closet from my graduation less than two years ago, and hardly qualified for this. Maybe if I paid more attention in economics class, instead of fighting every desire to fall asleep, I could be more prepared for this. But then again, I don't think even the teachers would know where to start if a company fell into their laps with no warning whatsoever.

I pulled my phone out of my back pocket and searched Google. There it was, the very first thing to show up, my stomach folding in on itself. The news article, posted by a local news station, explained it all. Curiosity got the best of me as I clicked on the link. The journalist got most of the facts right: yes, it was on Main Street, yes, there was a deadly collision, and yes, my dad was drunk, well past his limit.

I can't wrap my head around people who drive drunk in a time when Uber fucking exists.

Reading on, I searched for the victim's name, hoping for some sort of new information. The article stated it was a sixty-eight-year-old man, but no name was released, since the accident only happened last night.

His family might not even know yet.

Fuck.

I would have to wait a bit longer for an answer. But then another sentence stopped me from scrolling and made me straighten up, my spine tightening as I fisted my phone.

I read it, then reread it, and reread it again.

"The passenger of the oncoming car was also intoxicated, suffering minor injuries, and taken to a hospital for evaluation."

Passenger?

Someone was with my dad?

How the fuck did I miss that?

ANNA

We pulled up to a warehouse on the other side of town, the building as tall as the trees and the outside painted a dark grey. There were a few trucks lined up next to us as we slid into a parking space near the door. I moved in my seat awkwardly, not because I was uncomfortable, but because I wasn't sure how to read the situation.

"So, should I… wait here?"

"What?" He furrowed his eyebrows as he shifted the truck into park. "No. Come in."

I undid my seatbelt and followed him. The building was more extensive than it seemed on the outside. There were aisles of building materials, hundreds of planks of wood in all sizes, a station with all kinds of tools, and even a section with doors waiting to be installed. The place smelled of dust and wood shavings, tickling the inside of my nose.

"Are you sure you don't own a Home Depot?"

Diesel threw his head back and laughed. "With the amount of money I've spent there in my life, I *should* own one."

Following his steps closely, he led me to the left side of the building, opening the door to his office. There was a desk, worn and old, the metal rusting at the bottom of its legs, a small black chair accompanying it. On the desk, there was a desktop computer that looked to be over ten years old, the keyboard and mouse connected to it with a frayed wire. The walls were stark white, my pupils aching as they dilated from the bright blandness. Diesel walked over to his desk, sat down in the chair, and picked up a couple of papers that were left on his desk. I tilted my head, confused as to why he had such a run-down office. It wasn't falling apart, but it definitely didn't look comfortable. Maybe he didn't spend much time here, with most of the day working on-site, not feeling a need to have a fancy office. It was plausible, but then I saw the stack of papers to the side and realized there was no way he *doesn't* spend a good chunk of time here. Plus, I know he makes good money since he's the only construction company in town, so I know that's not the issue. My guess is he puts everything else first, with himself and his office last on his list of things to worry about.

Trying to pass the time, I walked around the office, but there wasn't much to explore since it was so small. I stepped out, feeling Diesel's gaze on me, letting my legs take me where my mind wanted to wander, trailing my fingers along the aisles as I studied everything. It was all foreign to me, a new language that I've never needed to know. Measurements and blueprints, drywall and insulation, tile and cement. Being here was like being in a world that I was unfamiliar with, a career that I never paid attention to until now.

After spending a decent chunk of time out of the office, I came back in and stood at the far wall directly across from him. I rested my back against it, with the door off to my right, tucking my arms behind me.

There was something in the way he worked. I couldn't help but notice a little crease in his forehead as he read intensely, his fingers holding the very edge of the papers, my heart doing a little leap at his small quirks. I bit the inside of my cheek, trying my hardest not to show a smile.

After a few minutes, Diesel took a deep breath and sighed. "I can't do this."

My stomach dropped. "Do what?"

He dropped the papers back on his desk, tossing a pen down with them, and leaned back in his chair as his arms crossed over his chest. His muscles pushed out through the sleeves of his shirt. "I can't focus when you're standing there, watching me."

Normally, I would take a statement like that and assume the person would want me to leave. But as soon as his eyes met mine, I felt the desire from him spread down my legs. It was an invitation. Our eyes stayed connected as I cocked my head to the side.

"I can go, if you want."

"No."

Not a second of hesitation. His answer was quick and firm. My breath hitched.

"Hey, Boss." A loud, booming voice came barreling into the office. "Did you check out the papers I left?"

A man, probably in his late forties, walked in without knocking, not noticing me standing on the other side of the door.

"Yeah, Darrell, it's all good."

Diesel picked up his pen, signed his name on some inventory papers, then stood up and handed them back to Darrell.

"Thanks, TD. See you tomorrow." As Darrell turned to leave, he stopped as soon as he saw me. I saw his eyes flick up to my forehead and widen, almost as if he'd seen a ghost. I didn't move as my face curled up with a smirk.

"Boss, you know there's a girl in your office, right?"

Diesel's eyes left Darrell and landed back on me. "Yeah, I know. This is Anna."

"Nice to meet you, Anna." He shuffled toward the door, papers tight in his grip, lifting his hand in a swift wave.

"Same to you." I smiled as he exited, shutting the door behind him.

Diesel still stood behind his desk, his set of fingertips brushing along the surface. Although he didn't move, I could see the debate weighing on him to say something, his chest rising and falling with each breath. He pressed his lips together. All of the looks he gave me, the way he says my name, the craving for me to stay with him, it was clear.

It was more than just desire, it was a need to dive into the connection we shared that neither one of us could come close to explaining.

My eyes shifted back and forth, waiting for him to say something. "What?"

It was like my voice broke some sort of seal, a barrier in his mind, because without missing a beat, Diesel walked around his desk, his stride toward me strong. He didn't say a single word as he closed the gap between us, his eyes sharp and never leaving mine. I could see a hint of daze swimming in his deep blue irises, a need, a want for more.

He brought one hand up, his palm flat on the wall behind me, keeping me rooted to the spot. His other hand pressed under my chin, lifting it, my throat stretched and exposed like a wolf's prey. My heartbeat became faster with each second, unsure what his next move would be. I watched his eyes move down to my lips, my gaze heated under my hooded eyelids, his thumb trailing along my bottom lip.

Back and forth, it ran along my skin, slowly, heavily, with each movement sending me deeper into his clutches.

There wasn't a single part of my body that wasn't in a tremble. The heat from his chest radiated onto me, mixing with the warmth that was growing inside me. Just a simple touch from him gave me goosebumps, almost as if a shock ran through my body, aching for more.

"I'm headin' out, Boss." Darrell's voice echoed through the warehouse. His heavy footsteps passed the office door and made their way outside. Diesel never broke his gaze with me, never said anything back. I could feel my heartbeat in my throat as I swallowed, my pulse making its way down between my legs, the area slick and wet.

Finally, he dropped both his hands and took a step backward.

"Ready to go?" His voice was solid, without even a hint of a quiver.

The sudden change had me frozen. It was as if he had broken out of a trance, sucking me out with him. I was afraid to answer because I knew my voice would shake, so I simply nodded. He made his way back to his desk, pretending to fumble around with some papers. Or maybe he was actually straightening things up, I'm not sure. I was too engulfed in my own feelings to care.

The moment he turned his back to me, I brought my own fingertips to my lip, the feeling of his thumb still lingering. After a minute, he casually made his way to the office door and swung it open, allowing me to step through first, both of us quiet. He switched off the lights, both in his office and the rest of the warehouse, and we walked out the main door as he locked up.

I did my best to remain neutral, even though my system was in overload and my knees still felt weak with each step.

The air outside had a bite to it. My arms instinctively crossed over my chest as the wind grazed against my skin, bringing goosebumps to the surface. There were no words spoken between us, the silence deafening in my ears, as we made our way to his truck. He opened the passenger door for me and I climbed inside, then he walked around the hood and made his way in as well.

More silence, more eye contact, all part of a song and dance that I've come to expect.

I didn't feel like entertaining this anymore, so I looked down at the bandage on my sprained wrist, pulling the corners off and placing them back on repetitively. The truck started, and I had no desire to talk on the ride home. He must not have either, because the wind thrashing through the windows was the only soundtrack playing on the drive. My mind was still spinning in circles, and the mixed signals he was giving me were throwing me in a loop. I watched the town pass by, my thumb still pulling my bandage, my hair dancing against my flushed cheeks.

When we arrived at my apartment building, I expected Diesel to pull up to the steps and drop me off, letting me go back to my place alone. But he surprised me by pulling into a parking spot and turning the truck off.

I looked at him, searching for an explanation as he locked his gaze in my eyes, trying to find the right words to say.

"Anna…"

I squeezed my eyes shut, dropping my chin. I wish he wouldn't say my name. With his dark voice and strong tone, it just sent me back to where I started. Melting in the palm of his hand.

He paused, then sighed. "Can I explain?"

About time.

Finally, I'm brought back to reality, away from the trance he held over me. The truck windows were still down, the breeze passing through the cab from one side out the other, the trees rustling in the distance.

Fearlessness seeped through my words as I lifted my head. "Do you have a girlfriend?"

"No."

"A boyfriend?"

He choked back a laugh. "No."

"A wife?"

"No."

"Then tell me, what's going on here?" Surprised by my own bravery, I asked the question that had been at the forefront of my mind since the moment we met. "Don't act like it's nothing. You brought me food. You took me to look at the stars. I can see it in the way you look at me. Diesel, you just had me against a wall…"

The last word fell off my voice, my confusion rising in my throat like acid.

I could see the muscle in his jaw flex, the bone sharp as he exhaled. For the first time, I could see the emotion in his eyes, the glisten that imitated fear. His eyebrows tilted up as I leaned closer, his lips parting as he tried to speak.

"Anna…" His voice cracked as his body remained frozen. He swallowed, his perfectly sculpted throat sliding up and then down.

I moved closer, the space between us shrinking. There was no centerpiece between our seats, only one connecting bench, so my body easily slid over to his side of the truck. Wind blew my hair across my cheeks. "Tell me."

Reaching out, he brushed his fingertips along my cheek. It was a movement I'd come to expect, but it never lost its power. His eyes trailed up to my forehead, his fingers following close behind. The cut was now entirely scabbed over, the stitches dissolved, and only a bright red, bumpy line was left behind. The feeling of his skin on mine was surreal, like he was a part of me, breathing in me, pulsing through my veins. I closed my eyes, letting the sensation wash over me as he ran his fingers along the scar.

I wanted this *so badly.*

"Tell me, Diesel." I opened my eyes to see his, the same look still written in his expression.

"I can't." The whispered words struggled to find their way out, cutting like knives through his voice.

It felt as if there was a large sheet of glass between us. I could see him, I could hear him, but there was something keeping us apart, something wasn't letting us get all the way through to each other.

My lungs exhaled. "Can't what?"

"I can't hurt you."

I dropped my shoulders. It was *such* a cliché thing to say. A guy who has broken hearts before, afraid he's going to get bored of me and break up with me in time, leaving me crumbling in misery. Great. It's the same story that's been told a million times, the same line being used on every girl. I had to fight the nagging urge to roll my eyes.

But then I thought of the look I saw earlier, the fear in his eyes, the astonishment when he watched me and my lips.

I thought of the quiver in his raspy voice when he spoke to me.

I thought of all the times he tried to say something but then stopped himself, his nerves getting the best of him.

On the outside, he was closed off and reserved, but when *I* saw him, whenever he was around me, I could see him using all his energy to keep himself together.

That's what told me he was *really* scared.

"You won't hurt me."

"You don't know that for sure." He shook his head.

I groaned, growing tired of trying to convince him, and fell back over to my side of the cab.

"Anna, please. You don't get it."

"Then help me understand. Because I like you, Diesel."

His posture softened, but his words hardened. "God, you have no *fucking* idea."

My eyes snapped up to his. His face was filled with angst, like everything was about to come pouring out of him, his ability to keep it together now broken.

"You have no idea how badly I want you, Anna. I've wanted you this whole *fucking* time. There's not a single moment that goes by when you're not on my mind."

His eyes narrowed as the desire was etched in the stone of his voice. "You're all I want."

There it was, in his own words, with his voice, the admission I'd been waiting for. And there we were, sitting together in the truck, our eyes locked. I shifted back over, touching my leg against his, causing him to tense. I could hear his breath quicken. He wanted this as much as I did, I could feel it. Our chemistry was undeniable. Just being in the same place, same car, same room together built the tension between us.

I inched closer to him, my hand moving to his forearm.

His eyes closed at my touch. "Anna…"

His voice was tired, needy, and desperate, giving me the fuel I needed. I leaned in closer, pressing my hand to his chest, feeling his heartbeat. It was practically jumping out of his body.

He growled. "Anna, be careful."

No. I was done being careful. I was done playing nice.

I brushed his nose with mine, finally closing my eyes.

If he wasn't going to shatter the glass, I would.

I pressed my lips to his.

He didn't stop me.

I could feel the electricity run through my blood, the kiss pulling my body in all different directions. My stomach dropped and heat began filling the area between my legs. I've never felt a kiss this alluring, this captivating.

After a soft release, the kiss only lasting a few seconds, he quickly opened his eyes to look at me, my lips still lingering over his. He searched me, his eyes scanning every part of me, his hand moving back up to my face, cupping my jaw. There was the look again, the look of wonder, like I was the answer to everything. I let my lips curl into a small smile, waiting to see his next move. His breath was even faster now.

Once he had the first taste of me, he didn't hold back.

He kissed me, bringing his lips to mine with a thirst he needed to quench. He ran his hand through my hair, grabbing and tugging, as he pushed his lips on me harder. I could feel myself aching for him, for more, for everything. He slid his tongue into my mouth, my lips eagerly opening to welcome it. He reached over and grabbed the back of my thighs and, with a swift movement, swung my body over his lap, forcing me to straddle him. His hands moved desperately over me, from my hips, tracing up my back, to my shoulders and back down again. His touch made its way under the hem of my shirt, moving higher, his fingertips caressing each ridge of my ribs, our embrace becoming more passionate by the second. Before I could control it, I let a soft groan escape me, my lips vibrating on his. I could feel his smile on our kiss.

There was a charge between us, something unexplainable, indescribable. Just the thought of it left me speechless.

His lips moved to my jaw, then down the side of my neck, ending at my collarbone, trailing kisses the whole way. I stayed on his lap, my arms wrapped loosely around his neck, feeling a pressure from his jeans pushing into my leg. The thought of it hypnotized me, my mind slipping into a deep fog where only he and I existed. Right here, with him, was the only place I wanted to be. Everything else faded away.

Wrapping his arms around me, he flipped me on my back, laying me on the seat of the truck, his arms holding himself up above me. It was the first time I looked into his eyes, *really looked*, since we kissed. There was a change in him, there was no fear or hesitation this time. I moved my hand up to his hair, sliding my fingers through the dark golden locks, wrapping my legs around his hovering body. He pulled my hand to his lips, kissing each of my fingertips.

I wanted to stay in this moment for eternity.

He leaned down to steal another kiss, his lips soft and lush. "Come inside," I said, nipping at his bottom lip and pulling it into my mouth.

His hand slipped under my head, pushing me harder against him, our kisses unable to get any closer. After a moment, he broke the kiss and whispered, "I can't."

I stopped, his words catching up to my thoughts, my thoughts catching up to the rest of my body. He moved to sit up, but I kept my legs wrapped around him, keeping him from doing so.

"There's a meeting with land surveyors tomorrow and I… *fuck*. I haven't even begun to prepare, and I—"

"Diesel." I stopped him, placing a hand on his chest. "It's okay. I get it."

His eyes searched me, drinking me in as I lay under him. The sun was beginning to set, casting a yellow-orange glow in the cab, the descending rays warming the skin that already felt like it was on fire. His gaze moved to my hair, which was draped over my shoulder. He moved it away, letting it fall over the side of the seat, clearing it off my collarbone.

"God, I'd do anything to stay right here, with you."

He leaned back down and planted another kiss on my lips. My thighs squeezed his toned waist, my hips grinding on the throbbing rise in his jeans.

"*Fuck*, Anna," he growled, unable to keep his composure.

His voice was more desperate than I'd ever heard it, making me smile against him. I moved my hands down to the top hem of his jeans, running my fingers along the seam. Every time my skin would accidentally brush against him, his muscles would tense and tighten, sending a jolt through his body.

I could easily spend the whole night teasing him, pushing him to his limits, but I know he has work to finish and responsibilities to fulfill. Releasing him from my legs and sliding out from under him, I smoothed out my clothes and hair. After a quiet moment of mentally talking himself down, he did the same.

"When can I see you again?" he asked, the question taking me by surprise. He was the busy one, the one that could barely breathe without getting a phone call.

"Whenever you want," I said, my voice breathy, my hand on the door handle. Before I could prop it open, his hand grabbed my thigh, directing my attention back to him.

"Just so you know," he began, leaning in toward me. "I think about you every damn night."

His hand moved up my thigh and in between my legs, caressing me tenderly.

My lungs started to shrink, and my chest refused to let me breathe.

"Tonight will be no different."

I was positive his hand could feel the heat radiating from under my jeans, making my face turn a deep red. His sky-blue eyes were pinned on me, and his gaze was seductive and persistent. I opened the door, his hand slipping away from my thigh, and climbed out.

"Goodbye, Diesel."

The purple hue from the sunset illuminated the side of my face as I shut the door. I turned and walked back to the building, feeling his eyes on me as I stepped up the stairs and went inside.

THOMAS

I could barely sleep at all last night. I read the article over and over, my bed sheets tangled up in my legs, trying to figure out who would be in the car with my dad. It could have been one of the guys from work, but whoever it was would've been seen leaving, and someone would have spoken up when I broke the news.

After hours with no answers and no update to the article, I decided to find out for myself.

Back at the county jail, I passed through security, and the same guard from yesterday took me back to the same visiting room. This routine must be torture for him since it was only day two and already hell for me. I sat at one of the tables, alone again, staring at my hands on the cool plastic surface. My mind was so focused on the mysterious passenger that I didn't even register the humming of the air conditioner. After a few minutes, the guard brought my dad into the room. He looked worse than he did yesterday. The circles around his eyes began to sink in, the stubble on his face was turning to scruff, and his slow saunter toward the table looked frail and weak. He fell into the chair across from me, not making eye contact.

"Twenty minutes." The monotonous guard picked up a newspaper and sat in a chair in the corner of the room.

I stared at my dad's face for a moment, studying him. He looked as if he was about to fall asleep right here in front of me.

"You look like shit."

He said nothing.

"Did you sleep?"

He shook his head, his eyes still glued to his lap. "Can't."

There was a timid squeak as I leaned back in my chair, the plastic aching under my large frame. I looked around the room, the bland walls doing absolutely nothing for my angst. God, this place was a hellhole. The empty tables acted as a silent audience for the conversation I was about to have.

"Do you know why I'm here?"

He shrugged.

"The article on your accident came out yesterday."

Silence. No reaction, no impulse, not even a twitch of a finger.

"Who is it?"

The question made him finally look up at me, and the look in his droopy eyes told me he knew what I was referring to. His mouth opened, but he stumbled on what words to say.

"Who was with you?"

"She's, uh," He rolled his shoulders and sniffled. The cut on his lip looked swollen, as if he had been chewing on it. "She's someone I've been…"

I waited for him to continue. I was done filling in his blanks, speaking for him, and trying to figure out his answers. I wanted him to tell me himself with his big-boy words.

"I've been seeing her for a couple of months now."

There was another woman in the car with my dad. It was the answer I was expecting. "Why didn't you tell me about her?"

His tone was tired, as if I had already asked him a hundred times. Or maybe, he's been practicing a hundred different ways to tell me. "I don't know, Tommy. It's hard. And I wasn't sure if it was anything serious."

"Is it?"

"Not anymore. Now that I'm here, I don't think she wants anything to do with me."

"Did she try to stop you from driving?"

There was a long stretch of time between my answer and the shake of my dad's head, as if he was debating on covering for her or throwing her under the bus.

"She's not innocent. She was drunk in the car, too. She's technically an accomplice."

He looked back down at his legs, either nodding in agreement or nodding so I'd stop my lecture, as if he was a teenager being grounded.

"Did she get arrested with you?"

He shrugged again. "I'm not sure. I don't know."

I sighed, the reality of everything still sinking into my chest. Any sympathy I felt for my dad, all of it being about two cells in my entire body, was fleeting. Nothing could justify drunk driving in my eyes.

"Who is she?"

He apparently wasn't in the mood to talk today, because he remained quiet making this conversation a fucking picnic.

"Tell me."

My dad rolled his head and sighed, clearly tired of this. But the funny thing is, he's going to be dealing with this shit for a long time, so he better get used to it.

This is just the beginning.

"Her name is Laila."

Staring at him, I waited as he furrowed his eyebrows, trying to remember details. "She's young, a few years older than you…"

The statement embarrassed my dad, the skin around his neck turning a shade of crimson. My mind went back to the awkward encounter with my classmate in my kitchen, causing me to slightly wince.

"…and she has a steady job. Good money."

"Doing what?"

"That doesn't matter." He was quick with his response, as if I fucking cared.

"Come on, what? She some sort of drug dealer?"

"No, *no,* no no no." My dad let out nervous laughter as he glanced over his shoulder at the guard, hoping he didn't hear. The guard didn't even look up from his newspaper. "She's…a dancer."

"A dancer?"

He nodded.

It clicked in my head. Money. Dancer. "Like a stripper?"

He nodded again.

"You're dating a stripper?" I raised my eyebrows and couldn't help but laugh.

He didn't think it was funny and quickly jumped to her defense. "She's a great person."

"Yeah, she's a great person who lets a guy get behind the wheel when he's drunk."

It wasn't the fact that she was a stripper that I was hung up on. I couldn't care less if that's how she wanted to make her money. Who gives a shit? It's her life, and people obviously enjoy it. It's the fact that she let my dad drive and ruin his life, take someone else's, and in turn, ruin a bunch of other people's lives.

His head hung down between his shoulders. He deserved everything he was getting, and he knew it.

But just as he was about to speak, something occurred to me.

"Wait. She works at Stoney's?"

Considering it was the only strip club in Kittanning, I was asking myself more than I was asking him. But he still nodded.

"What does she look like?"

It took a moment, but my dad's eyes lit up at the sight of her in his memory, the faintest smile beginning to show. "She's tall. Perfect skin from head to toe. Long, fire-red hair."

I swallowed hard, a wave of sweat breaking through my pores.

No way.

No *fucking* way.

"You said her name was Laila?"

"Yeah, well, that's her real name. Her 'stage name' is Eve." He used air quotes in his last statement, his expression insisting that he lay claim to her, acting as if he was better than the other men who lick the women with their eyes.

It took everything inside of me not to tense up. My insides were filled with confusion, anger, and maybe even a touch of disappointment, if I'm being honest. She was someone I had dreams about, at night and during the day, fantasizing about her body, her eyes, and her lips.

But she was with my dad.

Sleeping with him.

The thought sent a flood of nausea through me. And even worse, she turned out to be a shitty person. All the ideas I had of her in my head were thrown out at that moment.

Then I thought, was my dad under her little spell too? Was he given this "gift"? There was no way I could come out and ask because if he didn't have it, he would think I was crazy for even believing it. Then again, if he killed a man in a car accident, I'm sure he could have stepped out and saved him when given the chance, right? Maybe I'm giving him too much credit. Maybe he wouldn't have used it on a stranger. But either way, the man was dead.

My head ached from running in circles. I stood up from my chair and began pacing back and forth across the tile.

"What is it, T?"

Here I was, thinking I had my shit together on the outside, only for my dad to notice my jitters as if it was written all over my face. I knew this was the moment I had to take control, switch the narrative, and let him know that he didn't totally knock me on my ass with this new piece of information. And there was only one card I could play to get me ahead.

I turned to face him, planting my palms on the table, leaning in. "I want the company."

"I told you, it's yours while I'm here. I know you'll do fine while I'm gone—"

"No." I cut him off. "I want the company. Now. Without you. Even after you're done here."

He stared at me, his eyes unblinking.

"All of it."

The room was silent. Even the guard noticed the tension and looked up from his newspaper.

It was something that had crossed my mind last night after reading the article for the eleventh time. I can do this without him. I've been doing this for him long enough, and now that I've officially been pushed out of the nest, I don't need him anymore.

Ever.

"Thomas…"

The use of my full first name surprised me, but I didn't let it show. He hardly ever used my first name. Back when I was eight, I was riding my bike up and down our road. I came back home a little too fast and turned too hard into our driveway. I skidded right into my dad's truck, leaving a nice scratch down the side of the driver's door. When he heard me and stepped outside, he used my full name when he yelled at me. That's when I knew he was mad.

His tired eyes turned hard, fury rising up in his chest.

"…you know I can't do that."

"Why not?"

"Because *I* built that company from the ground!" His voice was growing louder. The guard watched him, sitting up straighter, making sure the conversation didn't get out of hand. My dad took notice and toned it down, his nostrils flaring.

I looked into his eyes, trying everything to get my message across. "But I'm a Diesel. It's my name on that company, too. You think I'm going to ruin something that has my name on it?"

That didn't convince him. He wasn't going down without a fight. "No. I can't."

I knew how to play his game. He had no outside source besides me, and I hadn't told him I already talked to the guys at work about taking over.

"Fine, then I quit."

His eyes widened. Finally, I was getting through, and he was getting scared.

"Good luck telling all the guys they're out of a job when there's no one to run it for you."

I straightened and pushed in my chair, making moves to leave. All the color drained from his face. It's almost as if losing his company hurt more than killing another person.

Just as I turned my back, his voice was forced out with a growl.

"Dammit, fine. Take it. But I swear to God, Thomas, if you fuck it up, I will come for you as soon as I'm done here."

His threats did nothing to me. If anything, it was soothing to hear that my father could be threatened. But he knew I wouldn't let the company fail. I wouldn't have taken it if I didn't care for it and wasn't serious. He's just a stubborn asshole who needed to face his new reality, and that reality consisted of nothing but himself in this jail.

I motioned for the guard, signaling that we were finished, and gave my dad a single nod.

"See you around."

It took a few weeks to sign the company over in my name. There was an enormous amount of paperwork I needed to fill out, including all the extensive laws I needed to read and understand to the best of my ability. Everything there was to know about hiring contractors, insurance on employees, the company, the things we build, the finances, the taxes, licensing, payroll, safety protocol, I knew it all. My dad's lawyer, Kurt Young, combed through every detail on every paper until our eyes were bloodshot. Finally, when we reached the end, I did it. After I lifted my pen off the last line of the last paper, I felt myself relax, my shoulders loosening away from this ongoing burden.

I became the sole owner of DCC, Diesel Construction Co.

Half of me felt like a weight was lifted, not having to rely on my dad to keep things running, and not having to answer to him even though I called most of the shots already. The other half of me dreaded the amount of work that was now my full responsibility. I was now in charge of things I never had a hand in before. And since everything was my obligation now, I had little to no time for anything else. My friends would ask me to go out and meet up with them at the bar, but after a full day of work and the new tasks on top of it, I had no energy to do anything. Work, shower, sleep, repeat. After declining a few times, they started asking less and less. Now, I see pictures of them online, out and having fun, while I can barely keep my eyes open. It's not what I had pictured in my head at twenty years old.

It was as if my dad going to prison pushed me into being the adult I wasn't ready to be.

I've gone in circles thinking about all this, time after time, sending myself into a nightlong pity party, and all I get in the end is pissed off. There are nights when I lay in bed, thinking about the life I'm living, thinking about the dad I'm supposed to have, and I bounce between feeling sorry for him and hating him. Either way, I need to keep this business afloat. And I was doing it all by myself.

There were just a few loose ends I needed to tie up.

ANNA

"Holy shit."

There was no hiding my expression as I walked through the doors.

Olivia echoed the words again, this time drawing them out, her eyes glued to me, following me. "*Holy shit.*"

I furrowed my brows as I walked to my workstation and set my bag down on the floor. I could feel Olivia's eyes burning into my back, and her words were starting to draw attention from the other students. I set up my station, pulled out my styling tools from my bag and plugged them in, letting them heat up. The mannequin head in the client chair stared at me in the mirror, a blonde bob wig resting on the scalp. Olivia's footsteps echoed through the room, the sound growing louder as she moved closer to me. She switched her gaze from the back of my head to my reflection in the mirror, then reached out and grabbed my arm. I turned to her, biting the inside of my cheek, trying not to smile too hard. The second she saw my face up close, her mouth dropped.

"Holy shit!" This time, her voice was as quiet as a whisper, but her excitement was so loud.

"Olivia!" I shushed her with a smile. "Shut up! Are you fifteen years old?"

"You guys kissed, didn't you?" she asked with a smile while ignoring me and keeping her voice down to a whisper.

I nodded, blushing. "How did you know?"

"It is written *all* over your face. I saw it as soon as you walked in. You're glowing."

I let out a sigh. I wasn't sure if being this easy to read was a good or bad thing, but I was too entranced to care.

"Did you…"

She didn't need to finish her question for me to know what she was asking. I shook my head.

"Did you *want* to?"

A smirk spread across my lips as I nodded. Our teacher stepped out of her office, ready to begin today's lesson.

Olivia was absolutely loving this. "You need to fill me in after class." She walked to her station and tousled her mannequin's wig with her fingers. "I can't believe you didn't text me." We both laughed under our breath and turned our attention to the work in front of us.

Once class was over, we packed up our things and left the building. Stepping outside was like walking into a sauna. The humidity was ruthless, the temperature was well above an average summer day, the skies a deep grey above us. It felt like the air was glued to my skin, and I was unable to peel it off. With the clouds darkening by the minute, time was running out before a storm was about to hit.

Our cars were parked on separate streets today, but I wanted to talk with Olivia, so we both stood against the exterior of the building. I told her everything. Reliving it all, saying it all out loud to someone else made it feel extremely real. I could feel myself floating back up to the cloud I was on all night last night after Diesel left my apartment.

"Have you talked to him since?" Olivia asked, and I shook my head.

I stared at my phone for hours last night, debating. Every part of me wanted to text him about anything and everything, as long as I got to talk to him. But I knew how busy he was and didn't want to interrupt him. I had no idea what running and owning a business was like, but from what I saw with Diesel, it was a lot of work. So I left him alone, and he didn't text me either. I brushed it off, knowing he was busy, but I couldn't help but feel a tiny sliver of disappointment.

There was a subtle rumble of thunder in the distance. We both looked up as I felt a raindrop on the back of my hand.

Olivia flung the hood of her jacket up, shielding her from incoming rain. I silently cursed myself for only wearing a tank top and jeans, forgetting my rain jacket at home.

"Text him. And text *me*, dammit!"

"I will," I said through a giggle as another raindrop landed on my cheek. She turned and took off running in the direction of her car. More raindrops began to fall as I shouted goodbye to Olivia and began walking in the other direction. Once I reached my car, my hand on the handle, I looked up and noticed a familiar truck parked across the street.

Diesel's truck.

And leaning against the bed of the truck, was Diesel himself.

My heart thudded to my toes.

The raindrops became more frequent as we locked eyes. He had his typical work outfit on, his brown work boots, dark blue jeans and a grey t-shirt, which was now sprinkled with wet droplets. For such a plain, generic outfit, he sure knew how to make it look incredibly attractive.

As he pushed off his truck and crossed the street, an infectious smile turned up on the corners of his lips. He walked around the back of my car and met me at my car door, my hand letting go of the handle and my body turning to face him. He stepped closer to me until my back was pushed against the frame. I couldn't help but return his smile.

"Whenever I want, right?"

It took me a second, but I realized he was echoing my answer from last night after he asked when he could see me again. I nodded, unable to speak. Thunder rumbled even louder, moving closer.

"Right now."

The assertive side of him made my knees go weak and I had to make a conscious effort to keep myself standing.

He pressed his body onto mine, my back still pushed onto my car. Placing his hands around my neck, his thumbs stroking my cheeks, he wasted no time in leaning down to kiss me. I had barely enough time to catch my breath after seeing him, and now, the feeling of his lips on mine was making it even harder to function. I wrapped my arms around his neck as the raindrops went from sprinkles to heavy, staggard drops, giving no sign of letting up and passing through. I pulled away for a second, even though Diesel kept trying to kiss me, clearing a laugh out of me.

"Your place or mine?" he asked, small drops of rainwater sliding down his cheeks.

"Yours." I planted my hands on his chest, the mix of cold rain and his body heat swirling through my fingers. "But give me an hour. I have some things I need to get."

He narrowed his eyes in suspicion but knew better than to ask me any questions. After he planted a kiss on my forehead, he turned to go, and I watched him the whole way as he ran back to his truck and climbed in. From his stride, to simple things like pulling his keys out of his pocket, everything he did was effortlessly sexy. I got in my car and watched him pull away.

Down around the corner and a few blocks west was the grocery store. It was smaller, not nearly as big as a supermarket, but it was still stocked with all the essentials that anyone could need. I slipped inside with a mental checklist and tracked my way down the aisles. There were a handful of other people throughout the store, almost all of them glancing in my direction and then looking away promptly after seeing my forehead.

I sighed. Is this what the rest of my life was going to be like? Unwanted stares, whispered questions, avoided eye contact? Despite the friendliness I've encountered since moving here, I still felt like I was being treated like a monster, like someone who didn't belong, and all I was trying to do was get a fresh pineapple.

After gathering everything I needed, I made my way to the checkout, where the cashier gave a courteous smile and then didn't look at me again. I'm not sure what's worse: having people terrified to look at you because of a brutal scar, or having people stare at you until they have to remind themselves to blink. Either way, it was unwanted attention, and I couldn't get out of there fast enough.

I arrived at Diesel's apartment and knocked on the door. I could hear his yell, muffled but loud enough to discover he left the door unlocked for me. As soon as I stepped inside, I could feel hot steam surround me, smelling like teakwood and fresh citrus. I looked down the hall, and sure enough, there he was, wearing a clean, dark grey t-shirt, dark wash jeans, barefoot, walking toward me. He had a white towel in his hands, rubbing the fabric against the back of his head, drying any excess water from his shower.

I froze, dead in my tracks, watching his steps come closer. Whether he's dirty from work or clean after a shower, he looks so good *all the time.*

He stopped only a foot away from me, his eyebrows pinched together. "What's that?" He nodded to the bag that I had gripped in my hand, the straps tight against my palm.

His question snapped me out of my daze and brought me back to reality. "Oh. I stopped at the store." I motioned to the kitchen. "May I?"

The puzzlement stayed on his face as I brushed past him and placed the bag on the counter. He followed me, his presence undeniably intense behind me. As I pulled all of the ingredients out of the bag, I said, "It's honey garlic chicken with pineapple. My specialty."

Diesel pressed his hands on the kitchen island, his voice mute, something burning in the way he studied me.

I continued to open packages and tear off plastic seals, trying my best to tame whatever reaction he was giving to my back.

"You said you haven't had a home-cooked meal in a while. That's going to change."

I set everything together on the counter, lined up and ready to begin, and reached over to preheat the oven.

"But I'm going to need your help."

I didn't really need him. I've done this recipe a million times and could cook it with my eyes closed. But I didn't want Diesel to feel like I was shutting him out by doing this all myself. I wanted him to stand with me and be with me, even if it was for something as simple as chopping pineapple.

And within the next hour, he not only did just that, but he also proved that he knew his way around the kitchen, sneaking kisses between steps.

"Have you been lying to me, Diesel?" I asked once we were finished. I set our full plates of food down on the table, ready to eat. "Do you cook for yourself? Are you secretly a chef?"

A grin appeared as he brought me sparkling water and a beer for himself. "Just because I don't have time to cook doesn't mean I don't know how."

I took a bite of the dish, a sigh deflating from me, proud of myself. It was so good for being so simple to throw together.

"Holy shit, Anna. This is amazing," Diesel said through bites, clearly satisfied.

"Better than The 87?"

"Hey, now, I wouldn't go that far." His tease was accompanied by a smile, and I reached over and punched his arm, which turned out to be rock hard and probably hurt my hand more than it hurt him.

"It was my dad's favorite," I said. I didn't mean to drop the mood, but there was a shift once the words were out.

Diesel straightened, catching the change in tone. "Well, he had very good taste." He took another bite and looked back at me. "And you were right. Nothing beats a home-cooked meal."

My insides warmed at the thought of taking care of him. He's been fighting his own battles for so long with no one else in his corner. It was time he had someone to give him a break, if nothing else.

"I'm glad you like it." I swallowed a sip of my water. "Although, getting this stuff was interesting. Everyone at the grocery store looked at me like I had five heads. I'm assuming because of my scar."

"No," Diesel shook his head. "They just aren't used to having someone new in town. Especially a pretty girl like you."

I stopped chewing mid-bite, a flush spreading on my cheeks.

"But they're all a bunch of fuckers anyway," he said with his beer pressed to his lips. Was that a hint of jealousy I heard? Maybe a pinch of possessiveness? I scrunched my face, quickly throwing that thought out of my head. Yeah, we might have had one of the hottest make-out sessions of my life yesterday, and even good kisses today, but that didn't mean he wanted anything more than that. And that's something I needed to remind myself of.

We finished the food way too fast, not realizing how hungry we both were. We laughed and joked through the whole thing; our company to each other so easy and came naturally.

Despite Diesel's demands for me to sit and relax, I helped him clear our plates and clean up, and I hesitated at how domestic this felt. Cooking him dinner, doing the dishes, it all felt normal, and I had to keep myself from falling into a mind trap, thinking this could be my life. I wanted him, yes, I could see myself living like this, yes, but I wasn't about to dream when I didn't know where his head was at.

Once I put the final dish in the dishwasher, I felt Diesel's arms snake around my waist and pick me up. I squealed, laughing as he carried me to the couch and laid me down, my back flat on the cushions. His body hovered over mine as he leaned down, whispering in my ear.

"Do you know how much control it has taken for me to resist you tonight?"

I closed my eyes, his words seeping into my pores and diving right into my bloodstream.

"To not grab you and throw you on the counter and *fuck* you right then and there?"

I could feel my breathing speed up. My legs instinctively bent at the knee, becoming more restless with his unruly speech. With his body unmoving and still lingering over me, he grabbed my leg and pushed it down, his grip tight on my knee, controlling me. If it was an attempt to keep me levelheaded and calm, it did everything but.

"To not have *you* for dinner instead?"

The hand that gripped my knee moved up, sliding along the inside of my thigh, climbing to the button of my jeans. He popped the button open with a flick of his wrist.

"Because, let me tell you something. I'm still so fucking hungry."

I whimpered, unable to speak, screaming on the inside to keep going.

His mouth drifted away from my ear and found my lips, his kiss sweeping across me in fierce ambition. He wasn't lying, his hunger for me was evident. I could feel it in his lips, his hands, even in his breathing. His hands grabbed my jeans and pulled them down, and I lifted my hips to help strip them off my legs. He continued to kiss me as his fingers trailed along my underwear, teasing the skin and making me shudder.

"Let me taste you."

He didn't let me respond before moving his head lower, pulling my underwear down past my knees. His hands pushed my legs open, exposing me for all that I have, his heated gaze took me in, drinking me, swallowing me as his jaw hardened. His mouth moved to my inner thigh, nipping at all the sensitive spots, making his way inward until he reached the center. Once there, the warmth of his breath made me curl my toes, writhing in need for him to please me.

His tongue circled my clit, sending the sensation up my entire body. His lips caressed every inch of me, from top to bottom, and his twisted grin between licks showed me that he was *enjoying* this. His irises flared with desire as he glanced up at me, with no signs of stopping.

My hands found his hair, long enough to run my fingers through but too short to get a good grip. A slight tilt of his head sent me into a whole new direction, my back arching and my hips lifting to meet him there, to guide him where I needed him. One of his hands moved up to my breast, gripping and pinching my nipple, adding to the intensity. There was no way to describe it, the way he took me higher than I had ever been, all while keeping me grounded and level with him. It was like the dense fog around me swirled with the brightest clarity.

My grip ached for him as his mouth moved in deeper, my body on the cusp of breaking. I could feel the waves beginning to wash over me, and soon enough, the orgasm completely ripped through, a heavy jolt working its way through my body. My chest was tight and my breathing was scattered as I looked down at Diesel, his mouth glistening of me. He didn't smile, he didn't look away, and he didn't even blink. All he did was take his own bottom lip into his mouth, tasting and licking away any remainder of me, all while never breaking eye contact.

With his knees on the floor, my legs still open, he moved up to my face and kissed me. I could taste myself in him as our tongues danced, the heat between us not shrinking in the slightest. His kisses were filled with fervor, as if this was the last time he would ever do this.

I went to move my hands to his jeans but paused, stopping myself right above his waist.

"Wait, wait."

He looked at me, surprised, his breath panting. "What? What's wrong?"

There was a moment of hesitation on my end. The orgasm I just had was bringing my previous thoughts to light. "What are we doing?"

"What do you mean?" His eyes shifted, confusion filling his body. It was pretty clear what we were doing, what we just *did*, and I could understand why he was thrown.

"I mean…" I began, covering my hands with my face, inwardly groaning at myself. Why did I have to stop and say all this now? "I *like* you, Diesel." I dropped my hands to see his expression. There wasn't one. He stared at me, his eyes boring into mine, his chest still expanding in every breath. I waited for him to say something, anything, but when he didn't, I elaborated.

"I don't… I'm tired of being used for sex. I don't want someone who uses my body as their hand, then forgets about me the next day."

I thought about the guys I've been with in the past, all of them now blocked contacts in my phone.

"I've had too much of that, and I don't want to do it anymore."

Closing my knees together, I shielded myself, trying to hide pieces of me.

"I like you, Diesel. A lot. And I want you. *Trust me*, I want you. But I'm not ready to be forgotten. Not by you."

After a minute to digest what I told him, he stood up and quietly walked over to the balcony doors, nudging his head in their direction. "Come here."

I obeyed, my tank top hanging loosely over my body as I pulled my underwear back up and cautiously made my way over. He slid open the doors and motioned for me to step out. The rain was coming down harder now, but there was a small awning above us, shielding us from the downpour. He followed me out and slid the door closed behind him, keeping the humidity from entering his apartment.

The last time I was on this balcony, all I could do was stare at the spot below, eyeing the circle of blood that stuck to the pavement like glue. But now, as I approached the railing and looked down, I could see the rain had erased it all. There was nothing, no red streaks, no leftover stain, nothing. It was like it never happened.

"Get out of your head," Diesel whispered in my ear from behind me. I flinched, not knowing he was already that close, but then felt the warmth of his chest close in on me.

"What?" I asked, ignoring his heat and focusing on his words.

"Anna," his voice was dark as his arms gripped the railing around me, caging me in, the exact same position and the exact same spot we were in before. But this time, I didn't turn around. I was mentally begging for a different outcome.

"I don't think you get it." He moved closer, and now his whole body was flush with mine, from the top of his chest down to his thighs. "You say you like me, but I don't think you understand my side of it."

I could feel a nudge against my tailbone, and my body tightened.

"You drive me absolutely *fucking* insane."

I pushed myself against him, his words a catalyst for the heat spreading through my body. His hips pushed back, and my need for any reassurance faded fast. All I knew was that I wanted him, I wanted this, and I wanted him to want this too.

"You showed up completely out of nowhere," he began, his mouth moving down to my neck, his hushed words warm on my skin. "And now that I have you, you're not going anywhere."

I closed my eyes, listening to him. It was a big jump, going from uncertainty in this to him keeping me, claiming me, but I was too caught up in the arousal to care.

His one hand moved to my arm, sliding his fingertips up to my shoulder, then to my neck. He lightly brushed my hair away, leaving my skin exposed to the damp air. His other hand slid around to my stomach, grazing over my hips, making its way to the bottom of my shirt.

"Look over there."

I opened my eyes and followed his aim as he briefly pointed down the road. It was deserted and quiet, with the streams of rainfall the only movement in the street. I didn't see anything other than pavement and trees. The hand on my stomach slid up my shirt, feeling my skin the whole way up to my bra, and I could already feel the build-up swirling in me.

"That's where I first saw you. Walking this way."

I sharply inhaled. It never crossed my mind to think about the moments leading up to the accident since it didn't change anything. But getting Diesel's play-by-play of how *he* remembers it tells a whole new story.

He slipped under my bra, his fingertips grazing my nipples, which were already firm. I could only muster out a small cry from the sensation, the feeling sending shockwaves all through my body. It felt *so* good.

"I couldn't take my eyes off of you."

After caressing my breasts, my nipples fueling the fire inside me, he slid his hand back down my stomach, stopping at the top of my underwear.

"And then everything happened, Anna."

My breathing increased as I remained frozen, longing for more of his touch, ready for him to move faster. But he didn't. He slowly maneuvered his way into my underwear, his hand having no trouble finding its path. His other hand still rested on my neck, but now he wrapped it around the front of my throat, giving it a squeeze. Knowing how strong he was, a surge of fear sparked in me, but I still had my complete trust in him. My body was bouncing between the ideas of panic and alarm, to craving and yearning. He forced my body forward just a few inches, but it was enough to lean me over the railing. I gripped the bars for balance.

"Right there," he whispered in my ear. "You were laying right there."

My eyes flickered down to the road below, his hold forcing me to look into the memory. The pavement was dark and wet, but I could still picture myself there, covered in blood. I tried to swallow, my throat bobbing against his grip.

"And I didn't even hesitate. Not for a fucking millisecond."

His fingertips brushed against my clit, and the simple movement severed me. I tried my best to keep my groans to a minimum, but his touch was impossible to ignore. He slowly added more pressure, moving up and down, and I bit my bottom lip in an attempt to control myself.

"I will run through fire to get to you."

His words were spoken through gritted teeth, as if this was setting him off as much as it was for me. Letting go of the railing, I pushed my underwear down, kicking the thin fabric off and to the side to give him more room. I had no thoughts or cares about anything else except for him. His hand moved lower, my legs opening more to accommodate, my wetness the only thing covering his skin. With his fingers resting on my entrance, he slid one finger in, then another, loosening a gasp from my mouth. My knuckles turned white as I gripped the railing again, squeezing the metal as he worked inside me. I could easily grab his arms, make him stop, and slow things down. But there wasn't a single part of me that wanted this to end.

"I will run over broken glass for you."

His fingers circled in all the right places, pushing and sliding and driving me close to the end. As soon as he added his thumb to the mix, the new pressure rubbing my swollen clit, my hips bucked and my body thrust with waves of ecstasy.

"I will find whoever did this to you, Anna."

The thought of it made him angry, causing him to snatch his hand away, right as I was about to come. My pussy squeezed, aching for his hand to come back and continue. I tried to drop my head down, my breathing ragged, but his other hand was still locked around my throat, keeping my head upright.

"Diesel," I muttered through a rasp, a plea for him to finish me. My legs were shaking, my need so heavy that a piece of me wanted to finish things myself. But his touch felt so good, so intimate, that all I wanted was him to do it for me.

I reached back, my palm searching then finding his cock, which was already rock hard. Taking the hand that was just knuckle deep in me, he helped me unbutton his jeans, the denim falling past his knees. I didn't have a choice but to stay facing the road since his grip on me was too tight to turn around. I could already feel the little marks that were sure to show up on my neck tomorrow.

I felt the waistband of his boxer briefs, then eagerly slipped my fingers underneath. The tip of his cock was dripping, his juices making the skin slick. I bit down, trying to suppress any noises that were about to slide through.

But Diesel didn't hold back.

As soon as I grabbed him, his mouth moved to my shoulder, his teeth close to biting my skin in passion. His voice let out a deep moan, coming up from the depths of his chest.

His underwear dropped, the length of him springing free. I grabbed him and began stroking, only to realize his size was more than I could've imagined. I could feel his breathing become heavier with every pump. His hunger for me grew as he pulled off my tank top and unclipped my bra, freeing my breasts and baring all of my skin. I would have felt exposed if I thought there may have been someone around, but there wasn't anyone even close.

After a minute, he pushed my hand away and I obediently placed it back on the railing. He pulled off his t-shirt and then guided himself to my entrance, my wetness practically dripping down my leg. The tip of his cock rested on my skin, and through it, I could feel him *throbbing*.

"That's where I saved you, Anna." The hand on my throat jerked me, forcing me to look down again. He slid into me, my eyes on the road but my focus on how good he felt inside me.

Oh, my God.

"I saved you once…"

He thrust in me, burying himself as deep as he could go, an uncontrollable groan rumbling in my voice.

"… I'll save you again…"

His hips slammed into me, his grip growing even tighter, and my vision was beginning to turn black.

"And I'll do it every time, forever."

His words were quiet but intense, his meaning loud and clear.

"But that means you're mine, Anna. No one else will ever save you but me."

A single tear slid down my cheek and onto his hand. If he felt it, he ignored it, too taken by the pleasure. My heart felt like it was about to combust, not only from the sex but also from his want for me, his demand for me, his emotion matching everything I've felt toward him.

He finally released his grip on my throat and I immediately inhaled, the rainy air more than welcome.

"I need to see you," he demanded as he pulled himself out of me, only for a split second, then spun me around to face him. My back was to the railing as he propped my leg up and pushed himself back inside my wet pussy with ease, his pulse raging in his cock.

He paused as his eyes did a complete sweep over my naked body.

"*Fuck*, Anna."

His grip moved to my hips as he continued to thrust in me, taking all control, his fingertips squeezing the skin around my bones.

I have a feeling there will be bruises there, too.

I released a broken sigh, my breasts rising and falling with each breath as my knees buckled. His eyes never left my body, his gaze even passing over the cut on my forehead. My pussy tightened around him, purposely compressing his entire length, and I could feel him stiffen.

"Be careful." A growl escaped him as he moved in and pressed his forehead close to my ear. "Or else you'll send me right over the *fucking* edge."

Knowing he was close was all it took for me to go. A flood ripped through me, my body rocking to the waves of the orgasm. The one leg I was standing on would've given out if Diesel wasn't there to keep me up, his cock still buried deep inside me.

"Diesel," my voice managed to squeak out his name. In a chain of events, my orgasm was what set him off. His arms moved up and tightened around me, his smooth skin hot on my chest as I could feel him tremble. His moans became more sporadic as his thrusting slowed.

Instead of pulling back, his chest stayed pressed on mine, with our bodies still connected and him uneager to pull out of me. His warm lips kissed the side of my neck, and I tilted my head so he had better access. He ended with a kiss on the side of my head, resting his cheek there as well, with my hair fanning out along my shoulders and down my back.

The silence between us was comfortable as we both came down from our high. My mind was clear, my smile was wide, and my body was relaxed, content with everything we did and everything I was feeling.

The rain continued to pour as we stood together, our embrace unbroken. The sound of the raindrops hitting the leaves of the trees around us soothed me, freeing me of any thoughts that didn't involve anything outside of Diesel.

As I replayed everything he said to me, his words etched into me like stone, I whispered, "Did you mean it?"

Without moving, he asked, "Which part?"

I opened my mouth to answer, but he stopped me.
"Doesn't matter. Yes. I meant all of it."

THOMAS

Jackson Diesel went to trial, pled guilty, was convicted of vehicular homicide, and was sentenced to six years in prison. I couldn't say that I was surprised. The trial didn't bring a lot of media attention; yes, we were in a small town where word spreads fast, but it wasn't the first fatal drunk driving accident, and unfortunately, it won't be the last. I attended the trial, sitting in the last row of the courtroom with only a handful of other witnesses, his guilty plea speeding up the process tremendously. I could barely recognize my dad as he was ushered into the room from the side door, his cheeks had hallowed out and his skin was beginning to sag.

Jail time can ruin a person.

Thankfully, I sat in a spot that was out of his eyesight and my presence never caught his attention. As the judge was reading the police report, the mention of the victim, Gerald Reeves, caused a loud cry from an older woman in the front row. My dad's posture immediately tightened, the tan jumpsuit gripping his shoulders, bowing his head in shame. I looked over to the woman who was dabbing her eyes with a crumpled tissue and instantly recognized her. Back when my dad first told me what he had done, I had a nagging interest in finding out who the victim was. A once-over of the police report and a quick internet search led me to Gerald Reeves, Jerry for short, and his wife, Marilyn Reeves. They were both older, Jerry was sixty-eight and Marilyn was sixty-five, married with two children, Everly and Lucas Reeves. Jerry worked at the power plant right outside the town up until he retired. The pictures showed them both happy, in love, with a life filled with joy and prosperity. Now, Marilyn Reeves was a widow, thanks to my father and his idiotic, selfish decisions.

When looking for information on the victim, I noticed they had multiple addresses. One was a ranch house close to the center of Kittanning, the other was a large building a few miles out, right along the forest that ended the town, tucked away from the noise and traffic. I figured Marilyn would be at the ranch house, and a few days after the trial, I drove over to offer my condolences. The lights were off, with no car in the driveway and snow barricading the doors as if the house hadn't been touched in weeks. I tried my other option, driving to the building on the other side of town. Once I found it, I noticed the parking lot hadn't been plowed, so I parked alongside the road. There was a sign in the frozen ground that read, "Apartments Available," but the wind had pushed the snow so it was covering most of the letters. Stepping out of my car, the winter's wind like little blades of ice on my skin, I looked up and studied the apartment complex. It was a decent size, three stories tall, wide enough to house units with multiple rooms. The poor woman had walked through the snow at ankle height, her footprints the only path to the inside, leading me to the apartment she was in. I did my best to make some sort of clearing, my boots brushing away snow from side to side, slowly making my way under an awning to the very first door. There was a number two on the outside, the metal beginning to rust away leaving streaks of brown, my fist tapping lightly on the door.

"One moment." Her fragile voice echoed on the inside. I brought my fists to the heat of my mouth, exhaling and rubbing them together to keep warm as I waited. Small, quick shuffles became louder as the woman made her way to the door, opening it.

"Are you here for the furnace?"

Before I could answer, she gently tugged on my arm to bring me inside, then closed the door behind me.

"It's so cold outside. I can't leave the door open or else I'll let all the warm air out."

When she spoke, I could see the vapor escaping her mouth. Her breath. There was no warm air in here. It was almost as cold inside as it was outside.

"Poor Teddy, he's probably freezing his boots off." She motioned to the black and white cat lying on the couch. The cat looked to be perfectly content, with its body curled into a ball, sound asleep. Clearly, his fur was acting as a blanket and keeping him warm. He was fine, but I said nothing.

"Come, the furnace is back this way."

I could have stopped her and told her the real reason why I was here, but I've worked with heating and cooling in houses before. I wasn't a professional by any means, but I knew enough to at least look at it. And judging by the temperature in this place, it needed to be fixed fast. I looked around briefly as she walked in front of me. The apartment was in major need of help; the carpet had frayed and torn at the seams, the ceiling had water stains, the switch for the light in the kitchen was missing, a gaping hole in the wall where it should've been. These were all things that were easily fixable, but it wasn't a job for a widowed elderly woman.

I followed her to a back closet door in the corner of the apartment, which led down to a cellar. The hinges on the door were rusted, a metal-on-metal scraping sound causing me to cringe as she pulled it open. I stepped in front of her and walked down the stairs, pulling a string above me to turn on the light. A damp, musty smell filled my nose, puddles of water on the floor grabbing my attention.

"You have a leak down here?" I asked as I looked up the stairs to her.

She shrugged. "I think so."

I rubbed a spot above my eye as I thought to myself. There's no way this woman will be able to survive on her own in a place like this.

There's too much that needs to be done and no one to do it for her, unless she hires an entire team of people, which would cost more than just selling the whole complex. I took a deep breath, forcing myself to focus on one thing at a time, starting with the furnace. It was across the cellar, and with only one look, I could tell the thing was older than me. I walked over and kneeled down, noticing a crack running along the bottom, most likely the cause of the problem. I studied the sides and the top, trying to get a good idea of the issue at hand without being able to open it.

With my focus stuck on the furnace, I did my best to yell up the stairs to her, making my voice clear. "So, I could go out to my truck to get my tools, but I'm going to be honest with you. It's worth getting a new system. This thing can probably be fixed, but you'll just have problems with it again next year."

There was a long pause.

I walked back to the bottom of the stairs and looked up. She was still standing by the door, but now she was silently crying.

I cleared my throat awkwardly. "Are you okay?"

She nodded, her hands trembling as she pulled her sweater tightly around herself. "I'm so sorry."

Making my way back up the stairs, I shook my head. "Don't be. Is there something I can help you with?"

"My husband was so good with these things. He could fix anything. But now he's gone, and I don't know what to do with myself."

Now was my chance. I had to tell her the truth.

"Ma'am, I didn't come here to fix your furnace."

Her eyes immediately looked at mine, her pupils widening in fear. She took a step away from me to the side.

I held my palms up in innocence, hoping she could let go of her panic. "No, no. Please, don't get the wrong idea. My name is Thomas Diesel."

Her hesitation was still holding her, her body frozen. "Diesel? Why does that name sound so…"

"…familiar?" I said, finishing her question. "Because my father is Jackson Diesel."

The statement felt like I ripped off a band-aid. The name clicked in her head, her fearful expression turning to anger.

"I think you need to go."

"Of course, I'll go, I'll go. But I just wanted to come by and talk to you."

"And say what?" Her voice quaked, nerves etched in her vocal cords.

"How sorry I am for what he's done."

She was silent, waiting for me to continue. I didn't think this far ahead, so at this point, I was scrambling to say the right thing.

"It should've never happened. Never. And I'm glad he's in prison. It's where he belongs."

More silence. But the silence meant she was listening.

"I'm going to make it up to you. I know that won't bring your husband back, but I'm going to help you as much as I can. I'll do whatever you need around here."

It was a thought that crossed my mind earlier when I noticed how much more work needed done. I wasn't sure if I wanted to commit to it by saying it out loud until now.

Her tears started flowing again as she slowly moved to sit on one of the wooden chairs at the small kitchen table. "We were married for forty-four years. He was my lifeline." She rested her head in her hands, her elbows propping herself up as she tried to control the tremor in her voice. The skin on her hands was dry and began turning a lighter shade of blue. She had to be freezing in here.

"I miss him so much."

A piece of me felt uncomfortable since I didn't know her that well, but she was still human. She was grieving. I knew how that felt.

I took a few steps to her and crouched down at her side.

"I'm sorry, Mrs. Reeves."

After slowly dropping her hands, she turned to face me, her eyes red with tears.

"You look nothing like him," she said after studying my face for a minute, her voice soft and sincere.

I smirked. "I take after my mom."

A few hours later, the furnace kicked on and was temporarily running, the tips of my fingers frozen solid. Mrs. Reeves was sitting in the kitchen, a steaming cup of tea nestled in her hands, waiting for me to finish. I climbed back up the stairs and noticed the room was a few degrees warmer.

"It feels better already." I wiped my dirty hands on an old, ratty cloth. "You might smell some dust for an hour or so, since the heat hasn't been on in a while. But it's normal. I can stop and pick you up a new furnace tomorrow after work if that's okay with you."

"Yes. Thank you, Thomas."

I nodded and looked around the kitchen, noticing the wallpaper that was beginning to peel. There was a running list in my mind of things that needed done. I could see her studying me out of the corner of my eye, prompting me to speak my thoughts.

"May I ask you something?"

She nodded.

"Why are you here?"

Her puzzled look caused me to explain, choosing my words carefully.

"This doesn't really seem like an ideal place to stay."

She thought for a moment, tapping her fragile fingers against her cup of tea. "Jerry and I bought this building as an investment. He would come here and fix up things when he had the time, but there was only so much he could do. It took too much of a toll on his body. Now that he's gone…" her voice began to crack as her eyes filled with tears. "…I don't like being at our other house. I can't. It reminds me of him, and it hurts."

I could feel the guilt rising in my chest, making me think that maybe I shouldn't have asked. Maybe I shouldn't have come here at all. But before I could process another thought, she spoke up, a heavy change in her tone.

"I want to live here. I want to sell our house."

I raised an eyebrow. "Do you want to rent out these other apartments?"

She waved a hand. "Oh, eventually. Once they're fixed up."

Then she looked at me, her eyebrows raised as if a light just went off in her head.

"Unless you're looking for a place to stay? Did you see the sign out front? You could fix up your own apartment and rent it."

I rubbed the back of my head and forced a small smile. "That's very kind of you, Mrs. Reeves. I'll consider it."

Grabbing a piece of scrap paper from my tool kit, I wrote down my cell phone number and placed it on the kitchen table.

"I'll be back tomorrow with the new furnace. If anything else goes wrong before then, call me and I'll be over."

As I pointed to my phone number, Mrs. Reeves placed her hand over mine. "You don't know how much this means to me, Thomas."

Here I was, cleaning up my father's messes. Feeling guilty for something I didn't even do. I gave her a nod, grabbed my tool kit, and walked to the front door. As I opened it, I noticed it had snowed another inch, accumulating against the side of the door frame.

"I'll bring a snow shovel, too."

I marched outside, pulling the "Apartments Available" sign out of the ground and tossing it into the bed of my truck.

ANNA

After a few minutes in his bathroom cleaning off what was left of us, I stepped out to see the apartment still vacant. I walked back to the balcony doors, slid them open and stepped out, the floor-length shades ruffling in the wind behind me. Now that the storm had passed, the air smelled like fresh earth and rainwater, and the aroma filling my lungs felt almost as good as what happened moments earlier.

I closed the door, eyeing Diesel as he sat in a patio chair, my hair getting caught up in the light breeze. He had nothing but gym shorts on, the skin on his arms and chest lined with a perfect glisten. He leaned back, a cold bottle of water clutched in his hands. As soon as he heard the door close, he turned to face me.

The sight of him brought a smile to my lips, as it always does. "Hi."

"Hey," he said quietly, as if the storm would come back if he were too loud.

I could see his eyes scanning me, head to toe. While in the bathroom, I found one of his t-shirts hanging to dry and put it on. It was light grey, almost white, and came down to my mid-thigh, covering just enough of me while still being comfortable. It was soft and smelled so clean, I wanted to take it home and keep it.

I approached him, and suddenly he stood to his feet, offering me the seat.

"I only have one chair. You can sit."

I shook my head, ignoring his request, and pushed him back down on the cushion. His skin was warm under my palm, his sweat spread in a thin layer between us. He kept his eyes on me as he sat down, obeying my simple order. I placed myself sideways on one of his thighs, my legs resting across his, his body melded perfectly with mine. It's been a while since I've been with anyone else, not only in the romantic sense, and it felt good to have someone with me. Even if it was just sitting and talking, or watching the storm clouds drift away, I missed having someone to be close to. It was the thing I longed for most in life, companionship. Friendship. Love and community. Without it, I was alone, and when I was alone, I was unhappy.

But now, I have Diesel. And although this thing between us is new and fresh and unexpected, I have every reason to be happy.

Taking the water from his grip, I opened the bottle and swallowed whatever was left, then placed the empty bottle on the ground below us.

We sat in silence for a few minutes, his thumb stroking my arm, the warm air comfortable around us. I loved the first few minutes after a storm. The Earth was replenished. The grass, the trees, and the leaves were drinking the rainwater with their color more vibrant than before. Everything felt peaceful. Although, every moment was bound to be calm on this balcony since there was only a forest to watch, sunrises and sunsets to see, and no one ever came around.

Besides me.

And besides the car that hit me.

"Thank God you were out here that night," I spoke the unfiltered thought, breaking the silence.

Diesel didn't say anything, but his thumb stopped stroking my arm. I took notice but didn't move.

After a minute, I asked, "Do you believe in God, Diesel?"

He arched an eyebrow. "Is this your idea of pillow talk?"

I looked at him, squinting my eyes, pushing his sarcasm away. "Answer me."

He looked at me, then away. "I don't."

"Why?"

His chest grew with a deep inhale before he could form a sentence. "Because I saw all the shit my mom went through. There's no way a God would make someone suffer like that."

I winced. A piece of me felt the same way.

"What happened to your mom?"

He looked down at one of my hands, took it, and began mindlessly stroking my palm with his fingertip.

I hoped he didn't mind me asking, but since he opened the door by bringing it up, I figured he was open to discussing it. I could see the wheels turning in his head, trying to relive it without the emotional toll.

"She was diagnosed with breast cancer when I was fourteen. She sat me down and told me about it, but of course, at fourteen, I didn't think it was that serious. And if it was, I knew she could beat it. She was my *mom*. She was invincible in my eyes."

I watched him speak. He still didn't look up from my hand.

"She did well with chemotherapy for a while. Then, when I was sixteen, it all went to hell. She became so weak, so helpless—"

His voice trailed off at the last word, an ache forming in my chest at the sound.

"She was in so much pain. She would get migraines for days, her joints were always swollen, and she could barely walk. I remember sitting with her in the hospital room, holding her hand as she lay there, barely breathing. The machines were doing more work for her than she was for herself. And then, finally, she was gone. Her body gave up. No more pain, no more suffering."

There was a silence, a moment passing that felt necessary.

"So, no, I don't believe in a God that would put someone through that. Or, selfishly, take a mother away from a sixteen-year-old."

With his fingertips still swirling aimlessly, I grabbed his hand and looked into his eyes.

"I'm really sorry, Diesel."

His blue eyes looked even more saturated as they met mine. I could see the love, the hurt, and the longing for his mom. And that thought stabbed me in the gut, as I wondered if people could see that in me, too.

Even though he had already opened up to me this much, I took my chances and asked another question. "What about your dad?"

He let out a laugh that sounded more like a hack. "What about him? He's a piece of shit. Started a good company, but after my mom died, he couldn't run it to save his life."

So, everything in Diesel's world came crashing down after his mom died. That's completely understandable. Grief affects everyone in different ways, forcing them to cope in different ways as well. His dad apparently didn't cope very well. My heart broke a little, thinking about how Diesel must've taken losing his mom *and* pieces of his dad at the same time. It's no wonder why he can be so closed off.

I leaned into him, resting my head on his shoulder, continuing the conversation. "He started the business? Why do you run it now?"

"Long story," he clipped out, and that was that. I got this much out of him, I wasn't going to press the topic any further.

It's funny how humans think sometimes. Diesel was okay with sharing the story of his mother with me, with all his hurt and grief, but didn't want to talk about his father. Maybe the pain was too fresh. I shrugged it off, knowing I'll probably get an explanation someday.

"What about you?" he asked, resting his chin on my head. "Do you believe?"

I took a long, deep breath, inhaling his natural scent before choosing my words carefully.

"Yeah. I do." I began with my most straightforward answer, then carried on. "I've always felt connected to the world, ever since I was a little girl. The sun, the moon, the stars, everything about the world intrigued me. The way people and animals live together. The way the Earth supplies us with everything we need to live, but we still rely on things like love and happiness to keep us alive. I could lay in the grass forever, watch the clouds and smell the fresh air, and the feelings I would get completely surpass any explanation."

I stopped, a smile spreading on my face.

"I sound like a hippie."

I could feel Diesel's cheeks move on my head and I knew he was smiling, too.

"Anyway, there was always something deep inside me that knew there was something bigger. I call it my 'seventh sense.'"

"Don't you mean 'sixth sense'?" Diesel choked out, his grin unwavering.

"No," I replied teasingly. "That's a movie. This is my seventh sense. The feeling I have knowing there's more to life than just this. There's something beyond the things you can see. There might not be cut-and-dry Heaven or Hell, but there's no way this is the end. So, even if I don't know exactly how everything plays out, I know there's more out there waiting for us."

Diesel tucked a lock of hair behind my ear, and I had to keep my thoughts from glitching.

"So, you're one of those people that hears about something awful and says 'everything happens for a reason,' with a smile, right?"

I could tell he was being playful with his tone, but it was an actual question.

"Not in the hallmark sort of way, no."

I sat up to look at him, debating on if I should say what I was thinking. But with one look at the softness in Diesel's face, I knew I could.

"Take your mom, for example. She was an amazing mom, I'm sure. And what happened to her was completely unfair. Not just to her, but to you too. I went down the same road with my dad. There was no doubt in my mind that he was the most incredible person I've ever known. I was so angry and lost and *broken* when he died, and a big part of me still is, but I know that it's not the end. My dad still lives in everything he taught me, just like your mom still lives in you."

He shifted at the mention of his mom but let me continue.

"Life has a continuous flow, through us, through nature, through science, through the unexplainable. It never ends, and it definitely doesn't get easier, but sometimes we get these rare glimpses of moments where something happens that we can't explain."

Something must have struck a chord in Diesel because my last sentence made his body stiffen. He gently pulled his arms away, his hand rubbing the stubble on his jaw, avoiding eye contact with me.

"What's wrong?" I asked, his head turned away from me, his eyes on the trees.

I knew I shouldn't have used him and his mom as an example. It was too much of a touchy subject, and I should've left it alone.

He shook his head. "Nothing. You just…"

I watched him, waiting for what felt like an eternity.

"…you're smart, Anna. You know that?"

A subtle smirk forced its way onto my face. I knew that's not what he was going to say, but I'll take the compliment anyway. "Thanks."

"What about your mom?" His question mimicked mine from moments earlier. He couldn't get it out quick enough, impatient to get the attention off of anything to do with him.

"Long story," I answered and smiled at our little game. There was an effortlessness in the way we teased each other so naturally, lifting the sobering mood.

Diesel raised his eyebrows in response. "Oh, so you have mommy issues…"

"…and you conveniently have daddy issues?" I finished his thought, pointing a finger at him.

"Trust me," he said, his teeth clenched, threading a hand through my hair. "There are plenty more issues with me than that." His fist tightened in my hair, pulling hard on my scalp. My lips curled up, enjoying this far too much. The intensity he instilled in me only pulled me closer to him, my fever for him climbing with each and every moment.

His eyes drilled into mine, and before I knew it, my vision was flipped upside down as he picked me up and threw me over his shoulder.

My legs dangled over his chest, my hips dug into his shoulder, and my hair draped down his back.

"Diesel!" I shrieked. "Put me down!"

He stood up, holding me effortlessly with one arm, and opened the sliding glass door with the other.

"I've lasted as long as possible with you in my shirt." He gripped the bottom of my butt that was now peeking out from the fabric, a singeing heat tingling on my skin. "Time to take it off."

As he carried me to his bedroom, my laughter was unstoppable, and my heart filled more and more with each step. Even though we were alone, he shut the bedroom door and we made love until we couldn't keep our eyes open any longer.

THOMAS

I had spent the last few months at Mrs. Reeves' apartment complex, fixing up multiple projects that needed to be done. The electric running to the living room ceiling light was now working, I applied new caulking to all the windows, and I paid some of my guys at work to put in new carpeting, replacing the old, stained one. The apartment was really coming together, just a few coats of paint and it will look forty times better than before. Mrs. Reeves offered to pay me, of course, but there was no way I would ever accept it after what my father had done to her. Day after day, I could still see the heartbreak in her eyes, but there was a small trickle of hope as time progressed. Her smile beamed when I would show up at her doorstep, as if she was looking forward to having the company. Sometimes, I would stop over just to bring her dinner, not even worrying about fixing anything that night. As the months passed, she grew more used to me, treating me like I was a part of her family. I could feel her trust in me, and I never led her off course.

One night, after I was done fixing a doorframe in her apartment, I asked her if I could look at the apartment above us. I pointed to the water stain on her ceiling and wanted to double-check to make sure there wasn't any severe or permanent damage done. Without hesitation, she gave me a ring with a key to each apartment. Upon inspection, I found a small leak in the second-floor apartment, right above hers. Thankfully, it was an easy fix. As I looked around, I noticed that all the problems in this vacant apartment were all similar to the ones downstairs. Tedious, yes, but nothing I couldn't handle. Still holding the ring of keys, I walked up to the third floor and opened the door to apartment six. Once again, similar issues, simple fixes. I walked around, feeling the paint chipping off the walls, the dust kicking up and filling my lungs. I made my way to the doors that led out to the balcony and unlocked them with a flick of my wrist, but the doors were stuck closed. I pulled and pulled, shifting my weight behind me, but nothing came loose. Maybe the winter had sealed it shut, ice gluing the door to its tracks. Whatever the case, I knew I'd be back. I never leave anything unfinished.

After saying my goodbyes to Mrs. Reeves, I headed home. It was late, almost ten thirty, and I could barely keep my eyes open. These fourteen-hour days were wearing me down. My body ached and my hands were littered with blood blisters. I shuffled inside to the kitchen, opening the fridge to find an old, shriveling apple and some leftover pizza. I ate the pizza cold, downing it all in just a few minutes, then headed upstairs to take a shower. Once I was done, I walked out into the hallway and looked to the far door.

It was my parents' room.

A deep breath filled me as I walked to it. The door was closed, always closed, because I had wanted everything in there to stay there. It was like a time capsule, with pieces of my mom still trapped on the other side.

With my hand on the doorknob, I could hear my mother's voice on the other side.

Hi, sweetie! How was your day?

Fuck. I fucking missed my mom. I could almost feel her gentle touch through the metal under my palm.

There was a sharp pang in my chest, an ache for something I could never get back. It was a void that yearned for the one person who loved me unconditionally, who was supposed to be here, with me, guiding me, helping me grow up into the person she was shaping me to be. But the hole inside me couldn't be filled, and I don't think I'll ever come to accept that fact.

I opened the door, a relief sweeping over me as I took it in.

Nothing in the room had changed.

My mother's clothes still hung in the closet, and her earrings still rested on the top of her dresser. Even some of my father's things were scattered around, although he hardly ever came up here since she died. Moving to sit on the edge of the bed, the scent of old, stale bed sheets filling the air, I rested my head in my hands.

It was at that moment that I knew what I had to do, what I would have to push myself to do.

I needed to move on, be the adult I'd been forced to be, and sell this house.

I needed to give myself closure.

"Tommy D." My dad's hands rested on his thighs; a smile spread upon his face. "I didn't think I'd see you here anytime soon."

I wasn't in the mood to return the smile. I wasn't angry anymore, but the dynamic between us had changed. I wasn't sure if he felt it, but I did.

"What's going on? How's the business?" my dad asked as the guard made his way to his corner of the room. This time, two other tables were occupied with other inmates and their family members, their voices hushed and muffled.

"It's fine."

"Good. I'm glad to hear it."

I leaned back in my chair, my decision made, my mind clear.

No tiptoeing, no bullshitting.

"I want to sell the house."

My dad didn't flinch. He stared at me for a few moments, unblinking. I tried to read his expression, but there was none. Nerves began to creep up my chest, but I mentally talked myself out of it. I had to make him think that he was in *my* power, not the other way around.

He directed a quick and quiet laugh to me. "What makes you think I'd do that?"

"You're not going to. I am."

"Okay," he spat out as he shook his head, clearly annoyed. "What makes you think I'd *let* you do that?"

I can answer this in one of two ways.

One, I could tell him the truth. Tell him that it hurt to go home every night, alone, to a house that reminded me of a family that ultimately fell apart. To see the remnants of a mother who didn't deserve the ending she got. To live in a house that wasn't mine, but suddenly now my responsibility, and to only use it for two things: showering and sleeping.

Or, two, I could make it seem like selling the house would benefit him.

The choice was fucking obvious.

"Because it will hurt you if you don't."

He rolled his eyes, the condescending reaction I was expecting.

"I'm being serious. I'm barely there anymore. I go there to sleep and get the mail. That's it. I can't keep up with your bills on top of the business. Do you want your payments to fall behind? Do you want your credit score to tank so that the second you walk out of here, you're screwed? Do you want to have a foreclosure under your name?"

"There are worse things associated with my name."

A sarcastic laugh escaped me. "Right, right. Just add it to the list."

My dad leaned forward, his hands clasped together on the table, and his voice dropped to a whisper. "You took my business. Now you want to take the house, too? The home of your mother?"

"Oh, cut the shit. You haven't cared about the house long before the prison became your new home."

"That's not true."

"Yes, it is. Mom's room is still untouched, as if she just died yesterday. It's like we're waiting for her to come back, but she's not. We need to let go. She's gone, you're gone. We need to sell it. And you won't have to lift a finger to do it."

His eyes narrowed. "Where are you staying? You got a girlfriend you're living with?"

"No."

He was quiet, waiting for me to elaborate. When he realized I wasn't going to, he sighed. "Where am I supposed to go when I'm out of here? Where am I supposed to live?"

"You'll figure it out. You always do."

There was a brief silence between us as one of the other inmates stood to leave, the guard escorting him back to his cell. The future hung in the balance of my father's choosing. I could tell he was apprehensive by the way he was bouncing his leg, the way he looked anywhere except at me, and the run of his tongue over his teeth.

I had one last card to play.

"I'll put the money into the business."

He looked up at me, clearly not convinced.

"The house is almost paid off, right? I'm not pocketing the money. It will go straight into the business for whatever we need. Although, we're doing pretty good without any extra money."

I was being honest when I told him the company was doing fine. Truthfully, we were doing better than fine. We were hired by a neighboring town to build a church and a small cluster of houses behind it, and it paid *really* well. I had enough money to hire a few more guys and even hand out some bonuses at Christmas.

His shoulders slumped forward, still listening but not eager to jump on board with the plan. I sighed, growing impatient.

"I can save some of the money if you want to put a down payment on something when you get released."

I was reluctant to tell him the last part, especially since I wasn't sure if it was something I really wanted to do, but I wanted to persuade him somehow.

"Fine."

I grinned. Isn't It funny how he'll make sacrifices to help himself or his business but not for me?

About a week later, I returned to the prison with our lawyer, Kurt Young. Between this and signing over the business, Kurt and I had spent more than enough time together. My dad and I signed the papers to make myself his power of attorney, allowing me to sell the house in his name, since he couldn't do it while he was incarcerated. There was still reluctance on his end, but at this point, I didn't care. The house would be better off with a real family.

Over the next few weeks, I cleaned out the house, room by room, throwing away more than saving. I ended up hiring movers and cleaners to help since I was still strapped for time most days. The movers boxed every room except for one: my mother's room. I told them I would take care of it since I had to go through her belongings anyways. I donated her clothes, sold the furniture, and searched for the one item I wanted to keep the most.

Her ring.

I remember watching her slide it off her finger the day she began radiation, as her bones ached and her skin lacked the warm glow she once had. As much as I hate to remember her in that state, it was the rawest image I had of her in my memory.

I eyed the jewelry box on her dresser and noticed a flash of something glinting in the light.

It was the ring.

She never put it back on.

It was a beautiful, shimmering, square diamond on a single silver band. Timeless. I fished it from the box and slid it into my pocket, safely tucked away from the dangers of misplacing it.

The house sold after only a month on the market for a hearty two hundred fifty thousand dollars. The buyers were a married couple with two kids, looking for a quiet, forever home. At the signing, I wished them luck, handed over the keys, and closed that chapter of my life, never looking back.

I will always be grateful for the place I grew up, but like all things, I know nothing lasts.

Later that afternoon, I pulled the U-Haul up to my new home. I lifted the back door of the truck, revealing the last of my boxes. My bed, the couch, and the rest of the heavy furniture were already moved in and settled in their appropriate places, thanks to the movers I hired. I pulled out the first box, the plates and dishes clanging together with my every move, and began walking. The door to my right swung open.

"Welcome home, Thomas."

I smiled. "Thanks, Mrs. Reeves."

I climbed the three flights of steps to the top floor and opened the door to apartment number six. I walked past the living room and into the kitchen, placing the box on the countertop with a thud. After pushing through the next few rounds of hauling boxes, I finally brought the last one up, setting it on the floor next to the kitchen table. I headed straight to the fridge, grabbed a cold beer, and cracked it open. My mind was officially mush, so I decided to call it a night. I would deal with the boxes in the days to come.

Now, I could breathe.

I looked around at the first place I could call my own. So many nights were spent here, fixing up anything and everything, trying to make it fit into somewhere I'd want to live. There were still little things that needed fine-tuning, but for now, it was perfect.

The beer slid down my throat, the cold refreshing, as I walked to the glass doors and slid them open with complete ease.

ANNA

Leaning into the entrance of the warehouse, I crossed my arms over my chest as Diesel pulled into the parking lot, with his truck sliding evenly into his designated spot. The engine cut off as the driver's door opened, his long leg leading his step out of his truck. We've been together for two months now, and I still get lost in a trance every time I see him. From his boots and his slim jeans, to his black t-shirt and his aviators, everything about him is perfect to me.

As he stepped into the sunlight, I gazed at his light brown hair, which was carefully mussed, my fingers curling at the sight and aching to run through it. After locking the truck, he turned to the entrance, only to catch me standing there with a bright smirk plastered on my face. He stopped in his tracks for only a moment, then walked to me, the same sexy smirk spreading on his full lips.

"What are you doing here?" Once he reached me, he wrapped his arms around my waist, pressing a quick kiss to my lips.

I responded by lifting my arms around his neck, catching the specks of dirt sprinkled across his face. "I thought I'd surprise you."

"Didn't you have class today?"

"I finished early." It was true. I finished class around noon, giving me enough time to work out the real reason why I was visiting him.

He pulled my hips into him, the feeling of his firm body against mine sending a chill all over my body.

"I like when you talk about finishing," he whispered into my ear, the meaning behind his words creating heat between my legs. We were insatiable for each other and have been since the first time we crossed that line. Even though we had sex last night, and this morning before he left for work, I would happily sneak him into one of his back rooms and take all of him.

He kissed the spot right below my ear, then moved to my jaw, up to my cheek, then onto my lips, leaving a trail of kisses the entire way. With his cock throbbing against me and my hands mindlessly sneaking up under his shirt, I knew I had to pump the brakes.

"Wait, wait." I laughed through our kisses, but pushed him gently away with my hands on his chest.

"I don't know if I can." He pinned me against the doorframe, his hand moving and resting above my head. Even though there was no one around currently, he obviously didn't care about anyone seeing our lips tied together like this.

Why was he making this so hard? His want for me made me go weak, and my desires were ready to cave in. I shook it off and said it again. "Diesel, *wait*."

He looked at me, confused. "What?"

"I have something for you."

Grabbing his hand, I guided him to his office, a twist of excitement hot on my heels. The door was closed as we stood outside of it. He looked at me again as I opened the door just enough to switch on the light.

"Close your eyes."

He did as he was told, but I thought better of it.

"I don't trust you." I walked behind him, reaching up and covering his eyes with my hands. His skin was soft even though it was coated with a thin layer of grime and dust. I knew today was a day when Diesel would be out of the office, working on-site with one of his properties, so I seized the chance and came here while he was gone.

I kicked the door open all the way and nudged Diesel inside, my hands still covering his eyes. I stood on my tiptoes to whisper in his ear, but he was so tall that I could barely whisper into his neck. "I couldn't wait until your birthday."

I dropped my hands. There, in front of us, was a brand new desk and office chair. The desk was solid, dark wood to replace the flimsy, sixty-year-old card table. It was wide enough to hold his computer, a small stationary section for all his papers, and a plant that I secretly hoped he could keep alive. The chair was black and well cushioned, with all the swivels and levers he could need.

Diesel walked to the desk and examined it, his fingers trailing along the edge. He moved to the chair, gave it a twist, and looked at me.

He said nothing, even though his smile said it all.

"You like it?"

There was a pause. "No one has ever done something this nice for me before."

I walked over to his side, sliding an arm around his waist and giving him a squeeze. "You deserve it. I couldn't stand to watch you sit in that awful chair for another second."

He planted a kiss on the top of my head, his lips resting there as he whispered. "Thank you."

I smiled. It was such a simple moment that meant more than what it showed at face value. Diesel works so hard to keep the steady flow of things, always taking care of his employees first and himself last. He needed to know that he was appreciated, too.

My insides warmed. Treating him felt so good.

"Try it out." I motioned for him to sit. He did, his posture straight as he slid the chair up to the desk and ran a smooth hand over the wood. His smile beamed, the crinkles in the corners of his eyes bringing life to my heart.

"So *this* is why Darrell needed the keys to my office today?"

I shrugged innocently. I needed the door unlocked somehow, and Darrell was one of the few people Diesel could trust. All it took was a phone call, a forgotten tool at the warehouse, and Darrell volunteering himself to go back and get it. Diesel threw him the keys, and everything from there was a go.

"She did good, didn't she, Boss?" Darrell poked his head into the office as he walked by. He sent a wink to me, and I smiled in return, our execution flawless.

"I couldn't have done it without him."

It was true. When I opened the boxes and pulled out the booklet of directions, I took one look and gave up. With a small bribe of food from The 87, he was the one who put it all together, way faster than I ever could have.

He held his palm up to his heart, thankful for my words, then looked to Diesel. "I'm headin' out." He gave a salute, then shut the office door.

Diesel couldn't peel his eyes off me when he yelled to Darrell. "Have a good weekend."

After a moment, the place was quiet. Darrell was the last one to leave the warehouse.

Now, it was just us.

Alone.

Diesel was in a good mood, and I was in a giving mood. It was a dangerous combination. I couldn't help but pull in my bottom lip, biting hard.

"Come here." His voice was stern and demanding, leaving no room to guess what he wanted from me. I walked to him, and his hands found my hips once again as he remained in his chair, tilting his chin up to me slightly. "We're alone now. And I think I need to break in this chair a bit."

I lifted one leg up onto the chair, my knee pressing into the space beside him.

"And the desk, too."

I stopped, my face puzzled only a second before he lifted me up, placing me down on the surface of the desk. I laid down on my back as Diesel looked at me with hunger. His jaw flexed as he brought his hand up to my mouth, his thumb pulling my bottom lip down. He looked like he wanted to bite it, to rip it off and keep it.

I'd probably let him.

With a quick shoot of his arm, he grabbed my face and turned my head away, giving him full access to my neck. I whimpered quietly, both shocked and aroused. He leaned down and kissed the skin of my neck, trailing down until he reached my collarbone, where he then decided to suck. I always knew his mouth had power, but I underestimated his ability to peel me apart from a single draw through his lips. The layers of skin broke apart, my yelp quickly turning to moans as deep red circles appeared on the surface.

His hands moved lower as they found their way under my sweater, pushing the fabric up, my own hands pulling it over my head and tossing it to the side. I could feel his lips turn up in a grin against my chest. He knew I wanted this just as badly.

His lips made their way down to my breasts, his mouth stopping over my bra as he unhooked it, letting my chest free. His warm tongue licked over my nipple, an unstoppable rush taking over every inch of me. He didn't stay there long, despite my weak plea when he moved on. He kissed his way down my stomach, stopping at the button of my jeans. I knew how good he was with me, with the way he tasted me and savored me.

Trust me, I *knew*.

So, I wasted no time unbuttoning my jeans, his hands pulling the denim over my hips and past my knees. His eyes soaked up every inch of my skin that became exposed, his fingertips caressing me gently. He got up and leaned forward, his body hovering over mine, and kissed me. Those soft, full lips felt like heaven every single time. Without opening his eyes, he broke the kiss and moved to my ear, his voice hushed, his tone firm.

"Don't you *ever* think you can try to do something nice for me without expecting me to return the favor."

As soon as the last word left his mouth, I felt his fingers glide along the edge of my underwear. He slipped a finger underneath, tenderly brushing his skin on mine. Just the simple touch made a moan sit in the bottom of my throat, and my self-control was doing everything to find its way out of me. I kept my eyes closed as his fingers caressed me, circling my clit, my breath growing ragged as he kissed the side of my face. Then down he went, trailing his lips the entire way, landing at the spot right above my underwear. I smiled, knowing he was everything I had ever wanted, and I had him in every part of my body.

My heart, my mind, my soul, and in between my legs.

He grabbed the top of the fabric, pulling it down forcefully, his eyes watching me. My chest was rising and falling at a faster speed. I could feel his hot breath moving lower, my legs aching for his mouth to lick me, suck me, bite me, anything. I *needed* this, his love like water for my body, air for my lungs.

"Diesel," I managed to squeeze out, more for myself than for him. I wanted him, all of him, all the time, and just his name in my mouth could spark a flame in me that could never be put out.

"Say it again."

I arched my back as he dove in, desperation in my soul, his lips taking me to places I didn't know I could go.

"Diesel." His name came out broken, the lust in my voice cracking it in half.

Somehow my mind and body disconnected from each other, but still worked in a perfect rhythm to take me up in the clouds. I felt weightless, with Diesel's power over me unmatched by anything I had ever experienced before. My fingers grabbed his hair, my grip pulling him into me, his mouth never faltering. It felt *so* good.

Diesel managed to look up at me for a second, a smile forming through his taste. In the same breath, he stood to his feet and began to fumble with his belt.

"I need to fuck you."

His words were filled with a venom made for only me.

There was no time wasted as he dropped his jeans, then his boxer briefs, and closed the gap between our bodies. With my legs spread, completely vulnerable here on his desk, my body began to shake at the need for him.

"You taste so good. But you feel even better."

I let out a gasp as he guided the tip of his cock up and down, teasing me, his warmth pressing gently against me.

"Please, Diesel."

The smile on his face grew, knowing he had me right where he wanted me. He let go of himself, only for a moment, grabbing my hand and moving it down to replace where he just was. I grabbed onto his length, his pulse aching, his needs crystal clear.

He needed this, I needed this.

I guided him to my entrance, my skin soaking wet, only for him to pause and lean down to my ear once more. He held his weight in his hands, pressed to either side of my head, and I could feel his fingers lightly stroking my hair.

"Anna,"

There was a quiver in his deep voice, so slight that I almost doubted it.

My eyes met his, the cold blue irises a shock to my delicate system.

"I just want you to know…"

He brought a hand to my face, his thumb stroking my cheek gently.

"…I am so *fucking*…"

He moved his hand to my throat and thrust deep inside me, his eyes still locked on mine. My groan was stuck in my lungs, unable to claw its way out.

"…in love with you."

That's it. I was gone.

He felt so incredibly good inside me, but now my heart was on another planet, soaring through the stars at lightspeed. He only thrust a few more times before I tipped over the edge, my mouth speechless and my mind blank. Our skin was slick with sweat, his hips rubbing on mine, and just a minute later his thrusts began to slow as he finished deep inside me. He relaxed his upper body, leaning down next to me, his panting heavy in my ear.

I felt him turn his face to me. His voice was so quiet, I could barely hear him. "I love you, Anna."

My legs were still hooked around him, his pulse deep between my thighs. I faced him, my back still flat on the desk, my smile so wide my cheeks ached. "I love you, too."

I knew I wanted him from the first moment I saw him. I knew I liked him from the first moment we ever spoke. And I knew I loved him from the first time we kissed.

Minutes passed as we caught our breath, our bodies still connected, both of us in no hurry to move. We wanted this to last forever.

I could feel his hand stroke my hair slowly and gently. I wondered what he was thinking about right now. Us? Work? Sleep? I closed my eyes, the desk growing uncomfortable as time went on, before hearing Diesel take a breath, about to speak. I looked at him again as he stood back up, holding his hands out to help me sit up.

"Thank you, again, for this." He looked at the desk once more.

He had already made his thankfulness clear, but I could sense it meant a lot to him, so I welcomed his words. "Anything for you."

His fingers trailed up my arm, the tingling sensation creeping back into my body. "So, now that we broke in the desk…"

He slowly took a step back, the padding of the chair against his legs.

"…It's time to break in the chair."

He sat down, his jeans still down past his knees, and motioned for me. We both smiled as I climbed onto his lap, straddling him, our bodies fused together like perfect puzzle pieces.

THOMAS

NOVEMBER 5, 2016

There was a knock on my office door as I was typing on my computer.

"It's open," I yelled without looking up from the screen.

A flicker of light grabbed my attention as it made its way into the room. It was a candle, a giant "21" made of wax taped to the top of a bottle of Bourbon, carried in by some of the guys from work.

"Happy birthday, Big T!"

I laughed, sitting back in my chair, amazed that they remembered my birthday. No one has gone out of their way to do something like this in a long time. "Thank you."

"Now, you can come out and drink with us." Darrell placed the bottle down on my desk, the flame growing taller. "Legally."

I blew out the candle and grabbed the glass bottle, studying it. "Really, thank you. You didn't have to do this."

Jim chimed in, standing by the door. "Come on, of course we did. You only turn twenty-one once."

"You're going out with us tonight. We're not taking no for an answer." Darrell pointed his finger at me, not even giving me a chance to say no. "As soon as you're off the clock, we're going. And we're getting shitfaced."

"Aren't you guys a little old to be getting shitfaced?"

"Watch it, TD. I can still kick your ass." Darrell pretended to box me, his fists up, punching me in the shoulder.

"Alright, alright." I put my hands up in surrender. "I'll go. As long as no one calls off tomorrow." As soon as the words came out, I internally winced at how stupid I sounded.

It was easier to give in to the plans rather than fight them. Anyway, the only plans I had tonight were going home, heating up a frozen pizza, and watching reruns of *Bar Rescue*. I haven't gone out and celebrated my birthday in years, and it has developed into just another day. Getting any sort of break in my mundane life was refreshing, even if it was with my employees who were old enough to be my father.

"You got it, Boss."

The guys returned to their jobs as my eyes stayed glued to the dripping, now hardening wax on the candle.

It was after five o'clock before I had even realized the workday was ending. My muscles ached, signaling to the rest of my body to stand up and stretch. I had been working on the computer for most of the day, only taking a quick break for lunch and inventory. I stepped out of the office and looked around. The warehouse was quiet, but the lights were still on. The guys must have just left. I pulled my phone out of my pocket to see a missed text message from twenty minutes ago.

Darrell: Come to The 87! We are getting food.

I quickly typed a message back.

Me: Finishing up some things. Be out later.

There were some calls I had to make regarding a new subdivision. It was a far drive for us, about forty-five minutes one way, but it paid *really* good money. I contacted the developer, who was waiting for my call, and an hour passed before we hung up. I closed up my office and the warehouse and drove back to my apartment. After showering off the inevitable dust from work, I headed back out to my truck to meet the guys, only to realize it had been over two hours since Darrell texted me. I hopped in the driver's seat and pulled out my phone.

Me: You still out?

I figured they were probably done by now, on their way back home. A buzz came through the phone.

Darrell: Meet us at Stoney's.

Shit.

Stoney's was the last place I wanted to go. After my dad's incident, I tried, again and again, to go there and talk to Eve. Or Laila. Or whatever the hell her name was. But every time I would pull into the parking lot, I would back out. I would sit in my truck, fumble with my car keys, trying to think of things to say or ask her. Nothing ever came to my mind.

Then one night, sitting in the parking lot, I saw the back door open. Laila stepped out, her black stilettos swapped out for red ones, still looking as breathtaking as before. She put a cigarette to her lips and flicked a lighter, a small red circle glowing as she inhaled. The wind swept her fire-red hair as smoke exhaled from her maroon lips, a black wool coat draped over her shoulders. She was alone, and it was the perfect opportunity for me to talk to her.

But seeing her for the first time since my dad went to prison—no, since my eighteenth birthday—I realized I had nothing to say to her. I had spent so much time dwelling over my anger toward her and my dad, that I didn't realize there was no eagerness to speak to her.

I felt nothing.

No nerves, no fear, nothing.

It was as simple as this: I just didn't want to talk to her.

I watched her as she took another drag of her cigarette, then dropped it and crushed it with the toe of her shoe. Another woman opened the door to smoke right as Laila turned to go back inside, and when she did, I could have sworn I saw her look in my direction, the smallest of smirks turning up on her lips.

That was over six months ago, and I doubt she would remember me if she saw me. She sees so many people every night, I was probably just a forgotten face to her. But to me, she was someone I would never forget, for more reasons than one.

I pulled into the parking lot, turned off the truck, and walked inside. The place hadn't changed much; the red lights still illuminated the room, the music was still blasting, and the catwalk sat right in the middle of the floor. The tables had been replaced with new ones, bigger than before, and organized in a way that was less chaotic. I showed the bouncer my ID and scanned the room, searching for familiar faces. Finally, I saw Darrell over in the corner, his towering height sticking him out from everyone else. He was sitting with a few other guys from work, ever so conveniently at the same table I sat at for my eighteenth birthday. The sight of it sent flashbacks: Parker jostling my shoulders, Caleb pulling out a wad of cash for the dancers, the rumors of me hooking up with a stripper floating around school the following week.

The whispers died down, but my reputation never did.

Darrell noticed me and shouted, "Happy birthday TD! Get over here!" with his voice booming over the music. I smiled and walked to them, and Jim handed me a glass of beer as I pulled out a chair and sat down. I happily accepted and took a drink, raising cheers to the guys. I wasn't nervous, this being my first time back inside in three years, but I couldn't help but feel eyes on me. Watching me. I turned my back and looked around, examining the faces of all the women working. None of them was the person I was looking for. I turned back to the table and gulped down more beer.

"Drink up, Boss. There's more coming!"

They weren't kidding when they said they were getting shitfaced.

Anyone could tell this wasn't their first drink of the night, and only a couple of minutes went by before the waitress brought out more. I still had half a glass in my first drink, so I quickly downed it and grabbed another. I wanted to take advantage of this night, as I realized it's probably the only time I'll be away from work for a while.

"Atta boy!"

I felt a proud clap on my back as I continued to drink.

The night rolled on, the topic of work completely off limits, the guys treating me like one of their own. There was always a thought in the back of my mind, wondering if it was strange for them that their boss was only twenty-one, while most of them were old enough to be my father. But their acceptance and approval of me came naturally.

I tilted my head back, letting the beer slide down my throat. The drinks were steadily adding up on someone's tab, thankfully not mine. I had lost count of how many I had, five or six maybe, before there was a quick lull in the music. We had all stopped our conversation, turning our heads to see what was about to happen. A new song started up, the buzz in my ears keeping me from moving any more than I already had. The black curtains along the stage had ruffled, a slender leg sliding its way out with a white stiletto strapped to the foot. There were cheers and whistles from men at other tables.

I held my breath, trying to keep steady as I waited to see the person behind the curtain.

A hand peeked out, caressing the leg slowly.

More cheers, more howling.

I took another quick glance around the room. She was still nowhere to be seen.

With my back pressed against the chair, our waitress returned with a round of shots for our table. I didn't even look to see what it was. I grabbed one, clinked the glass with the others in cheers, and gulped it down in a single swallow.

Back when I saw *her* standing outside, I knew I didn't feel anything. But now, sitting here at the same table, with the same lights and sounds,

I wasn't sure if I would feel the same emptiness as I did when I was sitting in my truck.

I waited for the alcohol to send me deeper into dizziness while I watched the stripper tease the audience.

Her leg slipped out more, showing the top of her thigh.

Her arm, wrapped in a silk robe, made its way out from behind the curtain.

Soon enough, she was completely out from behind the curtain, but her back was to us, the hood of her robe hiding her identity.

Darrell and the guys were hollering, clapping their hands, waiting for her show.

She slowly dropped her cover, revealing jet-black hair and a flower tattoo on her shoulder.

I took in a sharp, deep breath, knowing it wasn't who I was waiting for. It was someone else.

As the dancer took the stage, I realized my grip was locked onto the shot glass in my hand. Thankfully, none of the guys noticed my white knuckles. I could stay here, enjoy the show and drink some more, but I needed to cool down for a minute. Standing up, I told them I was going to use the restroom and get some air, but no one heard me, and no one seemed to care, which was fine by me.

I rounded my way around the tables, making my way past the bar toward the restrooms, when I heard a voice shout at me.

"Hey, Thomas."

The words stopped me dead in my tracks. With the room tilted on its side, I tried to blame it on the beer, or my mind playing tricks on me, but it happened again.

"Thomas," a singsong voice called to my back.

No. *Nope.*

I'm *not* doing this tonight.

I looked over my shoulder, remaining as calm as possible, but I was an unsteady drunk. An emotional drunk. And when I saw her, wiping down the bar top with a rag, a knowing smile plastered on her face, I felt like I was in a movie.

Shit.

Looks like I *am* doing this tonight.

"Come here, have a seat."

There was an open stool at the spot in front of her. I walked to it and sat down, trying to keep my expression blank and my balance straight, but I knew she could see right through me. Her looks hadn't changed at all; her hair was still long, wavy, and bright red, her teeth were white and straight, and her skin looked as if she walked right out of a painting. This time, instead of undressing in a private room, she stood behind the bar, tending to those not seated at a table.

I blinked, hard and slow. Was it the alcohol messing with me? I knew she wasn't there before. There had to be someone else working behind the bar when I looked for her, or else I would have noticed her instantly. She wore a white tank top, her shoulders soft and beautifully rounded, her breasts holding a perfect teardrop shape as they brushed firm against the cotton. Her frayed jean shorts dipped right below her hips, revealing a black string thong at the top. She clearly saw me staring, my inebriated eyes lingering on her body for far too long, causing a smirk to grace her lips. I choked down my drunken desires and forced myself to study her face, trying to get a read on her.

"You're a bartender now?"

"No. Astrid is on her break. I'm filling in."

Astrid? I don't remember anyone in this town having that name. It probably was a stage name.

She pulled out two shot glasses and set them down in front of her.

"Pick your poison."

Thank God we were in the corner of the room, where the music didn't quite reach us and we didn't have to scream over it. I shook my head and held up my hand. "I'm good."

"Oh, come on, Thomas. You don't want to do a shot with me?"

Call me crazy, but I thought I sensed a hint of flirtation in her request. I brushed it off, just like I have every other time.

"I've already had enough to drink."

She took out a bottle of tequila from behind the bar and poured it into both glasses. "Are you sure?" Her eyes sparkled with a glimmer of a tease. She placed a small dish with two lime slices on the surface in front of me, eyeing me. "It is your birthday, after all."

My eyes matched hers, my adrenaline kicking in as the room continued to spin.

She must've heard the guys talking about it at our table.

Or maybe the bouncer told her after seeing my ID.

Or maybe she remembers me and remembers what happened three years ago.

She raised her eyebrows to me, waiting to see if I took one of the shots. I shook my head again and she shrugged, taking over both glasses.

First shot.

Downed it.

Sucked on a lime.

Second shot.

Downed it.

Sucked on a lime.

She flipped the shot glasses over and pressed her palms down on the bar top, acting as if she just took shots of water, completely unfazed.

"So, Thomas…"

I cut her off. "You remember me?"

"Of course I remember you." She brought a finger under my chin, and I was immediately brought back to this night three years ago when she did the exact same thing in the private room. "How could I forget?"

I continued to watch her as she cleaned off the shot glasses and wiped down the bar, my mind falling deeper into disorientation by the minute. It's as if the two shots she took bypassed her system and went directly into me. I squeezed my eyes shut, trying to right myself.

"You seem fine," I finally muttered to her as she handed a glass of beer to a man sitting a few seats over.

"I am fine. Why wouldn't I be?"

"You know why."

She crossed her arms over her chest. "Because of your father?"

I straightened my posture, trying my best to not give her any sort of reaction. But then I realized righting myself *was* a reaction, and she definitely took notice. She walked back to my section of the bar, leaning in close to me, as if she was about to tell me a secret.

"Listen, what happened that night was unfortunate, but it's in the past. No use dwelling over it now."

There was no remorse in her voice at all. None. I'm not even sure she knows it was exactly one year ago that it all happened.

"You don't take any responsibility for it at all?" I asked, my drunken speech stumbling over the word "responsibility."

She shook her head and frowned. "I wasn't the one driving."

"But you let him drive! You were drunk too, and you killed someone. Did you spend *any* time in jail?"

Her frown turned to a smirk. She shook her head.

"Un-fucking-believable."

She paused, then leaned her side against the bar and angled her shoulders away from me, her eyes scanning the room. I couldn't help but stare at the dip in her tank top, my eyes drifting lower and lower.

No. Snap the fuck out of it.

"See that guy over there," she said, pointing to the far side of the room. "The man in the white button-down shirt? With the buzz cut?"

I nodded, finding the backside of the man she was referring to.

"That's Anthony Harper. Chief of Police here in Kittanning. Divorced, no girlfriend, no kids, *loves* Fireball whiskey, and one of my best clients."

"Yeah?" I tried to play along. "Does he call you Eve or Laila?"

Her immediate eye roll told me she didn't care much about names.

"Eve is my show name. I gave you that one because it's my job. You were an eighteen-year-old boy, and I wasn't sure if you would run and tell all your friends about me. It's easier that way."

I stared down at my hands. I don't blame her for that. Dancers have fake names for a reason. Even so, I couldn't help but feel a small bit of disappointment. That night, that conversation, that *kiss* was so personal, such a raw moment between the two of us, I figured she would've had the decency to tell me her actual name.

I guess I was wrong.

"But yes, my real name is Laila. But Officer Harper calls me whatever he wants."

I knew where she was going with this.

"That night—well, that *morning*—I was sitting in the police station, waiting for someone to find me and tell me what was going on. It was agony, sitting in there alone. I overheard someone mentioning something about 'reckless endangerment.' Then, in walked Officer Harper, and he took one look at me and told me to go." She faked a dreamy sigh. "My knight in shining armor."

I squinted my eyes, her words spilling out like venom.

"I don't think he can do that."

She let out a bark of a laugh, as if she was amused.

"Oh, naïve Thomas. That doesn't matter at all. Small town, small problems. You see, Officer Harper comes in here at least three times a week. Sometimes more. He sits at the same table and orders the same drinks. He even rents out a room in the back when he's feeling extra generous. His life must be *riveting*. But honestly, it plays well in my favor. Not only is he one of *my* best clients, but he brings in a lot of money to this place. When he saw me sitting there, in the police station, I knew he wouldn't dare keep me. What good am I to him if I'm rotting behind bars?"

I could feel my face turning hot, and I wasn't sure if it was from her talking or from the alcohol.

"And, trust me, he's not the only man of power that comes here on a regular basis. Even if I were to get charged with something, it wouldn't go far. There are people from the courthouse that come here, too."

Fuck. She had the upper hand and she knew it.

"So, you're going to let my dad take the fall for everything?"

She shrugged. "Like I said, I wasn't the one driving. How is he, anyway?"

I had no idea, but I wasn't going to clue her in on our falling out. If you could even call it that.

"Fine," I bit out.

With a sigh, she continued. "Jackson Diesel. He really is a good man." She dropped her voice slightly above a whisper, barely audible with the music around us. "Even better lover."

I rolled my head back. I knew I shouldn't have entertained this stupid fucking conversation.

"What the hell is wrong with you? You know my dad is in love with you, right?"

"Most men are."

"No," I shook my head. "He really loves you."

I did my best to cut the slur from my words, but it bled through.

"Do you have any plans to visit him in prison?"

She furrowed her brows, deep in thought, as if she was contemplating her choices. "I doubt it. It was fun while it lasted, but I think our time has run its course."

The tone in her words suggested she had no problem never seeing him again. He could drop dead tomorrow, and she wouldn't bat an eye. It was clear that she didn't love him and that my dad fell for an act.

I stood up off the stool, preparing to leave. "I think *our* time has run its course too. Bye, Laila."

Three steps were all I took before she yelled after me.

"Do you still have it, Thomas?"

It took me a moment, the floor starting to give out from under me, to realize what she was talking about. I pinched the bridge of my nose, trying to feel an ounce of pain in an attempt to sober myself.

"Have what?" I asked, trying to play dumb, but a part of me hoped she would bring this up.

The Gift.

She mouthed the words so no one could hear, even though the music was loud and no one was close enough. My eyes watched her red lips, round and full, and I felt an unsettling stir in me.

I took those three steps back to the bar and rested my forearms on the tabletop.

"Yes."

She paused and I could see the wheels turning in her mind. "Interesting."

The more she talked to me, the more I felt like I was suffocating. I needed fresh air. I needed water.

"What is?"

"You haven't had any chances to use it yet?"

"Chances? What, like the opportunity to see someone die comes daily?"

There was no response to my sarcasm, so I thought back for a minute, scratching the back of my head, my drunkenness clouding my thinking.

"Uh, no. I hit a raccoon one night and saw it run off the road. I hit it pretty hard, so I was sure it died. But I didn't think following it and using it on an animal would be the best—or smartest—idea."

"Oof," she said with a wince. "You can't use it on animals, anyway. Only humans."

"Okay. Well, there was a time when I saw a guy choking on his food at the steakhouse down the road. But someone came and gave him the Heimlich, and he was fine."

She nodded. For the first time tonight, my stomach dropped when our eyes locked, her stare diving into the depths of my body. The hairs stood up on my arms, my skin crawling to find its way off me. The music faded, and for a sobering moment, it was only her and me. I thought back to three years ago when she told me she chose *me*. She made me feel like the luckiest guy in the world, simply by singling me out, and for a split second, I felt it again now. There was a glimmer in her eye, a sign of hope and promise that I was where I was supposed to be.

I let the moment pass before I spoke again.

"What?" I let a rare, drunken smile come to me.

"You're smart, Thomas. You'll know when it's supposed to happen."

Her words settled deep in my core before I realized they held weight. The gift wasn't something I thought about every day. I didn't feel physically different, there was no membership club I was attending, and there was no one else I knew that had it.

I wasn't sure if it was even real.

But there would be times when I would sit alone and it would pop into my head. Someone would mention something about death, and I would immediately turn my head and listen. It always caught me off guard and put me on edge. Something would spark my memory and remind me of my mom, and all I could wonder was… what if I had it then? Would things be different? Would she continue to fight her cancer and go into remission? Would she be here, with me now, celebrating my birthday? Would my dad still end up in prison?

In the end, the questions didn't matter because she's not coming back. She's *never* coming back.

I must have zoned out because when I looked back up at her, she was holding a clear cup of *something* out to me. I declined this drink, too, just like the shot.

She didn't take no for an answer this time.

"It's water. Sober up."

Oh, thank God.

My body was aching for some water. I downed it in a few seconds. As soon as I brought the cup down from my lips, a beautiful woman with dark, shimmering skin and dark, flowing hair walked behind the bar, clutching Laila's arm.

"Thanks, babe," the returning bartender said as she made her way over to new customers. What was her name again? Ashley? Ashton? I couldn't remember. She was almost as hot as Laila, and I know for a fact I've never seen her around town before. I wondered if every chick here was hot, but then I realized where I was. And in there was my answer.

Laila stepped out from behind the bar and leaned in next to me. Her gaze met mine as one of her hands rested on my arm, the other doing a quick, sensual run through my hair.

"Happy birthday, Thomas."

Her lips were warm as they pressed on my cheek, lingering a beat too long. I held my breath.

"Take care of yourself?"

She said it as a question, as a request, as sincere as she could possibly be. There were no words left in me. My only response was a blink and a slow exhale.

Turning on her heel, she left the bar and walked down the back hallway, past the private rooms and into the dressing room. I had no idea if her shift was now over or if she had more work to do, and honestly, I didn't care to find out. It was getting late, with my eyes growing heavier by the second, and the last thing I wanted was a mix of exhaustion with the buzz of alcohol still swirling in my system. The guys were still talking and laughing at the table when I turned to look at them, so I stood and began to make my way over to say goodbye.

The man sitting a few stools down at the bar yelled to me before I could take another step.

"Is she a good fuck?" he asked, motioning to the hallway Laila just walked down a moment ago.

The question caught me off guard, but I couldn't help but flash a quick grin, thinking about all the fantasies I've had of her the past few years. Her perfectly toned body on top of mine, her soft lips kissing her way down my chest, past my stomach as she popped the button on my jeans. Her shiny lips, not from makeup, but from her own spit sliding up and down my cock. Even a few minutes ago, with her tits spilling out of her bar outfit, I dreamt about bending her over right there, in front of everyone, burying myself deep inside her, her pussy milking me for every last drop. It was a picture that was constantly on replay in my dreams. I could feel my dick pulse, pushing hard against my jeans.

"Yeah. She is."

ANNA

I placed a box down on the floor, the red wrapping paper sparkling under the lights. There were a handful of other boxes, all wrapped by me, arranged neatly under the Christmas tree. I took a deep breath as I stood straight, proud of myself for finishing and wrapping all of Diesel's gifts on time. He was *not* easy to shop for, since he always bought himself whatever he needed, but some of the guys from work clued me in on things he could use at the warehouse. After I bought all that stuff, my head spinning from learning about four hundred different types of drills, I wanted to put my own touch on some presents. I bought fun things, like cheesy matching underwear for us. It was corny, it wasn't serious, but I knew he would get a kick out of it. I blushed at the thought of buying him underwear, only to strip it off him later.

Diesel opened his front door, snow trailing in from his boots.

"Hey, sorry about that." He shook off the excess snow from his coat and hat, taking them off and hanging them up by the door to dry. He knelt down to untie his laces.

"How did it go?" I asked.

Diesel shrugged. Even though it was Christmas Eve, he still had to work at least a half-day. If it weren't for my convincing protests, he would've worked the entire day. Now that winter was in full swing, his company moved from building houses to indoor jobs, such as remodeling, repairs, and installation. Sometimes, when we hit a warm streak of days, he could squeeze in some outdoor projects, such as roof repairs. But since the Pennsylvania ground was almost always frozen, they had to pause on the actual house building. Other times, he would fill odds and ends in the warehouse or do inventory, which is what he did today.

I trotted over to him, wrapping my arms around his neck. Even though it was the dead of winter, his skin was still slightly golden and sun-kissed, as if the sun had tattooed itself on his body.

I pressed a warm kiss to his cold lips. "You're freezing."

"You're warm," he replied as he placed his hands under my sweater, trying to rub the skin on my back. I squealed, because as much as I loved his hands on me, I hated cold hands more than anything. I squirmed my way out of his grip, but he chased me to the couch, pinning me down.

"No! No! Please!" Our laughter filled the apartment, bouncing off the walls.

It was a soundtrack to our first Christmas together.

It was my favorite holiday, and the greatest time of year, in my opinion. The white snow, the lights lining the streets downtown, the cookies, the crackle of a fireplace. The way families would come together and laugh and smile all day. My heart ached at the thought of my dad. This is only my second Christmas without him, and it doesn't feel any easier than the first.

My thoughts must've been spelled out on my face because Diesel stopped his cold-handed torment to look at me.

"You okay?"

I showed a pitiful smile and nodded.

"Bullshit. What's going on?"

Not that I was hiding it all that well, but I liked when he called me out. It was a reminder that someone still cared about me.

"It's hard." I paused, turning to look at him. "Missing someone."

"Your dad?"

I nodded again. I missed him so much, and there was nothing I could do about it. But this was also my first Christmas without my mom. And although we weren't close, she was still my *mom*. And this was Christmas. There was a silent ache in my heart that I couldn't shake away. She lost my dad, too, and now she doesn't even have me anymore.

"And my mom."

Diesel nodded. He sat on the couch beside me, his arm resting along the back. I stayed lying down, my legs crossing over his.

There was hesitation on both our ends.

"What happened?"

I had yet to tell Diesel the story of my mom, although there wasn't much to tell. I was afraid he wouldn't understand because he lost his mom so unfairly when he was sixteen. I didn't want to burden him with it. But now, since we've built our trust with each other, since we've been together and told each other our 'I love you's, I knew I could open up to him without a problem.

I began with a sigh, my shoulders dropping, as if it was all a weight too heavy to carry.

"You would think my dad's death would've brought us closer together. All we had was each other. But it didn't. My mom and I were never super close. I was a 'Daddy's Girl' through and through, so when he died, things changed. She loved me, don't get me wrong, but my dad was the one that really took care of me. For as long as I can remember, she was *always* working and hardly ever home. My dad was the one who would cook dinner, take me places, take care of me when I was sick, everything. So, once he was gone, our family kind of… fell apart."

Diesel nodded, looking down at my legs on his lap, understanding what that was like.

"He was the glue that held my mom and me together."

I looked at the Christmas tree, the fake snow dusted onto the branches, the warm lights illuminating the apartment, and the presents neatly stacked on the floor.

"And I'm almost positive she cheated on my dad."

I could feel Diesel's eyes flick back up to me.

"A few years ago, before he died, I saw her phone one night and saw some texts from a guy named 'Nathan,' and I just knew. Everything added up at that moment. All her late nights, work trips, the amount of time she spent on the phone, it was embarrassing. I think my dad knew but didn't want to deal with it. And he didn't want to hurt me."

The ways my father would protect me, even if it meant hurting himself, were the definition of unconditional love. He truly was my best friend, and talking about him, thinking about how my life was with him, I could feel my chest ache. I missed him more than anything.

"After I finished college, I told her I wanted to move out of Pittsburgh and go to beauty school. All I did was a quick Google search of beauty schools nearby, and Kittanning was the first one to pop up outside of Pittsburgh. My dad gave me more than enough money in his will to go, and my mom had no desire to stop me. And that was that."

I let my story settle, both of us diving deep into our own minds. Diesel had a mother who loved him more than anything, and she was taken away far too soon. I had a mother that was never really present, so losing her would be like losing something I never had in the first place. They were both losses in their own way.

Part of me also felt guilty about it. She deserved to be happy with her life after my dad. And besides cheating, she never truly did anything wrong to me. She never hit me, she never yelled at me or degraded me in any way. She just wasn't there. I guess you could consider that a form of neglect, but that seemed too extreme to me. Then again, maybe that's the wishful side of me, a daughter defending her mother, no matter what.

"And now," I began again. "Her and that Nathan guy are officially together. They're spending their Christmas in Bora Bora."

"Ah, fuck," Diesel chimed in, rubbing the stubble on his jaw. "I'm sorry, Anna."

I shook my head, now realizing I've been spilling all my issues with my mom to someone who doesn't have one. "No, I'm sorry. This all sounds superficial. And I know it's unfair, considering what you went through. Diesel, I'm sorry."

He put his hand on my thigh, instantly calming me and setting me on fire at the same time. "Don't be. You know none of this is your fault, right?"

I shrugged.

"Nobody's family is perfect. Anyone who says otherwise is lying. And I don't ever want you thinking you can't talk to me about something. Just because you don't have a good relationship with your mom doesn't mean you can't talk to me about it. I get it." Diesel reached out and stroked my jaw, his touch the only thing keeping me sane. "Trust me, I get it."

With an understanding focused deep in his eyes, I knew he did.

Thankfully, the memory of my mom didn't ruin the whole night. I wallowed in the flashbacks for about an hour, then forced myself out of it. I wasn't about to sacrifice my Christmas over something that couldn't be changed in a day. I was happy with my life and where I was now, and I did everything in my power to focus on that alone.

Diesel and I cooked and ate a perfect Christmas Eve dinner together. We laughed, kissed, joked, kissed again, and then cleaned our dishes. I washed while he dried, but it was really just me avoiding his towel whips to my thighs while throwing soap bubbles at him.

Moments like these were ones I tucked into my memory, vowing to never forget them. Here I was, with the one person I truly loved more than anything, our stomachs full, perfect white snow quieting the world around us, with nothing standing in our way.

Once we were finished cleaning up, I poured myself a glass of red wine and grabbed a beer for Diesel. I followed him to the couch, placed our drinks on the coffee table in front of us, and looked at the Christmas tree.

"You know," I angled myself toward him as he leaned into me. "I still can't believe you didn't have a Christmas tree."

He shrugged. Right after Thanksgiving, I told him I would help him decorate his apartment for Christmas, and he looked at me like I was crazy. So maybe a twenty-six-year-old guy who lives alone won't have a lot of decorations, but I figured he would *at least* have a Christmas tree.

Right?

Wrong.

In all his time living here at this apartment, he never bothered to celebrate the holiday. He had no one to spend time with, no one to watch cheesy movies with, and no one to buy gifts for or receive gifts from. It was something I could relate to, in a way, because if I hadn't met him, I would probably be sitting alone tonight, too. Mrs. Reeves would give him a few Christmas cookies that she baked every year, but that's all he ever got. The thought of him alone made my heart ache, so I made it my mission to give him an amazing Christmas, starting with buying a Christmas tree. We ended up getting a six-foot, pre-lit Christmas tree with fake snow brushed on the branches and a silver star on the top.

It was perfect.

And I could tell by the smile on his face after we put it up that he thought it was perfect, too.

I reached out and touched one of the branches, the fake pine needles poking my skin delicately. "Do you like it?"

Diesel brought his arm around my shoulders, squeezing gently. "I do."

The look in his eyes spoke volumes. It was a look of comfort, a piece of himself guarded by the loneliness that melted away. The tree was more than just a homey touch to his apartment for the holidays.

I sucked in a breath. "Okay. I think it's time to open some gifts."

"Aren't we supposed to wait until tomorrow?"

I shook my head. "We don't have to. Plus, aren't you dying to know what I got you?"

He smiled. "Of course I am."

I leaned down and grabbed a small gift bag, tissue paper poking out from the top. "Smallest presents to biggest presents. Here's your smallest." I went to hand it to him but stopped halfway. "By the way, you're *incredibly* hard to shop for. Especially since your birthday was just last month."

He took the bag from me. "So are you." Wasting no time in taking the tissue paper out, he reached in and released a wide grin, my smile matching his.

"Big League Chew!" He held the bag of gum in his hands, his excitement contagious. "How'd you know I liked this?"

"I saw you looking at it when we were in the gas station. You almost grabbed it, but didn't."

"Man," he sighed a delighted breath. "I haven't had this since I was a kid. Thank you."

Sometimes the little presents mean the most. My heart filled a little more as I watched him study the package.

Snapping out of his memories, he stood up, walking to his bedroom. "Alright. Your turn." His voice carried over his shoulder as he disappeared for a moment, then returned with a miniature gift bag. He held the bag out to me, the silver sparkles falling to the ground, a single piece of tissue paper along the top edge. It was so small, I don't think it could fit a golf ball.

"Your smallest."

I was intrigued. I took the bag, its weight close to nothing, as Diesel stood in front of me. I looked at him, his eyes burning my skin as he waited for me to open it. I pulled out the tissue paper and glanced to the bottom of the bag.

A key.

A shiny, silver key.

I looked back up to Diesel, whose eyes never left me.

"Move in with me."

The sentence made my stomach fall to my feet. I looked at the key again. It was brand new, like he just had it made, only for me. My cheeks grew red as I bit my bottom lip, my smile forcing its way out. The closest I had ever come to living with someone was my roommate in college, and that didn't really count to me. I had never *lived* with someone before. I had never paid bills with someone or shared a living room with someone, let alone with someone I was dating. But it made sense since I was here all the time anyway. This was an unfamiliar road, but with Diesel, it was something I desperately wanted. And with this key, he felt the same. He was opening his door to me.

I covered my mouth with my hand and let out a little laugh, joy spilling out of me like liquid. "Diesel…" I looked from the key, back to him, then back to the key. My smile wasn't going away anytime soon. I jumped to my feet and wrapped my arms around him, kissing him hard, my answer in our lips.

He tried to squeeze words out, but my lips wouldn't leave his. "So, is that a yes?"

I nodded. But then my lips stopped, and my kiss paused.

"Wait. What about my apartment? My lease."

Diesel moved his hands up to my face, stroking my skin as his gaze melted deep into mine.

"It's done."

Confusion filled my thoughts. "What?"

He didn't falter, he didn't hesitate. His voice was deep and firm, straight and to the point. "I took care of it."

My mind instantly flashed back to my first time on the balcony, with his arms caging me in, saying those exact same words.

When I didn't react, my mind still processing, he continued.

"I paid your landlord the remainder of the lease. And managed to get your security deposit back."

No way. No. Way.

He really went out of his way and did all that for me? So he could have me, here with him, all the time?

I was speechless. Even if I had something to say, my body wouldn't let me.

"When I want something, I get it. I want you here, Anna. There's nothing that will ever stand in my way of that."

My knees buckled as my heart raced.

He really did this.

For me.

For us.

I began to picture what living here would be like. Cooking pancakes in the morning in just a t-shirt, taking showers together after midnight, and sitting on the balcony watching sunsets in the summer. I couldn't imagine anything better.

I kissed him again, this time with tender lips, our thoughts together. We wanted this, we wanted each other, we wanted forever.

This was the first step, and I was all in.

"I love you, Anna." His whisper came out in a rasp, his words spoken against my lips, his eyes still closed.

"I love you, too, Diesel."

I took a deep breath, inhaling this moment. The tree, the snow, the words, the woodsy smell of his skin, the key, the way his arms moved down my body.

He picked me up with his hands under my thighs and my legs tightly wrapped around his waist. I looked at his face, his firm jaw tightening as he carried me to his bedroom, preparing to take me. Have me. Own me.

He placed me on his bed. I moved my arms up, taking my sweater off as he took off his shirt.

"This is so much better than gum," I said, pushing my messy hair out of my face.

He laughed, the smile that I loved more than anything returning, the crinkles by his eyes that I've come to memorize appearing. That was the best present of all. He pushed me down on the bed and climbed on top of me, the night slipping away with the snowfall.

THOMAS

There was a quiet knock at the door to my office. I glanced up, the phone still pressed to my ear, waiting to see if someone was going to open the door. No one did.

"Hey, can I call you back tomorrow? There's someone here to see me. Thanks." The phone call with one of my clients was supposed to be over twenty minutes ago, but he insisted on rambling on about specifics of his house that didn't need to be discussed yet. I was looking for a reason to hang up, and the knock on the door was a perfect excuse. I placed my phone on my desk and sat back in my chair, the metal frame digging into my side. I needed to upgrade soon.

"Come in."

I could hear muffled voices on the other side of the door but couldn't distinguish any words. A minute passed before I turned back to my computer, resuming my work, the voices still echoing in the space outside my office. Knowing the guys' work ethic, I trusted them and wasn't concerned if they were taking a break to talk, but I needed them away from me so I could focus on what I needed to get done. I was just about to get up and out of the office to tell them to go somewhere else when another knock sounded on the door.

"What?" It came out as more of a bark, growing annoyed with whatever was happening.

The door opened slowly, and Darrell stepped in, wariness on his face. "Hey, Boss."

"Yeah, Darrell?" I remained sitting at my desk, focused on the computer.

"There's someone here to see you."

I don't usually get visitors, but once in a while, someone will come in for a price quote. Usually, one of the guys will handle it, but sometimes people want to talk to the owner. It's fine with me. It's a slow day, and I could use the distraction.

"Okay. Send 'em in."

Darrell scratched the back of his head, his pause insinuating there was something clearly on his mind. There was an awkward silence. Darrell was not the type to be awkward or silent.

"What?" I asked, confused.

"You should probably come outside."

Something in his tone set me off. I stood up and left my office, shutting and locking the door behind me. There was access to a lot in that office: blueprints, employee payroll, and keys to vacant houses, just to name a few. I never took any chances leaving the door unlocked. I tucked the key into my pocket and followed Darrell to the front of the warehouse, the door propped open to let in fresh air on the hot summer day. Sunshine flooded the entrance, my eyes squinting as my pupils dilated to accommodate the brightness. I could see a shadow of a person on the pavement, but I couldn't see who it was until I was fully outside. I stepped out, rounding the corner, to see him standing there.

Jackson Diesel.

My dad.

Out of fucking prison.

Early.

"Tommy D!" He reached in for a hug, patting me hard on the back, as I stood there and did nothing. Even if I was expecting his return, I still don't think I would have hugged him back.

"My boy! How are you?"

I said nothing as I stared at him, my face scrunched in confusion. Thanks to the five and a half years spent in prison, he had aged at least twenty years. The skin on his cheeks was beginning to sag, his eyes were sunken into purple craters, the stubble on his face had flecks of grey, and his shoulders looked as if they were carrying an invisible weight. His clothes hung loosely off his body, and just one look at his arms ensured he lost weight. But even though he looked like he was in rough shape, he seemed awfully chipper. Then again, he was a free man now. I knew this day would come, but I wasn't expecting it to come five months early. And I definitely wasn't expecting him to visit me when he was out.

Darrell turned to me and dropped his voice. "I'll be back inside if you need anything." He gave my shoulder a nudge and waved to my dad. "Good to see you, JD."

"You too, Darrell! I see you still got the good guys workin' for ya." He said to me, but his voice was loud enough so Darrell could hear him as he walked back inside. Clearly, he was trying to earn brownie points with everyone now that he was back.

No, not back.

Visiting.

And here he is, still trying to charm anyone he encounters to cover all his mistakes.

"Look at you. You beefed up. You look so grown. So old. So much older than the last time I saw you."

I could've easily said the same thing to him, but instead, I cocked my head to the side and said nothing, shoving my hands in my pockets. I wasn't in the mood to squabble.

"Now when… when *was* the last time I saw you?" That chipper tone he had moments earlier vanished and was replaced with resentment.

I rolled my head back. "What do you want?"

He opened his arms in a grand gesture. "There he is! He speaks!"

I looked to anywhere else but him as he continued to make a show out of nothing.

"How about a '*Welcome back, Dad*' or maybe '*Good to see you, Dad,*' huh?"

He waited a minute for a reaction from me. If that's what he wanted, we could stand here all day.

"When were you released?"

"Earlier today. Got out on good behavior. Right in time for the fourth of July." His smile widened. "Independence Day for the independent man."

Prison changed him, and not for the better. I didn't realize he could be this annoying.

Propping his hands on his hips, he looked away from me and at the building, a whistle sliding out from his mouth. "Now her." He wagged a finger toward the warehouse. "She hasn't aged a day. She's still as beautiful as the last time I was here."

I stayed where I was as he took a step past me, looking up at the giant sign on the front of the building. *Diesel Construction Co.* I had the letters repainted last year, and now the logo looks even brighter than before. It was one cosmetic decision I made that I never regretted.

I cleared my throat, trying to move this along. I knew how this was all going to end, so everything in between seemed like a big waste of my time.

My dad spent a moment too long staring at the sign before turning back to me.

"You've done such a great job handling this while I was gone." He clapped a hand on my shoulder. I tried my hardest to not slink away from his grasp. "Really. I'm surprised this building didn't go up in flames!" He forced a laugh while my expression stayed blank.

I hated when he tried to be likable.

"But I'm back now. I'm ready to take back what's mine."

He rubbed his hands together in anticipation. There was only one explanation for this.

"Are you drunk?"

He shook his head. "Nope."

"High?"

"Stone cold sober."

"Then why, in your right mind, would you come back here and think nothing ever happened? That *I* would act like nothing happened?" I did my best to remain calm, but the fact that he was acting so self-righteous made resentment bleed through my voice.

"Because this business is mine, Tommy. It always has been."

"Not according to all the papers we signed."

"*Fuck* the papers."

Finally, the happy-go-lucky act was gone. Now, the real conversation was about to begin.

"You know you can't run a business by yourself."

His statement shocked me so abruptly, I couldn't help but laugh. "Are you kidding me? That's all I've been doing for the past five years!" I caught and corrected myself. "No. Longer. I've been cleaning up your messes for longer than five years."

My dad groaned, rubbing his hands down his face, as if my fight was an inconvenience to him. As if he didn't expect me to straighten my spine and stand the fuck up. He's skated by all his life, doing the absolute least and getting away with it. I wasn't about to roll over and take it.

"Come on, Tommy. You know it's only fair. The guys need a leader, not some kid telling them what to do."

"We do just fine without you." I quickly managed to get my voice back down to regular volume as I dug into my back pocket and pulled out my wallet. "Here, take this." I handed him two fifty-dollar bills, and he didn't hesitate to grab them. "I think you should go."

I looked around the parking lot for a running car, or even an out-of-place rental car. There was nothing. I had no idea how he got here. Considering how far the prison was from the warehouse, I don't think he walked all this way.

"Get an Uber."

"I'm not leaving until we sort this out."

"Sort *what* out? Everything's already in my name. What don't you understand?"

A wave of defeat washed over his face, but soon it switched to anger.

"You can't take my business *and* my house."

I paused.

The house.

Fuck, I forgot about that.

"By the way, where's my cut?"

I raised my eyebrows. "What?"

"My cut from the house. I want that money."

I placed my wallet back in my pocket, letting the stillness fill the gaps.

"You told me you'd save some money for me. I was *relying* on that money." His voice was starting to catch fire. He was right. I did say that. But after everything was said and done, that money was put to better use in other places. Most of it went to the business, and some of it went to Mrs. Reeves' apartment building. The rest of it, though not much, was stashed away somewhere safe. I'm sure I could give him enough to satisfy him, but right now, I didn't want to.

"You need to—"

Before I could finish my sentence, his right fist connected with my left eye, a crunching sound reverberating through my skull.

Fucking hell.

I took the blow by stumbling backward, my hand immediately covering my eye.

"What the fuck?" I yelled. He came toward me again, throwing another punch to my face, this time to the left side of my mouth. Before he could knock me completely on my ass, I flung his arm to the side with one swift move and gave him exactly what he gave me. His cheekbone felt like it chipped apart under my knuckles. I struck again, this time swinging right to his temple. He wavered, trying to steady himself and regain his balance. There was no letup before he tried lunging at me, his arms reaching for my torso to tackle me, but some of the guys ran out of the warehouse to break it up. Darrell grabbed my arms while Jim stopped my dad, their limbs tangled in each other.

"Ay, what the hell?" Darrell shouted as both my dad and I tried to catch our breath. Neither one of us wanted to answer for what we had just done. My dad's cheek was already purple and bleeding, with two lines of blood running down his face. My left eye was throbbing, and judging by the heat beginning to pulse in my eye socket, I knew it was minutes away from swelling.

Darrell looked at my dad, to me, then back to my dad. "JD, I think you need to take some time to cool down."

My dad peeled his eyes off me, flickering over to Darrell. His jaw clenched, making more blood pool out from his cut. Jim still held him back, but my dad managed to squeeze an arm out of his grasp. He pointed at me, the fifty-dollar bills still crumpled in his hand.

After all that, he still had a death grip on the money.

"You better figure out your shit, Tommy. We're not done."

He turned to walk away, out of the parking lot, Jim guiding him the whole way. As soon as Darrell let me go, I looked at my hand. There was a row of blood along my knuckles, a small scrape on the top of each one. I squeezed my hand into a fist, then released; the lack of sharp pain ensured me nothing was broken. I looked back at Darrell, who was still standing beside me, watching my father leave.

"Sorry."

He shook his head. "Nah, don't worry. I knew something was going on as soon as he showed up here."

We stood there, unmoving, watching Jim and my dad stand at the edge of the lot. They were talking, too far away for me to hear what they were saying, but my dad seemed to calm down. I stood for a few more moments before turning to head back inside. I gripped my hand, my heartbeat stuck in my knuckles, my attempt at massaging it doing nothing to help.

"You okay, Boss?" Darrell asked as he followed me in.

The fact that he still called me Boss gave me a surge of happiness, but I pushed it back down into my chest.

I didn't turn to look at him as I answered. "Yeah. Fine."

ANNA

"You ready?" A voice spoke over my shoulder. I stood up from my station, the leather from my chair sticking to the backs of my thighs. I looked behind me to my teacher, Mrs. Ang, giving her a faint smile, and her sending one right back.

"It's time." She glanced from me to the logging station on the wall.

I *was* ready, so ready, but after doing a quick scan of the room, I hesitated. I wanted to wait just a minute longer. I looked at the clock on the wall.

He was late.

Fourteen minutes late, in fact.

I took a deep breath, knowing my time was next, and smoothed down the fabric of my navy blue dress. My chest squeezed, knowing that my teacher and Olivia were the only people here to support me. But as Olivia wrapped her arm in mine, a giddy smile glued to her face, I relaxed a little. She's been right by my side through all this, knowing how hard I had worked these past eleven months. I tried, failed, tried again, and failed again, only to keep picking myself back up and finally getting the hang of everything. Being a hairdresser was a skill that I wasn't born with, but with constant focus and practice, I managed to get better as each day went on. My confidence was boosted with each class, and my hands became more graceful with the shears each time I picked them up. Now, I'm at a point where I'm not only confident in this field of work, but I'm confident in who I am.

Olivia tugged me toward the logging station, our heels clicking on the floor just as the door opened behind us. I spun around, the hot, sticky air filling the room as he entered, the door falling closed behind him.

Diesel.

We've been together for ten months, and he still makes my heart jump every time I see him.

But today, he ran in here wearing new shoes, a pair of slim-fit khakis, and a white button-down shirt with the sleeves rolled to the elbows. His light brown hair was styled and sat perfectly, and in his hand was a beautiful bouquet of white roses.

My jaw dropped. It was miles from the Diesel I had come to know. I didn't even know he owned a pair of khaki pants. My heart sank to the pit of my stomach, and my throat swelled with choked-back emotion.

"I didn't miss it, did I?" His voice was nervous as he gave me a once over, the corner of his mouth lifting into a smirk.

I shook my head. "You're just in time."

We locked eyes. We could have stared at each other forever if it wasn't for Olivia elbowing me in the ribs.

"Let's do this."

Olivia had already finished her final class last week, so she was only here for me today. I hugged her, and she let go of my arm as I turned and walked to the logging station. I was officially done with beauty school. I worked all the hours I needed to and passed every quiz, exam, and hands-on training experience required of me. There was nothing more to do other than log out of today's class, closing the door on this chapter and opening the door to the next.

I entered my student code and logged out. I exhaled, my shoulders dropping, and felt a strong, warm arm wrap around the top of my chest.

"I'm *so* proud of you."

I smiled and turned around, Diesel's eyes beaming with the same joy I had in mine. I kissed him quickly, wrapped my arms around him in a hug, and took the flowers he had brought for me.

White roses, my favorite.

They were beautiful, and he was more than perfect. I was floating.

"Thank you," I managed to squeak out, everything leading up to this moment.

Olivia walked up to us and draped her arm on Diesel's shoulder. In the few times they've met, she seemed to like him. There were times when Diesel couldn't get out of work before dinner, so Olivia and I would go out to eat, and he would end up meeting us there. They would talk and joke around, and even though Olivia looked like a supermodel, he never looked at anyone else the way he looked at me.

"Hey." She smiled at Diesel. "Congrats on the free haircuts."

He laughed. "Thanks."

Olivia turned to me, keeping her arm on Diesel, as if they were lifelong friends. "So, I'm leaving on Sunday."

"What?" I dropped my arms, disappointment taking the flowers down with me. "That's in two days."

"I know, I'm sorry. I already have a job lined up in Harrisburg with my aunt's salon. I start next week." She moved in to hug me again, knowing this would be the last time we saw each other. I could always count on her to be there for me day in and day out, no questions asked. She cared for me, the day I walked in with the giant gash on my forehead proving it. Everyone else stared and whispered about me, but all she wanted was to make sure I was okay. Her heart and her friendship got me through the class, and I don't know what I would've done without her. Even though we weren't close outside of beauty school, I knew I could always text her and she'd be up and there for me.

Everything worked out for us, but I was still sad at the end of it all.

"You're gonna kick ass out there, Anna. I *know* it. And not just as a hairdresser."

My arms ached as they squeezed her back. My voice was a quiet muffle in her shoulder. "Thank you for being my friend."

I felt her head nodding on my shoulder, her voice quiet. She released me, her hand giving mine a quick hold as she said goodbye to me and Diesel.

I sighed and looked at Diesel, my sad spell broken as I was reminded of how nice he looked.

"You clean up so good." I couldn't help but pull him to me and kiss him again.

His hands squeezed my waist, his hips moving in to find mine. "Let's get out of here."

I happily obeyed, took his hand, and walked toward the front door. I stopped to give Mrs. Ang one last hug and said goodbye to the school that helped me find where I wanted to be these past eleven months.

ANNA

AUGUST 23, 2022

The phone on Diesel's nightstand buzzed, the light from the screen illuminating the room. I blinked my sleep away a few times to look at the clock. 12:56 AM. The phone continued buzzing, and Diesel was still so deep in his sleep that it wasn't waking him. I sat up and nudged him a few times until he stirred, turning to me.

"Your phone's ringing," I whispered. I tried to see who was on the caller ID, but my vision was still trying to focus. He reached over and grabbed his phone, not even looking to see who would be calling this late, and answered it.

"Hello?"

A pause.

"Yes, this is him." His voice was groggy as he rubbed his eyes.

Another pause, this time longer.

"Okay…yes…thank you. I'll be right there."

He clicked off the phone and fumbled out of bed, searching for clothes to put on.

"What's going on?" Now that I was more awake, my nerves started creeping into me. No one calls in the middle of the night without good reason.

"Someone vandalized one of the properties down in the Red Hill subdivision. I have to go meet the police there."

He slid on a pair of jeans as I pushed the covers off of me. "I'll go with you."

"No. Stay." He pulled on a thin, long-sleeved shirt. "I won't be long. I just need to give them a list of anything that was stolen and figure out if anything is salvageable."

"It's that bad?" I asked as I thought about all the hard work Diesel and his guys do during the day, all to be wasted because someone felt like destroying it. It wasn't fair.

"We'll see." He leaned into the bed and planted a kiss on my forehead. "Go back to sleep. I'll be back before you know it."

I nodded and watched him walk out the door. There was a feeling, deep down in the pit of my stomach, telling me something was off. I sat and waited for the sound of his truck engine to turn on before laying back down.

He'll be back soon.

I said it to myself over and over, trying to subdue any strange feelings inside my body.

With the pillow still soft and warm under my head, I closed my eyes and tried to fall back to sleep.

I counted backward from one hundred.

No luck.

I mentally relaxed every part of my body, starting with my toes.

No luck.

The moonlight was streaming through the cracks of the shades in the bedroom window, casting a white, striped glow on the comforter. It felt weird to be in this bed without Diesel. He had always kept me warm, every night since I moved in, his soft skin pressed along the curve of my back, his shallow breath brushing along the nape of my neck. And now that he was gone, even if it was only for an hour or so, it was impossible for me to sleep.

After a sad attempt at trying to keep my eyes closed, I stood and padded to the kitchen. I pulled out a glass from the cabinet and filled it with water.

I took a long swallow right as a knock sounded on the front door.

My heart jumped.

Diesel wouldn't knock unless he forgot his key. But if he forgot his key, the door would still be unlocked, and he could just come right in. And I didn't hear his truck come back.

With moments like these, I found myself wishing the door had a peephole.

Another knock.

Who would be knocking on the door in the middle of the night?

At an apartment complex that only one other person lived in?

That was on the outskirts of town, away from any main roads?

I placed the glass down on the counter as quietly as possible. I didn't want anyone to know I was here, awake, and listening.

Four of the six apartments were empty, and this person chose to come to *this* door? That feeling, the one buried in the pit of my stomach, suddenly reared its head and came back to the surface. A wave of unease covered me, and I found myself bound in its ropes.

A knock sounded again, and this time a voice spoke through the door.

"Anna?"

I could feel my chest heave. It was a female voice, one I'd never heard before, and she knew my name.

"Anna? Are you there?"

My blood was pumping through my body so fast, my heart couldn't keep up. I thought of my phone and thought about calling Diesel, but I didn't want to bother him if he was with the police. Especially if this person turned out to be harmless.

I walked to the door and did my best to catch my breath, keeping my voice level as I spoke. "Hello?"

There was what sounded like an exhale on the other side of the door. "Oh, Anna. Hi. Um, is Diesel there? I'm… I'm…"

I stood there, waiting for her to continue.

"I'm his ex-girlfriend. I was driving through and got tired and wondered if I could crash here for a little while."

I looked down at my toes. So, she knew Diesel, knew he lived here, and was looking for a place to stay. I could feel an inch of give in my resistance. She sounded nice, but that sinking feeling still held tightly onto me.

"He told me about you." I could hear the plea in her words. "He loves you, Anna, and trust me, he and I happened a *long* time ago. There's nothing there for you to worry about, if that's what you're thinking. And I just need a couch to sleep on for a few hours."

A handful of thoughts sprinted through me. Why here? Why not a motel nearby? Who is she? Why didn't Diesel tell me about this?

"Is he there?" she asked.

"No."

I pushed away the running questions in my head and focused on getting more information out of her, even if it was through the door.

"Who are you?"

"I'm Diesel's ex-girlfriend."

"Yeah, I know. What's your name?"

"Eve."

Something in her voice sounded sincere and harmless. I looked down the hall at the bedroom door, picturing my phone again as it sat on the nightstand next to the bed. I could call him, ask him about her and if he knows her. But I've already talked to her this much.

My breath began to settle as I leaned back from the door. Her voice was calm; she didn't sound like she was being held at gunpoint or anything. I could hear the jingle of her car keys and the tapping of her shoes. There was something about this that felt okay, but the fact that Diesel wasn't here was the only thing holding me back from opening the door.

I eyed the doorknob.

"Anna?"

I blinked.

"Do you want me to call him?"

I shook my head, but then realized she couldn't see that. "No. That's okay."

With a quick pull, I opened the door, only wide enough for my body to fill the opening.

She was leaning against the doorframe, and I noticed how tall she was. She was wearing black pumps, and how she was able to drive in those, I have no idea. Her dark blue jeans hugged her long, lean legs, and a white, flowy tank top left nothing to the imagination. Her skin was smooth and creamy, and her tousled, fire-red hair reached down to the middle of her back. She was incredibly beautiful, and I was immediately hit with insecurities. Even though I don't know her and have never heard their backstory, if Diesel sees her, I don't know how he wouldn't want her back.

My plan was to hear her out a bit more, but after seeing her, I don't think having her stay here is a good idea.

"Oh, you are so cute." I could see her eyes scan me, starting at my bare legs, trailing up to my athletic shorts and Diesel's oversized shirt hanging off my body, to my messy bun tied to the top of my head. She took a loose lock of my hair between her fingers, twirling it softly. "He has a type."

She winked at me and pushed her way into the apartment with little resistance. I closed the door behind her and turned around. I noticed she didn't bring anything inside with her as she walked straight ahead to the glass balcony doors and peered out. There wasn't much to see outside, especially at this time of night, except for the streetlight on the other side of the road. I gently cleared my throat and scratched my head.

"Can I get you anything? Water?"

She shook her head, not making eye contact with me. "No, that's okay." She slowly walked around the apartment, slipping past the kitchen, passing me as she moved across the hall and into the living room. I watched her with my arms wrapped around myself. I was calm but nervous at the same time, unsure of what to think. This was *weird*.

"What a nice little apartment." Her fingertips glided along the back of the couch.

I gave a puzzled look. "You've never been here before?"

"No."

"How…when were you guys together?" I asked.

She moved to the arm of the couch and sat down, facing me. She took a deep breath, pursing her lips as her eyes trailed away, as if in thought. "It was a while ago. It didn't last long, but we still talk occasionally."

Her smile broadened, showing all her perfectly aligned white teeth.

"He's a good kisser, though, isn't he?"

Her nose scrunched in delight and her tone dropped.

I swallowed. Suddenly, I wasn't sure about this, about her, anymore. I shifted my weight, taking a step backward toward the kitchen. She took the hint and held a hand up in surrender.

"Oh, I'm sorry. I didn't mean to make you uncomfortable."

Nothing in her voice sounded sincere anymore. I should've listened to my gut.

I took another step back. "I think I should call Diesel," my voice croaked out, quiet and unsteady.

"How about we just wait here until he comes back?"

I nodded. Fine. As long as I could keep my eyes on her, watching her movements, I felt safer.

She went back to studying the apartment, her eyes scanning the walls. After a minute, she landed back on me and her eyes widened.

She stood up, her steps flowing toward me, her height towering over me.

"Woah."

I watched her as her ice-blue eyes dilated with amazement.

"How did you get that?"

She pointed to the scar on my forehead. It was still noticeable at this point, but in the right lighting, it stuck out like a sore thumb.

"Um…" I fumbled, wondering if I should spare her the story. I figured she was simply trying to make small talk, even if it came off as rude. "I… I was hit by a car."

Her hand moved to her heart. "Oh, you poor thing."

Our eyes held each other's gaze. The shine in her eyes was gone. There was a new fire in them, a deepening glow that I couldn't push past. She didn't blink as the corner of her mouth curled up so slightly. The hair on the back of my neck stood, and my skin felt like it wanted to crawl off my body.

Just then, a lightbulb went off in my head.

"How did you know I was here?"

"Diesel told me about you."

"No," I said, my voice firming up, my posture tightening. "You knocked on the door, asking for *me*. Why didn't you ask for Diesel?"

Her little smile grew.

"You already knew he wasn't here, didn't you?"

Her only answer was the smile that didn't falter.

"You came here for me." I didn't give her a chance to refute it, even though it seemed as if she didn't care to. "Why?"

She let out a snicker, turning her face away. "You're smarter than you look, Anna." Her heels clicked on the floor as she stepped around me. She circled me, studying me, and for a minute, I couldn't breathe. Her presence was wrapping heavily around me, weighing me down, pinning my feet to the floor.

My mouth took over before my mind could stop it.

"Who are you?" I asked, a whisper that was calling for her. She had more to tell me.

This person, this woman, standing in front of me, isn't who she claims to be.

But I have no idea what she wants. Or needs.

"Do you even really know Diesel?"

She stopped walking. "Yes. I wasn't lying about that. We really *do* have history together."

"Then what do you want? Why are you here?"

Her fingertips brushed the back of my neck, sending a hot shiver down my spine. The adrenaline that faded in the past few minutes came back in a fury.

I found myself mentally pleading with Diesel to come home and save me from this.

From her.

Fear overran my body, creating piercing signals from my head to my toes. Suddenly, I felt lightheaded, and the room began to spin.

Her mouth came only an inch away from my ear as she whispered.

"I came here to collect what's mine."

PART TWO

THOMAS

I opened the door to the apartment and slipped off my shoes. I had spent longer with the police than I intended to, but the damage was so bad that I needed to go through every piece of material to report a claim that would later be used for insurance purposes. It was a headache in itself, but this wasn't the first time it happened. Kids get the end-of-summer itch, don't want to go back to school, want to have one last send-off before they get tied down, whatever it is. This time, in my opinion, it seemed to be a metal baseball bat blasting through some framework. Whoever did it has a hell of an arm because that place was barely standing when I got there. One look at the framework had me wishing the weapon of choice was spray paint instead, which would have been an easy fix. But now, two and a half hours later, my body was screaming for my bed. And my girl.

I shuffled past the kitchen and into the hallway, stopping in front of the bedroom door. I went to reach for the doorknob but paused. Something isn't right. Something is off. The air filtering through the hall, through my lungs, was heavy. All the lights were still off, exactly as they were when I left, but something wasn't sitting right with me, and I couldn't place it.

Was this that "seventh sense" that Anna talked about?

It felt like the silence of a room right after you wake from a nightmare, or the quiet of a city after a deadly hurricane. It was eerie. There was also a faint trace of vanilla, so distant I almost doubted myself. I pushed open the door, only to see the bed empty and unmade.

"Anna?"

I glanced over to the living room to see if she was sleeping on the couch, even though I would have seen her as soon as I walked in. It was empty. I eyed the balcony doors over my shoulder, and those were also untouched. My heartbeat began to pick up the pace. I moved down the hall to the next door, the bathroom. Knocking twice, I leaned in to listen for any sounds coming from the other side.

"Anna?"

Nothing. I opened the door, darkness spilling out into the hall. She wasn't in there.

I quickly opened and checked the guest bedroom. It was untouched, the same way it's been for years. What the hell? My breathing began to match my pulse, gaining speed in fear. I took one last look at our bedroom in my walk toward the living room. A reflection of moonlight on Anna's end table caught my eye.

Her phone.

She's still here.

Maybe I missed something. She may have slipped out onto the balcony for some air and shut the doors behind her, even though we almost always left them open. I began to walk, my steps quick with nerves. It was the only place left for her to be. Holding my breath without knowing, I passed the kitchen and noticed a single glass of water on the counter. She must not have been able to sleep.

My eyes trailed to the floor when I saw it.

Her foot.

My soul crumpled in on itself.

Her sunkissed skin, blue painted toenails, there on the kitchen floor.

I lost all sense of the world when I ran to her, my knees collapsing on the floor beside her.

"Anna? Anna! Wake up!"

I tried waking her, shifting her body around a bit. When that didn't work, I grabbed her face, tapping her cheeks, her skin cold under my touch.

No.

Not again.

"Anna… dammit."

I pressed my fingers to the side of her throat, a vision of last year's accident rushing back to my memory. Her head on my lap, her face covered in blood, my lips on hers.

I couldn't find her pulse then.

I can't find her pulse now.

My pulse was fast enough for the both of us, and I found myself thinking of ways to give her some of my own heartbeat.

I pushed my palms flat on her chest and began to thrust down, trying to jump-start her heart. Her body shook from my force, but her eyes remained closed. I could feel tingles behind my eyes, my vision becoming blurrier every time I blinked, every time I pushed.

This couldn't be happening.

We were just lying in bed together.

We were sitting on the balcony after dinner, her laugh echoing off the trees, her strawberry hair tangling with the wind.

We were talking about her desire to open her own hair salon here in Kittanning.

Right as my hands began to soften, I felt a cold, firm grip slap onto my wrist. My bones jolted as Anna's hand was tight on me, her knuckles white, her fingers like snakes wrapped around their prey. My body was frozen, fear like ice in my blood. She pushed my hands off her chest, away from her body, acting as if I was trying to hold her down. With her eyes still closed, she turned on her side and immediately started to vomit all over the floor. There was a pool of liquid at her side, her spit trailing down her chin, but I couldn't help but smile through my relief.

She was *alive*.

I felt like I could run a hundred miles from this blissful adrenaline, knowing that she was going to be okay. I could breathe again. But I needed to tend to her first.

"What the hell happened?" There was worry coursing through me, but for some reason, my voice decided to convey my words with a hint of anger.

Her response was a groan as she tried propping herself up on her elbow, but failed, falling back down onto the kitchen floor.

"Woah, okay, easy." I threaded one arm through her arms and under her back, with my other arm under her legs, and lifted her. Her skin was still cold, with goosebumps coating her bare legs and small spots of vomit dotting her shirt. I carried her to the bedroom and laid her down on the bed. Besides a groan rattling her throat a time or two, she didn't fuss and kept her eyes closed. Maybe she hit her head and passed out, and now she's left with a headache. I could only hope that was the worst of it.

"Do you want water? Or Advil?"

Another groan released as she lifted her arm, her muscles weak, and shushed me with her hand, telling me to shut up with one quick motion. I obeyed, sliding the covers over her as she lay on her side, facing away from me.

This felt strange to me. I tried to tell myself that maybe she just wasn't feeling well, got up for water, and passed out. Maybe hit her head on the island. Fuck. But now, with the way she's acting, I felt like some of this was my fault. I left her here alone, not knowing something was up before I kissed her goodbye and left. I should've had her come with me. Or, I should've met the police in the morning.

I walked back out to the kitchen and grabbed a few things: a fresh glass of water, three Advil, and a bowl in case she needed to throw up again. I placed it all on her nightstand, then returned to the kitchen to clean the mess on the floor.

I washed up, doubled checked that everything was locked, and went back into the bedroom. She was sound asleep and hadn't moved an inch. I slipped off my clothes and climbed into bed next to her, knowing I probably won't be sleeping, but hoping the morning will bring more answers.

211

THOMAS

There was a stir in the sheets next to me, the cotton brushing my bare chest causing me to wake. I opened my eyes to the sunlight streaming in through the window, the room cast in a bright yellow glow.

Fuck, I slept?

I didn't mean to fall asleep, not after last night's scare. My plan was to keep an eye on her all night until the sun came up. I cursed myself for letting myself slip. As soon as I got my senses, I whipped my head over to look at Anna, who was shifting uncomfortably next to me.

"Anna, hey." My voice was quiet as I sat up in bed, my hands brushing away loose strands of hair from her face. "How are you feeling?"

Another groan. My shoulders dropped. I was hoping for an actual conversation this morning. Since she wasn't speaking, I decided to do the talking myself.

"Is it your head? Do you have a headache?"

She lifted her shoulders in a shrug.

"Your stomach?"

Another shrug.

I looked at the nightstand and noticed everything I had brought in last night was still untouched.

"I brought you some water. Do you want some?"

This time, she shook her head no, her eyes never opening. It could be from the sunlight, or maybe she didn't get a good night's sleep and was still tired. And here I was, not shutting the fuck up. There were more questions floating in the back of my mind, but judging by her current state, I didn't want to press. Maybe she just needed more sleep.

I looked at the clock. 8:22.

Fuck. I was late for work. I wanted to take the day off to spend with Anna, to make sure she was alright and I didn't need to take her to the hospital, but I needed to handle things with the vandalism. I'm sure the guys knew about it by now since they usually showed up to the work sites well before 8 AM, but they still needed to hear all the information from me. I climbed out of bed, put on my work clothes, and walked to Anna's side of the bed. Her head was still turned away from my side, the sunlight creating a golden glow on her skin. I crouched down so we were face to face and couldn't help but watch her for a moment. I stared at her delicate eyelashes, the sprinkle of freckles across the bridge of her nose, and the curve of her lips that were so perfectly round. I reached up and gently touched her cheek, careful not to wake her, my fingertips brushing her smooth skin.

There wasn't a thing about her that wasn't perfect.

I leaned in and kissed her forehead.

"I'll be back soon. I love you."

Every bone in my body was screaming for me to stay the fuck home.

She stirred but didn't come close to waking. I made sure her phone was charged and nearby in case she needed to call me. Which, to be honest, I'm sure I'll do at some point. As I was walking out of the room, I texted her and told her I was at work and I'd be home soon, in case she woke and didn't know where I was.

I hated leaving her, I hated her being alone, and I hated myself for not being able to stay here.

The dread that filled me stayed in me the whole time I was at work.

I explained to the guys what happened to the house, what our next steps were, and where it put us on the timeline of things. I was straight and to the point. No bullshit. They were frustrated, of course, that all their work was ruined and they would have to start over. But they also didn't ask any questions when I left around noon.

When I arrived home, I opened the door to see everything as I had left it. Everything seemed normal. I walked to the bedroom to check on Anna, only to peer in and see her still in the same spot as when I left her. She was still sleeping with her body facing away from the door. She didn't even change positions.

Doing my best to keep quiet, I stepped around to her side of the bed. Her hair was falling out of the hair tie, with pieces of hair falling over her shoulders. I reached down and brushed the hair away from her neck, allowing her skin to breathe. She inhaled, turning her face to me, and finally, her eyes fluttered open.

"Anna," I whimpered as I dropped to my knees, eye level with her, my heart beating hard. I grabbed one of her hands, and she pulled it into her chest.

God, I could stare into her eyes forever.

She tried to clear her throat, but her voice got lost in the growl.

"Want me to get you some ice water?"

She nodded her head, and I bolted to my feet to fill her needs. I came back moments later with fresh water, kneeling back down to the same spot, lifting the water to her lips. She lifted her head slightly, but a bead of water trickled down the side of her mouth. She seemed so weak, and my mind was begging for answers as to what happened.

"Do you remember last night?"

Another nod.

"What happened?"

She tried to clear her throat again, this time breaking through the barrier.

"I just…don't feel very well."

Holy hell. Her voice.

I didn't know how much I missed it until I heard it.

I tried to keep my composure, controlling my nerves to a minimum as I watched her lay her head back down on her pillow. As I studied her face, I noticed the bags under her eyes. They looked more purple now than they did this morning.

"Did you get enough sleep?" I asked, my fingers running through her silky hair.

"Maybe."

Obviously, she didn't. It was written all over her. But the fact that she was up and talking to me again meant that she was making progress.

I stood and moved to the end of the bed, sitting on the edge, her eyes following me the whole way. I rested my hand on her leg, the covers between our skin.

"Are you hungry? I can get you lunch. Or, if you're not hungry yet, you can sleep and I'll wake you for dinner."

She wrinkled her nose. "Don't make me anything."

No appetite, either, I guess. I don't blame her, since she *did* puke all over the kitchen floor last night.

"Okay, can I go and get you something like a milkshake? Or a smoothie? Or even just a coke?"

I could see her face turn pale, the rose color in her cheeks fading.

"Everything sounds gross."

I nodded, dropping the topic. I wanted to take care of her, but I was out of practice. I barely take care of myself. I wanted her to get better, to feel better, but I didn't even know where to begin. One thing was for sure, I knew she needed sleep, so that's where we'll start.

"Okay. Will you let me know if you change your mind? Or if there's something you need?"

Her lips turned up into a small smile, and for a split second, I knew, deep down, that everything was going to be fine. As long as I had her eyes, green as emeralds, locked with mine, everything would be okay.

"Absolutely." She tucked her hands under her head, between her and the pillow.

There she was. The spark in her was beginning to show through the cracks, and I grinned. If there was anything I would do right with my time on Earth, it would be to marry her. There was no doubt in my mind. I would do it tomorrow if she was up for it.

Grabbing the back of my shirt, I pulled it over my head in a swift motion. I walked to my side of the bed, slid my jeans off, and crawled into bed with her. With her back to me, I pressed my body to hers, our skin melding together perfectly.

A laugh escaped her, so small I almost missed it. "Diesel…"

"Shh…" I whispered, cutting her off, even though I loved hearing her say my name. I wrapped my arms around her body, pulling us as close together as we could possibly be. "I'm not going anywhere. Plus, I had a shitty sleep, too."

She probably thought I was doing this for her, to comfort her while she was sick, to be there if she needed me. But I needed it just as much as she did, if not more. She was everything to me.

I closed my eyes, my head resting just behind hers. I moved my face in close, breathing in the scent of her hair, as I did most nights. It smelled like fresh rainwater dripping off leaves, and I couldn't get enough of it.

I fell asleep breathing her in.

There was nothing better.

THOMAS

There was a deep rumble sound in the room. My eyes shot open, the sound waking me from my sleep. I looked around the room, but my eyes couldn't focus. It was too dark. Confusion flooded me, sleep jumbling my mind in the moments that passed. I tried to sit up, but my arm was pinned down. I glanced over at Anna, who was still sound asleep, lying on her back over my arm. I gently slid out from under her and pulled myself up, her sleep undisturbed. The clock was bright, the white numbers reading 1:43 AM, making me nearly choke on my own spit. We slept for twelve hours? There was no way in hell. Then, I heard the rumble again.

It was my stomach.

I was *starving.*

The rumble went all the way from the top of my ribs to the bottom of my bladder.

Which felt like it was about to burst.

Okay, maybe we did sleep for twelve hours.

After pulling on gym shorts, a t-shirt, and pissing for what seemed like ten years straight, I walked into the kitchen to find something to eat. The fridge was decently stocked, but I didn't feel like cooking in the middle of the night. Screwing up my sleep schedule wasn't something I was interested in making permanent. I pulled out the gallon of milk from the fridge and a box of cereal, making myself a bowl. I carried it to the bedroom, stopped in the doorway, and stood against the frame. My bones were aching to stand, to stretch, and I knew I wasn't going to be able to sit back down for a while.

Anna lay there, her back flat on the mattress, one arm hooked over her head, the other across her stomach. Unless she was up while I was sleeping, she's been in bed for almost twenty-four hours. Maybe she was sick with the flu or some sort of bug. But even after that thought, there was a punch in my gut, like something wasn't right, something I was missing, but I couldn't figure it out. I took another bite of the cereal, chewed through it and swallowed, all while never taking my eyes off Anna. The purple circles under her eyes darkened, and her skin didn't look as vibrant as it did the day before.

I didn't understand it.

One moment, she was fine, sleeping next to me, then I left and came back to her almost lifeless on the kitchen floor. There was a missing factor, and I needed to find it.

I finished the cereal, washed the bowl, and walked to the bedroom. Gently placing my hand on her shoulder, I tried to gently wake Anna with a nudge.

"Hey." My voice was quiet, but it was enough to wake her. She rolled back onto her side, and her eyebrows creased together as she swatted my hand away. There was that spunk seeping out of the cracks again. I smiled.

"Sleepyhead," I began, but she paid me no mind. "We slept a long time. You think you should get up and maybe get something to eat?"

There was a stillness to her before she shook her head. My chest let out a sigh, feeling more defeated as time went on. It's been a whole day since she's had anything to eat or drink besides the small sips of water. The thought made me uncomfortable. Even if she didn't have an appetite, she still needed *something* in her to give her fuel. Maybe if I could get her out of bed for a bit, she'd realize her body needed some calories.

Right as I was about to suggest it, she propped herself up on an elbow, casting a somber look to me. "I'd love to take a bath, if you'd run one for me?"

Her words fumbled up her throat and spilled out of her mouth with difficulty. I blinked and swallowed.

"Of course."

I walked to the bathroom and began running the water, not too hot but not too cold. Once it filled to the ideal amount, I walked back to the bedroom to find Anna sitting up, her knees brought up to her chest, her hands running down her smooth legs. She may be sick, she may be weak and frail, but she was still so damn beautiful. There was never a day that went by where I didn't want to just dwell in her existence. It was something I couldn't explain to anyone no matter how hard I tried, but I knew her and I had an unspoken understanding of it.

When I walked through the doorway into the bedroom, she turned her head to look at me, her eyes piercing into mine. My knees almost gave way to the glimmer in her irises, the green emitting a glow that was only intensified by the moonlight streaking through the room.

I made my way to her side, her head turning to follow me the whole way until I stopped at the bedside. Slowly, she lifted her arms, and I reached down and pulled her shirt over her head with ease, her nipples hardening from the cool air. Then, hooking my arm under her back, I lifted her and slid her shorts down swiftly. She helped me kick them off but didn't let me go once her clothes were off. I bent my other arm under her legs, swooping her up in my arms, the feeling of her cold skin filling my hands. She wrapped her arms around my neck, resting her head on my shoulder.

As I made the short walk down the hall to the bathroom, I looked down at Anna, her naked, smooth body cradled in my arms. Out of all the things we've done—kissing, fucking, cuddling, you name it—this felt the most intimate. With her skin in mine, my focus was so in tune with her that I could almost count every goosebump just by touching them. My heart felt like it was about to explode out of my chest, my bones barely able to contain the heartbeats. My grip tightened on her at the thought of our closeness, and how I knew she was it.

All I wanted.

I was *never* going to let her go.

I could feel the muscles in my face tighten as I continued to watch the woman I love suffer. There was only so much I could do to help her. I could alleviate her pain, but I couldn't make it go away.

And that was the hardest part of all this.

Last year, I was able to help her, to save her, to bring her back to life. Now, I don't know what to do, besides wait.

When I reached the tub, I slowly placed her in the water, making sure it was the right temperature before letting her submerge the rest of the way. She kept her head up, the water rising to the middle of her neck. A sigh escaped her lips and her body seemed to relax, even if just a little. I sat on the floor next to the tub, my back against the wall, our bodies facing the same direction.

She tilted her head to me, looking up at me through her eyelashes.

"My knight in shining armor."

I lifted a smirk. Even though I was only doing the bare minimum, I could tell this meant a lot to her in the look she gave me. And if it meant a lot to her, it meant a lot to me.

I brought my hand up to her forehead, brushing away loose hair. "My queen."

The sounds of water paddling around the tub echoed against the walls around us. Anna breathed in deeply, her face still toward mine.

"Do you ever think about our future together?" she asked with a gravelly tone, the water sliding through her boney fingers.

"I do," I said without an ounce of hesitation. "Do you?"

"Every day."

I rested my head on the wall, my gaze still fixated on her as she moved her hands effortlessly through the warm water. "What do you picture?"

Breathing in another heavy sigh, she let her lids fall closed over her eyes. A minute passed before she spoke, a small smile curling up on her lips.

"A big, white farmhouse, settled on a lot of land. Deep, green grass as far as you can see, with horses and chickens and cows grazing in the sunshine. Gardens lining the back of the house, both vegetable and flower beds so full of color. Oakwood throughout the house, in the flooring, in the walls and doors, and wrapping around the outside in our porch. Opal stepping stones in a path leading to the backyard, with wind chimes dancing in the wind above them. Daylight streaming through the windows of our home, the rays warming every room until nighttime when we sit by the crackling fireplace. Blueberry pie on the windowsill and fresh iced tea on the kitchen counter. You, beside me, every moment of every day. Even when we're old and grey."

I stopped breathing as I listened to her words, her dreams filling my mind with such clarity. We had talked about our futures before but never went in-depth with it, and we didn't discuss anything further than a few years from now. But with this picture she painted for me, a life so beautiful and valuable, I now couldn't see myself living any other way. Everything she pictured, everything she wanted, I was determined to give her.

She paused before opening her eyes, her visions fading as she fell back to reality.

My head was still turned to her, and she turned to meet me.

There were no words to fill this moment, nothing to say to compete with the hope she filled in me.

A single tear trailed down from her right eye as a small gleam of hope flickered in her gaze. My chest tried to rise and fall in rhythm, but the heat in my veins made my breathing uneven. I shifted to my knees, kneeled over the edge of the tub, grabbed her chin with a touch of my thumb, and pulled her into a kiss. Her lips were as smooth as melted ice as they gently pressed back into mine. The weight of my world was shifting with every passing day I was with her, starting from the moment I saved her.

THOMAS

After almost an hour in the tub, I drained the water and dried Anna's skin. I couldn't help but create a pathway of kisses starting from her neck to her shoulder and down her arms as I collected water droplets with the towel. My lips were beginning to feel numb from the number of kisses I'd been giving her, but I didn't want her to forget how much I loved her. Not even for a second.

Lifting her up, her skin still saturated as I wrapped her in the towel, I carried her back to the bedroom, her weight so light and delicate. I could smell the scent of jasmine wafting from her hair, her shampoo bringing the familiar fragrance back into my lungs with pleasure. It was a smell I could never get enough of. Washing her hair for her was another act I had never considered intimate until now. The feeling of the soft suds in my hands, massaging her scalp with her eyes closed, is a picture I'll have burned into my memory forever. Small moans slipped from her lips as the white soap slid down her wet, glossy skin. The closeness between us in that moment was indescribable, and my shorts grew tight simply thinking about it.

Once we reached her side of the bed, I gently sat her down and removed the towel. There were still stray drops of water running down her collarbone to her breasts, my eyes watching their trail the entire way. I tried to swallow the lump in my throat, unsure how to act in this moment. She still wasn't back to her normal self, I could see it in her face, but she was giving me unspoken cues. Her body remained open after I took the towel, her arms holding herself up as she leaned back slightly. There were goosebumps covering every inch of her skin, her nipples hard from the exposure. I licked my bottom lip without realizing, bringing it in and biting down hard.

She didn't move to cover herself.

Her eyes flicked up to mine, desire like flames igniting in her look.

I didn't want to be the guy that couldn't resist sex, even when the girl was still sick and recovering.

But *fuck*, she was making it hard to say no.

I turned away to grab her a clean shirt but quickly felt her hand on my arm, grabbing me. I looked at her expressionless face as she shook her head. She didn't want to get dressed. She wanted to stay naked.

I turned my body toward her as she lay back completely on the bed. In a split decision, I pulled my shirt over my head and crawled onto the mattress, my body hovering over hers. She tilted her chin up to me, her gestures worth a thousand words. The heat between our bodies turned red hot as my skin grazed along hers, our breathing growing heavier by the second.

All my needs are fulfilled by her, and her needs will never go untouched by me.

Reaching up, my fingertips brushed her jaw slowly, our eyes blinking to each other in unspoken hunger. My body fit perfectly between her legs, which soon lifted and wrapped around my waist with the help of my grip. I dipped my hips down to hers, my sight never leaving her flawless face as the tip of my cock teased her entrance. I ran the head up and down, our juices mixing to create the perfect slickness as I slid into her. God, she was so tight. We were both left speechless. The only sound in the room was the rocking of the headboard against the wall in the rhythm of my thrusts. Her round breasts bounced up and down, the sight making my cock throb as it pumped in and out of her.

A quiet hum released from her throat, her eyes rolling to the back of her head in pleasure.

This connection was exactly what we needed in this moment.

I gripped her hips, my fingers pushing into her hard, leaving small red marks on her skin. Her mouth fell open, her screams of lust silenced with the continuous shove of my cock. I picked up speed, the muscles in my stomach tightening as I neared my peak. Keeping my eyes locked on her, I watched as she gained momentum, her finish line approaching in pace with mine. I brought my body down to hers, my forearms holding my weight off her, my lips nipping and sucking her neck as my body began to convulse. Beads of our sweat mixed together, our panting in sync as we both reached our climax at the same time.

"*Fuck*, Anna. Fuck."

It was all I could manage to strangle out as my cock poured everything into her. Her hips bucked under mine, her back arching as her hands gripped the bedsheets under her. My body shuddered as my muscles released, the feeling making my head spin. She had that effect on me every time we finished. Her sexual grip on me was like super glue, and I wasn't getting out of it without ripping myself to shreds.

Squeezing my eyes shut, I tried to catch my breath, my face still buried in her neck. I shifted my weight and laid on the bed next to her with my head propped up under my fist, staring at her as she looked to the ceiling with a smile.

I would pay good money to know what she was thinking about right now.

Slowly, she turned her head to me, moving her hand up and resting it on my cheek. I closed my eyes at the touch, so gentle, so simple, yet so fulfilling. I breathed in the smell of her skin, forcing my heart to remember her scent.

Without opening my eyes, I opened my mouth to speak. "Want me to lay with you?"

It was more of a question for me, since I was so relaxed I could barely move. I felt the nodding of her head against the pillow and smirked, knowing I wasn't going anywhere anytime soon. The cotton sheets hugged us both as our legs intertwined, drifting off into another sleep.

225

THOMAS

Jogging down the stairs of the apartment building, I heard a door open as I reached the bottom step. Mrs. Reeves stepped out of her apartment, shutting the door behind her with a fragile hand.

"Good morning, Mrs. Reeves." I smiled at her as I passed her, making my way to my truck.

"Good morning, Thomas. Can I talk to you for a moment?"

I stopped, my keys resting in my hand, and turned to her. "Sure. What's up?"

I could see a look of hesitation on her face as she shuffled toward me, her slip-on shoes rubbing along the concrete.

"I know this is a lot to ask, but I don't know who else to turn to." She took a breath, pausing. "I already talked to my children about it, and they think it's the right thing to do."

Confused, I cinched my eyebrows.

"I'm moving in with my daughter, Everly, and her husband and my granddaughter. I'm getting too old, Thomas. I can't be here alone anymore. I don't *want* to be alone." Her hands shook as she brought them up to her chest.

I pressed my lips together, still confused. "Okay, that's great. What's this have to—"

"She lives in Nevada."

"Oh, wow." I leaned back on my heels. "That's far."

She nodded. "I want you to have the building."

I nearly choked on my own tongue, my eyebrows raising high in shock. "What? Why? I can't—"

"When Gerald died, I held onto this building so hard because it reminded me so much of him. And it helped me for a while. But *you* also helped me, and now this place reminds me of *you*. Everything you did, all the fixes you made, they were all things Gerald wanted to do but never got the chance to."

I could hear her voice start to crack, her bottom lip trembling.

"I can't thank you enough for everything you've done, Thomas. You deserve this."

I scrambled to find the right words, fighting through the chaos in my head. But before I could open my mouth to stop her, she stopped me.

"Both Everly and my son, Lucas, live in Nevada, so they can't move here to take care of the place. They have families and jobs that they can't leave. I already talked to them about it, and they agree that passing it to you is the right thing to do. I wouldn't feel right giving it to anyone else."

In my head was a whirlwind of questions. I struggled but managed to ask the most obvious. "Why don't you sell it?"

She shook her head as if it wasn't even an option. "The amount of work you put into these apartments is worth more than I could ever sell it for."

Well, I'll be damned. History really does repeat itself. First, my dad's company was given to me, even though my dad's back was against the wall. There was a learning curve at first, but I quickly got the hang of owning a business. Now, the apartment building is being handed to me, this time in better circumstances. I'm sure there will be a lot to learn here as well, but a piece of me feels oddly optimistic.

It almost seems like life is guiding me into a path I'm happy to go down, my future with Anna easily slipping into place.

"I…don't know what to say."

While still looking at me, she slowly grabbed my empty hand and turned my palm up, placing her set of keys in them. I already had a master set to the building, but the significance of this was clear. She was passing everything along to me.

"Take it, Thomas." She turned around, heading back into her apartment. "I already talked to a lawyer about it."

She already had her mind made up, even without talking to me first.

"I'm leaving in a few days. I'll be sure to see you before then."

I gave a single nod, my hand frozen where she had left it, her keys still resting in my palm. It might take me a while to process this.

Right as I was about to turn and go, she perked up at a thought. "One last thing."

Raising my eyebrows, I waited for what she needed to say.

"These apartments are ready to be rented, Thomas. I saw what you did with them, and they are easily up to code. Make some money and rent them out. And use that money to give Anna what she wants."

A wide smile struck my face as she slipped back into her apartment, closing the door behind her. I turned and walked to my truck, setting her keys in the cup holder in front of me. I stared at them, the purple carabiner clip holding them together, and released a small laugh.

We had the same thought.

Anna was going to be my wife.

Mrs. Reeves wasn't joking. When I returned home from work a couple of days later, there was a U-Haul in the parking lot with the back door rolled to the top. There were multiple boxes lining one side, with furniture along the other. Right as I closed the door to my truck, a man came out of the apartment carrying another box.

"Hey, you must be Thomas, right?" He dropped the box on the edge of the U-Haul and extended his hand to me.

"Yeah, hey." I took his hand and shook it.

"I'm Lucas, Marilyn's daughter." He hitched his thumb over his shoulder toward Mrs. Reeves' apartment just as the front door opened.

As Mrs. Reeves fumbled with a box, I glanced to the space that was now empty and bare, and my lungs deflated a bit.

"Thanks for everything you've done here."

Looking back to Lucas, I shrugged it off. "It was nothing, really."

He shook his head. "It definitely wasn't nothing."

A wave of unease washed over me, unsure how to take the compliment. I instinctively rubbed a spot under my eyebrow.

"You know…" he began, briefly looking over his shoulder to make sure she wasn't in earshot. "It was absolute hell when my dad died. One day, she had her husband, and the next, she was alone. Everly and I flew in for the funeral but couldn't stay much longer after that, so she would call us at night and just let it loose. I've never heard her cry so much. We honestly thought, for a minute there, that she might die of a broken heart. Right there, alone in her apartment. It killed us to not physically be there for her, but Everly was pregnant at the time, and after a certain point, her doctor didn't want her traveling anymore. And there was no way I could leave work. But then, one day, she stopped. She told us about a man who volunteered himself to fix up the apartments. And it changed her. She was still sad, of course, but we could hear the pain ease up little by little. She loved having you around. She said you reminded her of my dad."

I paused, my eyes moving to the concrete below me, my eyebrows meeting in a crease.

I didn't know any of this.

It was a quick reminder of how everyone is fighting some sort of battle, and most of the time, it's not visible.

"So, it's not nothing. Thank you."

He clapped a hand on my arm right as Mrs. Reeves stepped out of her apartment, a small pet carrier in her hand.

"Thomas."

It was the biggest smile I'd ever seen on her, and it made my mood skyrocket. She deserves to be happy. She always has.

She quickly trotted over to me and placed the carrier down, then engulfed me in a hug. "Oh, Thomas. I can't thank you enough. For everything."

"Of course," I said as I squatted low to return the hug. "Is there anything I can help you with?"

She released the hug but kept her grip on my arms. "No, we're all done." She looked to Lucas, who gave a nod and closed the back door to the U-Haul.

"Nice to meet you, Thomas." Lucas gave a salute as he climbed into the driver's side of the U-Haul and shut the door.

"You be good, okay?" She looked into my eyes, and knowing what I know now, I understood why there was a film of tears coating hers. I grinned, giving her one last hug.

"You know, I'm going to miss your Christmas cookies."

I could feel a laugh escape her as she pulled away. "Oh, honey. I know where you live. You'll be receiving a box of them every year, don't you worry."

And with one final pat on my arm, she picked up the pet carrier.

"See you later, Teddy." Leaning down, I poked a finger through the grated door and got a simple meow in return.

With a smile, she turned and made her way to the passenger side of the U-Haul and got in. I stepped into the stairwell and watched them drive off, waving as they pulled onto the road, a sliver of me going with them.

Without realizing it, she helped me too.

She offered me a place to stay while knowing who my dad is. She took a chance on me, even with the chance that I could turn out like him. She filled a small part of a void that appeared when my mom passed away. Even though nothing could take my mom's place, Mrs. Reeves did a good job playing the role when I needed her to.

I rolled my shoulders, regaining my composure, and jogged up the stairs to my apartment.

THOMAS

I leaned against the doorframe of the bedroom, watching her sleep with her back to me. It's been six days since I found Anna on the kitchen floor. She was still spending her entire days in bed with no return of her appetite. Yesterday, before leaving for work, I placed a peanut butter and jelly sandwich next to her bed, and it was gone when I came back. That gave me some hope, but it was only a band-aid on a bigger problem. She refused to say much to me, and when she did, her words came out in broken fragments, like she couldn't place her wording or simply didn't feel like talking. She won't tell me exactly what happened or how she's feeling, and if I mention going to the doctor, she shuts me out, making it clear there's no way she'll go. I told her I could bring one here, I could find a doctor that makes house calls, but she refused.

The more I thought about it, the more frustrated I became. I didn't understand what was happening, and the fact that she won't talk to me about it made me want to pull my fucking hair out. I was only trying to help, because watching her suffer like this felt like the deepest cut in my skin.

Normally after work, I would head straight for the shower to wash all the grime off my body, but there was something nagging in me to figure this out. I needed to get to the bottom of this, and if she wasn't going to let me in, I was going to take her to the doctor. Even if that meant carrying her out of here, kicking and screaming.

I made my way into the bedroom and stood at the end of the bed, my height towering over her as she remained on her side.

"Anna." Her name came out as a whisper from force of habit. But I was growing tired of being gentle with her when she wasn't letting me help.

"Anna." This time, my voice was sharp, a deep growl coating her name. She turned onto her back, blinking her eyes at me slowly, waiting for me to say whatever I had to say.

"What's going on? Why are you still in bed?"

"Laying down is the only thing that feels good." Her voice was still hoarse, making my skin crawl.

Proceeding with caution, I spoke firmly, making my worries known, but kept concern in my tone as well. "Anna, I think it's time you go to—"

"I'm *not* going to the doctor," she cut in, a fierceness to her I haven't seen before.

"Then you need to tell me what's wrong. It's been almost a week and you haven't gotten out of bed. You've barely eaten anything, and you aren't acting like yourself."

She turned her head away from me, with one arm under her acting as a pillow and the other resting on her stomach. Her gaze floated out the window, her eyes pointed in that direction, but her focus was on nothing.

"Let me in, Anna. Please."

Her eyelids were heavy. I could see the hesitation on her face.

"Letting you in will only hurt you."

I could feel my heart squeeze in need. Her voice sounded so broken, so cracked, and I almost lost my shit at that moment.

"The only thing that's hurting me is seeing you like this. I need you to get better. I need you with me because I can't stand to live without you."

She inhaled, her throat and chest expanding, and finally turned her head to me again.

"I think you need to talk to your ex-girlfriend."

My face snapped up into confusion. What? Ex-girlfriend? I've only had two ex-girlfriends, and based on our breakups, they both probably want nothing to do with me. Also, last I heard, they don't even live in Pennsylvania anymore.

"What… Who are you talking about?" I asked as I walked to her side of the bed and sat on the edge.

"The one with the red hair, really tall, could pass as a supermodel."

My blood instantly pooled to my face, and my cheeks grew red. There was only one person she could be referring to.

Laila.

I balled my hands into fists, the rage in my body beginning to rear its ugly head. I wish I could correct her, tell her she's *not* my ex-girlfriend, not even in the slightest sense. But that's a problem for a different day.

"What did she say?" I asked, keeping my voice low. A spontaneous visit from Laila couldn't mean anything good, and if she said anything to Anna to knock her into this state, I wouldn't hesitate to knock her right out.

Anna cocked her head slightly. A single tear slipped out of her left eye, falling down her temple and into her smooth locks of hair. I reached down and grabbed the hand that was resting on her stomach, squeezing her fingers gently, my heart aching in return.

It felt as if she was slipping from me, and there was no way I could catch her.

After a minute passed without her answer, I asked again, this time with more force.

"What did she say?" My words spilled out of gritted teeth, even though my voice cracked on the last word.

My increase in anger seemed to have no effect on her as she continued to stare at me, her eyes drained and lifeless. Whatever was going on, it was going to take a while to fix, but there wasn't a single part of me that was going to give up on her.

Anna reached her hand up, my fingers still entwined with hers, and pressed her palm to my cheek. Instinctively, I shut my eyes. The feeling of her caress was the only thing fueling me. It was a loving gesture, one that we've done a hundred times, but today it also held an ounce of sadness. It seemed like she was doing anything to resist answering me, anything to stall for time.

Finally, her voice croaked up, my eyes snapping open to her answer.

"How about you go and ask her."

Her lips curled up into a small smile, unable to reach her eyes and push past her weakness. I leaned into her hand, kissing each finger, then let her go. Every piece of me hated leaving her even more than I already had, but I needed to get to the bottom of this. And this was the first time she clued me into whatever was bothering her.

I stood up, still dressed and wearing my boots from work, ready to go. There were silent curses in my head for not having Laila's phone number. This could have been an easy phone call, but instead, I have to go out and find her.

It's a good thing I know where she'll be.

I began walking out of the bedroom but turned back to Anna before fully leaving.

"I'll be back. I love you."

She was still lying on her back, but now her face looked up at the ceiling. She glanced my way, giving me the same small smile, with a look I couldn't quite trace in her evergreen eyes. It almost looked like empathy.

I bolted out of the apartment, locking the door behind me, desperate to find an answer.

THOMAS

It was only 5:45 PM, but the parking lot to Stoney's was already littered with cars. My truck was parked in the back row, discreetly hidden by low branches from a tree line behind me.

Watching the doors, I sat in the driver's seat, my hands fumbling with the keys. I wasn't sure if Laila was here yet, or if she was even working tonight.

Maybe she didn't work here at all anymore.

The last time I saw her was almost six years ago, at this very bar, for my twenty-first birthday. I was drunk off my ass, looking at her in ways I shouldn't have been. And, honestly, I wouldn't be surprised if she got a job somewhere else, somewhere better. She's an incredible dancer with a face most women would pay for. She could easily make more money at a place that's not in the middle of smack dab, small-town Kittanning, Pennsylvania.

Squeezing my eyes shut, I shook my head. Fuck. I needed to stop seeing her in that way. She was an accomplice in my dad's drunk driving accident. There was no way I could give her the benefit of the doubt, especially when Anna had mentioned her when I asked what was wrong. Laila had a part in all of this, and I needed to find out what it was.

There was some unspoken pull between me and Laila, yes, but I don't love her like I love Anna.

I never have.

I owe *everything* to Anna.

My loyalty, my trust, my love, everything.

I watched a few people enter the front doors. There were three women, laughing together at something one of them said. They looked close, like they were friends, and based on the small duffel bags looped over their shoulders, I'm assuming they were dancers here.

But none of them had red hair.

None of them were Laila.

Two men followed behind them, dressed in suit pants and button-down shirts with their ties loosened. They opened the door and entered with ease, with no bouncer acting as a buffer. The club opened at five for food and drinks, then tightened up security when the dancing began at nine. I decided to take my chances and try to find her now, hoping to get this over with.

I kicked open the door of my truck and hopped out, shutting and locking it behind me. To most people, it looks like I'm just getting off work and grabbing a bite to eat, since I'm still dressed in my work clothes and dirty from head to toe, but the last thing I want is to sit down and relax.

Opening the front doors, I stepped inside. The lighting was brighter than usual, with the red lights dimmed and the main overhead lights on, since there was no entertainment on stage yet. The place still reeked of musty wood, as if the building hadn't been checked for mold in ten years. But now, there was an added bonus smell of hot sauce and chicken wings filling the air. Immediately to my left was the bar, with two women stocking items and paying me no mind, neither one of them being Laila. I scanned the room, searching for more employees, but none of them were who I was looking for.

A waitress stepped in front of me, her hand carrying a tray of drinks. Her straight, brown hair was cut to her shoulders, and her big, brown eyes darted to me. "Hey, sweetie. Go ahead and take a seat wherever you'd like."

I took a half step toward her, trying to block her path. "I'm sorry, mind if I ask you something real quick?"

"Sure," she said with a pause, a small squint of suspicion in her eyes. She lowered her tray, taking the weight off her one wrist, and waited for me to continue.

"Is Laila working today? Or tonight?"

Her eyes lowered even more, unsure of my intention, but then quickly snapped back to normal. I know they are wary of people who come in, searching for their favorite dancer, especially before and after their shifts. They don't want creeps hanging around, stalking them, waiting for them, clinging onto false hope that they have a shot with them. But that's not why I'm here.

"What's your name?"

"My name is Thomas. I'm a friend, and I just wanted to say hi."

She nodded once, a graceful smile spreading along her cheeks. "I can check for you. If she's not here, I'll leave her a note. Sound good?"

Before I could reply, she walked past me, taking her tray of drinks to a table across the room. It was obvious her answer was code. She would go to the back, or wherever Laila was, and ask if she knew me. If not, the waitress would pretend Laila wasn't here in hopes that I would leave. Hopefully, Laila won't pull some shit, and she'll make this easy for both of us.

I rested my back against the bar, my hands deep in my pockets as I waited. Within seconds, I felt a presence near my back.

"Can I get you a drink?"

I turned to see one of the employees from earlier eyeing me, thinking I was waiting to be served, her freshly stocked glass bottles resting in her hands.

"I'm good, thanks."

Just as I turned back around, my body facing the long hallway of private rooms, I watched the waitress walk all the way down to the main dressing room. She looked to be only a few years older than me, but I didn't recognize her.

Weird.

In fact, I didn't know the other woman working behind the bar, either. Since this was such a small town, I usually recognized anyone within a few years of me that would have graduated from my high school. There were only around one hundred kids in each graduating class, and when you see them almost every day of your life, you get to know who they are whether you want to or not.

Do that many people move here, to Kittanning, to work at a strip club?

The waitress closed the door behind her, a streak of light illuminating the floor underneath. I watched as the shadows of her feet faded away, her footsteps taking her away from the door. A few minutes passed, my annoyance growing and my patience wearing thin.

A quiet thud hit the bar top behind me, and I turned around to see a tall glass of beer sitting on a napkin, bubbles climbing in a perfect stream to the top of the glass.

"On the house."

The same employee looked at me, her blonde hair sliding past her shoulders as she snapped her gum in a smile, sending a wink my way. Arching an eyebrow, I looked to her, to the drink, then back to her. Didn't I say I didn't want a fucking drink?

"Thomas Diesel."

A chill ran down my spine at the sound of that voice. That rich, smooth, silk voice.

There she stood as I turned to her, my back still against the bar. With her signature black stilettos, dark skinny jeans hugging her long legs, and a white v-neck shirt neatly tucked under a black blazer, she dressed even better than she used to. How I didn't hear the click of her heels walking toward me, I'm not sure. Her red hair was gently curled into waves, the tresses running past her shoulders and dipping to the middle of her back. She crossed her arms over her chest, sticking one leg out, tilting her chin up slightly.

She was a woman of power, and damn, it showed.

"Laila."

"It's good to see you."

I swallowed, my mouth suddenly dryer than the Sahara, and did everything to keep my face neutral. Whatever hold this woman had over me would not take me today.

"You as well."

After uncrossing her arms, she slowly took steps toward me, her gaze locked on me the whole time. It was only when she was close enough to me that I could see her skin, still flawless and creamy, not a single blemish in sight.

"Look at you, Thomas."

The wood behind me dug into my back as her hands moved to either side of me, resting on the bar, enclosing me in her trap.

"All grown up."

I couldn't say the same about her, since she still looks exactly the same as when I was eighteen. The woman drinks from the fucking fountain of youth, apparently.

Our eyes connected, neither one of us looking away, refusing to break the stare.

"How long has it been? Three, four, five years?"

Almost six, said the voice in my head, my mouth closed shut.

With her heels, we were almost at eye level with each other, her height only an inch or two lower than me. I watched as her eyes trailed down to my lips, studying them for a moment, unknown thoughts flickering through her mind, then moved back up to my eyes. I kept my hands in my pockets, ignoring the game she was trying to play.

"To what do I owe the pleasure?"

My lungs squeezed out an exhale. "I think you know why I'm here."

She cocked her head to the side, a playful smile shadowing her lips. "Do I?"

With another step toward me, she firmly pressed her hips into mine, our bodies melding together like clay in an art piece.

Fuck, I said I wasn't going to do this.

I turned my eyes away, scanning the room, but not a single person seemed to notice. Or care. Maybe she did this shit so frequently that it's just another day in the life of Laila.

Aware of my hand placement, I grabbed her waist and gently pushed her off me. "Back off, Laila," I said with gritted teeth, my annoyance seeping through. "I'm with someone."

Smiling, she let her straight, white teeth shine, and lifted a finger to my chin. With the slight breeze from the upward motion of her arm, I caught a whiff of her perfume.

Vanilla.

The scent in my apartment the night I found Anna on the kitchen floor.

"I know."

Laila dropped her arms and moved to the stool next to me, taking a seat. I sat next to her, the bar top at our sides as we faced each other. Our long legs had nowhere to go besides between each other, and I was doing my best to keep our knees from connecting like magnets.

"You gonna drink that?"

She motioned to the untouched glass of free beer. I had no idea what kind it even was. I slid it to her, giving permission for her to have it. She lifted it to her lips, closing her eyes as she swallowed a few times. A sheer coating of foam left a gloss as she placed the glass back down, her tongue sliding along her lips, cleaning the residue.

Laila looked at the two women still stocking the bar. "Emma. Polly. Go. Make sure the dressing room is ready for tonight."

The girls dropped what they were doing and scrambled out from behind the bar without protest. The blonde who gave me the drink slipped me a smirk as she walked past, but I didn't return it. I had no idea why she told them to leave since there was a room full of other people around us, still close enough to listen if they wanted to.

"You run this place now?"

She nodded, satisfaction etched in her expression.

"You still dance?" I asked, layers of reasoning in my question. Although, I wasn't sure why I was still making small talk when I had a reason for being here.

Lifting one shoulder in a shrug, she looked down at the glass, mindlessly twisting it. "Sometimes. If I feel like pulling in extra money."

Now I understand why she was still here. She was the boss. Of course, she could get a job anywhere, and she could probably be a boss anywhere, too, but you have to climb the ladder to get there. Sometimes.

"She's a beautiful girl, Thomas."

I could feel the muscles in my back tighten, her words snapping me out of my train of thought. She was right, Anna is beautiful, and anyone could see that. But Anna also led me here. I know there's something Laila's hiding.

"Is something wrong?" she asked, picking up on the fact that I wasn't talking as much.

"Why did you come to my apartment?" I returned, getting right to the point.

"I wanted to see you."

"Bullshit."

Fire lit her eyes, but from anger or desire, I wasn't sure.

I silently rubbed the spot under my eyebrow. "Laila, Anna's not…"

My voice trailed off, trying to find the best way to explain it.

"Anna's not doing well. And she told me to ask you about it."

Laila froze, her hand iced to her glass. "She did, did she?"

I swore I saw the corner of her lip curl with a hint of a smirk. I said nothing and gave no reaction, waiting for her to explain. When a minute passed and she didn't, I sighed. I'm sick of beating around the bush, waiting for answers.

"Laila, you have five fucking seconds to tell me what the *fuck* is going on."

She crossed one leg over another, her gaze almost softening to me. I didn't scare her. I could scare everyone but her.

But she didn't scare me either.

"I wanted to visit you. But you weren't home, and she was."

"Yeah, I get that. But that doesn't explain why she won't get out of bed anymore."

She sighed, probably just as tired of this as I was. "When did this start?"

"A week ago. The night you fucking saw her!"

A few heads turned our way as my voice grew louder, but neither one of us paid them any attention.

"What was the date, Thomas?"

I squeezed my eyes shut. "I don't know." My brain twisted, trying to think of the dates of today and last week, but honestly, I couldn't even remember what day of the week today was.

"Think." She brought the glass of beer to her lips once more, throwing a knowing look at me over the rim. It was hard to think with sparkling shades of blue staring me down.

Was it the anniversary of her father dying? Did her mother try to contact her? But what would any of that have to do with Laila?

I glanced at Laila as she lowered her glass back to the bar top, drips of condensation sliding down.

Laila.

Fuck.

In an instant, everything clicked in my head.

The accident.

The kiss.

"Did you tell her?" My voice was quiet, every cell in my body growing hot.

This is what Anna was talking about.

I watched as Laila chewed the inside of her cheek, fighting some sort of internal battle, trying to think of the right thing to say. She reached to me, grabbing my hand, an electric current running up my arm at her touch.

My chest heaved at the thought of Anna knowing the absolute truth about everything. It was something I thought about every day, every night, as I watched her live and breathe, but I was never sure if I could tell her. I wouldn't even know where to begin.

How do you look someone in the eye and tell them you brought them back to life through some supernatural kiss? How would they look at you and *not* think you're batshit crazy?

But Laila must have done it for me. And now, Anna is probably upset that I didn't tell her first, and now I have to go home and explain everything. Of course, I'll gladly grovel if that's what it takes to make her feel better. I just wish Laila would've stayed the fuck out of it.

I went to stand, pulled my hand away from hers, and pushed the bar stool out from under me. That's when Laila stopped me.

"Close your eyes."

I groaned, rolling my eyes instead. She stood up as well, moving her face only inches away from mine.

"Close your eyes," she said again, this time softer, her velvet tone brushing across my ears.

I did what I was told and closed them. I could still hear the bustle of the club around me, silverware clinking against dishes and the laughter of men sitting around after their shifts. The front door opened beside me, letting a breeze of fresh air glide across my side. Laila's warm hand grazed my cheek, her palm flat on my skin, another current stinging my body.

That's when the background noises ceased. Everything stopped. Even though my eyes were closed, everything turned blacker than black. I knew that if I were to open my eyes, I wouldn't be able to see anything.

For a minute, I forgot everything. All I could do was feel her touch and smell her perfume. I could envision nothing but her red hair, a waterfall descending and turning into a pool of blood at her feet. She didn't have a body, only an outline of one from her hair. Slowly, she turned and looked over her shoulder to me, a black void of where her head should be, and motioned for me to come closer. In my head, I took a step toward her, but my physical body remained unmoving as my complete trust was placed in her. My feet stepped into the warm blood, and with each step, I fell deeper until the liquid was up to my knees. She lifted her hand to me, and although I couldn't see it, I knew it was there, outstretched to me. I felt myself sinking lower into the blood, the surface at my chest. Her hand rested atop my head, drops of blood trickling out of her sharp fingertips. She pushed me down, the blood rising up to my collarbones, to my throat, to my chin, to my nose. She pushed me completely under, my entire body engulfed in the liquid at her feet, filling my lungs. Then, she pulled me up, every inch of me covered, the pores of my skin filled. Stepping out of the red puddle, I looked at the void where her body should be, her voice speaking in a language I couldn't understand. Whatever she was saying wasn't for me.

Physically, I slowly leaned my head into her hand, my heart quickening, my breathing shallow. Wherever she took me was where I wanted to stay. I felt like I was in another universe, with no gravity weighing on me. There was nothing else in the world but here, now, her and me.

Laila dropped her hand and I was immediately catapulted back to Earth.

My eyes snapped open, my equilibrium completely disoriented as I tried to find my balance.

What the fuck was that?

It felt like I was gone for hours, sucked into her palm, somewhere far off planet Earth.

Laila leaned in and kissed the side of my face, patted my chest with her hand, then walked back to the long hallway of private rooms.

Without looking back at me, she yelled over her shoulder.

"There's your truth."

THOMAS

I reached the top of the stairwell when it hit me. What was that? I crinkled my nose in disgust. Was there a dead animal in apartment five? God, that smelled awful. I bet there was a dead raccoon or opossum over there. Sometimes they could sneak in the walls or find an open space somewhere for shelter, and then they can't get out. And the summer heat only makes everything worse.

Stepping to the front door of my apartment, the smell only got stronger, triggering a cough. What the fuck? There were no storage rooms on this side of the building, and I couldn't think of anything else that would cause the odor. I unlocked the front door and swung it open, the putrid smell hitting me full force.

Holy *fuck*.

Why does it smell like fucking death in here?

That's when my eyes opened wide, despite them watering, and my shoulders stiffened.

No.

No.

No.

No.

I slammed the door and ran to the bedroom, my heart falling out of my ass, and grabbed the knob, flinging it open.

I didn't think the smell could get any worse, but it did.

I looked to the bed to see Anna, lying there, lifeless and dead.

Dead.

Immediately, I turned and threw up all over the floor, the river of vomit feeling like it would never end as my stomach launched itself up my throat.

After there was nothing left in me, I forced myself to look at her again. Taking small steps closer to the bed, she slowly came into view until I was right at her feet.

Her skin had a greenish-brown hue with unknown liquid oozing out of her, making her body look almost slimy. It was coming out of her pores, her nose, mouth, everything, including her eyes, which were basically liquified. Her skin was bloated, her insides a cesspool of whatever gases were concocting. Her hair was thinning and falling out. What once was soft, beautiful strawberry-blonde hair was now stringy, brittle, and sparse. Her eyes, what was left of them, looked up to the ceiling in what seemed to be fright, but her eyelids were just plastered open, making it appear that way. Her teeth and nails were on the brink of falling out, with her pinky finger already missing a nail. Looking at the sheets, her body was oozing the liquids into the mattress, staining them a deep brown color. Flies danced around her, landing and feasting on whatever part of her they could find.

I covered my mouth with the back of my hand, my eyes too shocked to look away.

Her hand was still resting on her stomach, in the same spot where I left it.

I...*Fuck.*

She was dressed in my t-shirt, the same one from the night I found her on the kitchen floor.

The. Same. Shirt.

It was her favorite shirt of mine, so after I had undressed her and given her a bath, she wanted it back on.

Judging by the shirt, and how far her body has decayed, that means…

Anna's been dead for a week.

And *that* fucking means…

I closed my eyes and replayed the last week in my head.

Carrying her to bed.

Sleeping next to her every night.

Giving her a bath.

Kissing her.

Fucking her.

No.

I turned to my side and threw up again, even though barely anything came out. Strings of bile fell to the floor, only adding to the putrid aroma of the room. There was no stopping my body's reaction. I fell to my knees, my hands clammy on the cold floor, and threw the fuck up.

I fucked her dead body.

Trying to stand but failing miserably, I dashed out of the room, my legs neglecting to keep me upright, and launched myself to the kitchen sink. I needed to get my fucking head on straight. I turned on the faucet and stuck my head under the water, making sure it was as cold as possible. The water parted, and half of it slid down the back of my neck in rivulets while the rest soaked my hair, ran down my face, and fell off the tip of my nose. I tried to close my eyes, but every time I did, all I saw was Anna's dead body. I didn't even have the ability to envision her alive. The only thing my mind was letting me see was her fucking corpse.

I turned off the water, my skin sweating through the cold, the collar of my shirt soaked. I didn't want to turn around because I knew I would have to face her again.

But I had to.

I pushed off the edge of the counter and walked back to the bedroom, stopping at the doorway. As if hoping for a miracle would change anything, she remained in the bed, her mouth hanging wide open.

She was *gone.*

Her laugh, her dreams, her future, it was all gone.

Without thinking, I slammed my fist into the wall next to me, leaving an indent in the drywall. There was no pain registering in my hand, so I did it again.

And again.

And a-fucking-gain.

My fist went flying into the same spot in the wall, the hole growing wider and deeper with each punch. Each of my knuckles tore open, leaving heavy traces of blood along the wall. Once I couldn't punch with my right hand anymore, I switched to my left and sent it flying, making a new hole in the wall. The adrenaline in my veins kept me going, my fist unrelenting until it went numb.

I felt numb.

Anna was *gone.*

I bent at the waist, my bloody hands resting on my knees as I tried to catch my breath. There was a tidal wave of thoughts and questions flooding me now that the shock had worn off.

How did I not know?

My mind hit rewind, taking me back to the night I found her lying on the floor. She was out cold, but alive. I remember her groaning, puking, and breathing. I slept next to her that night. I bathed her, and she talked to me.

How did she die?

Of all thoughts in my head, this puzzled me the most. I didn't get a clear look at her when I came in, but I knew I had to in order to see what had happened.

I stepped farther into the room and slowly made my way to her body.

Dammit. *Fuck.*

I ran my hands over my face. Seeing her wasn't getting any easier.

But as I studied her face, I noticed something. The scar on her forehead was split open, the fleshy skin completely unhealed. Old blood and pus oozed from the gash as if stitches were never there. I furrowed my eyebrows, confused. The last time I saw her, well, the last time I saw her *alive*, the scar was healed. So why was it open now?

My eyes drifted down her decaying body. Bruises and deep discoloration lined her arms. Her shirt was lifted slightly at her hip, skin peeking out from under the cotton. Carefully, I pinched the cotton and slid the shirt up, exposing her stomach. It was a dark purple, to the point where it was mainly black. Her bones were broken into fragments, the pieces scattered all around her torso under her skin. Her ribcage was completely demolished. No wonder why she didn't survive this.

I pulled the shirt back down and took a step back. I forced my stare on her, to burn this picture in my mind so I'd never forget it, a punishment for myself. It's what I fucking deserved for not protecting her from this.

Why couldn't I see that she was dead?

What filter was over my mind and eyes?

A picture flashed in my vision. Laila. Her hand on my cheek.

There's your truth.

The realization dawned on me as I stared at Anna's body.

The accident.

The kiss.

She had all the same injuries as the night of the accident.

She died from those injuries.

The date.

I shut my eyes, trying to think of the date I found Anna on the floor. *Come on, think.* I wrote it down a hundred times for the insurance claims.

August 23, 2022.

Then, I tried to think of when Anna was hit by the car. I was sitting on the balcony. It was nice outside. It was summer, or the end of summer.

Near the end of August.

One year ago.

Fuck me.

My legs couldn't carry me out of the apartment fast enough as I slammed the front door behind me.

251

THOMAS

My truck screeched into Stoney's parking lot, nearly tilting on its side. I pulled into the same spot I was in earlier, hidden under the trees, and flung the door open. By this time, it was close to nine o'clock, and the place was filling up with people waiting for the dancers. There was no way to keep the fire under my ass to a minimum. I knew what I was about to do, and I didn't care who saw me do it.

Stepping out of the truck, I glanced to the back of the building. There were a few dancers standing outside, looking as if they were finishing their cigarettes. Perfect timing. I jogged up to where they were, the scent of smoke lingering in the air as they opened the back door to the dressing room and trotted back inside. I waited until they were most of the way in, then grabbed the door to prevent it from closing. I thought I was being discreet, but one of the girls turned and looked back at me.

It was the blonde bartender from earlier.

She slid me another wink as I stepped in behind her. Just as I was about to demand for Laila, the handful of dancers made their way across the room to leave, giving me a perfect view.

There she was.

She was still in the same clothes from earlier, with the blazer and jeans and stilettoes, sitting on the desk of a vanity, with her feet on the chair and her back to the mirror. She was facing me, as if she's been expecting me. The door to the main floor clicked closed behind the dancers, leaving just the two of us.

Here.

Alone.

I wasted no time and rushed to her. Both of my hands grabbed her neck and my thumbs pressed firmly under her jaw, forcing her to look at me.

"Oh, shit. You're sexy when you're angry," she pushed out, my grip squeezing the air from her throat.

Rage pulsed through me, my blood heating. With one thrust, I smashed her head back into the mirror behind her, producing a crack in the glass. She blinked at me, unfazed.

"What the *fuck* did you do?" I asked, my teeth grinding so hard they felt like they were going to crack. It was taking everything in me to not twist her head all the way around her neck.

She pulled her red lips up in a smile. "If I knew you liked it rough, I would've fucked you instead of your daddy."

I cracked her head back into the mirror again, the lines in the reflection growing wider, and this time a circle of blood stained the glass.

"What the *FUCK* did you do to her?"

My shouting was sure to trigger security. It was only a matter of time before I expected them to come charging in here, so I needed her answers *now*.

She placed her hands on my forearms, but her grip was loose. Not a single one of her muscles was trying to get out of my grasp. She was almost *relaxed*. Her grin stayed, and now she let out a shallow laugh, her breathing still constricted.

"I see the veil has been lifted from your eyes."

My hands squeezed her throat harder, causing her face to turn a dark shade of red. There was sweat pouring out of every part of me as I watched her silently lose the ability to breathe.

"So let me get this straight," I began in a hiss, leaning into her face, my nose brushing against her cheek. "You gave me this gift, I used it to save Anna's life, then you waited a year and took her from me?"

She nodded, my fingertips leaving bruises on her neck.

"Why?"

The question came out in a shout as I smashed her head into the mirror again, the spiderweb of broken glass spreading wider. Her eyes rolled back only for a brief moment, then she gathered herself and looked back to me.

"You should've let her die, Thomas."

With a roar, I used every muscle in my arms and threw her head back in the mirror once more. She had finally had enough, as she brought her leg up and kicked me in the stomach, the heel of her stiletto digging into me as she shoved me off of her. I took a step back and my hands released her throat. Even though I had backed away, my body was no less tense.

"So, what? This was all just one big fucking test?"

It wasn't a rhetorical question, but she took it as such.

"Take me instead. Take me and bring her back. Now."

It was a plea filled with every ounce of sincerity I had. I meant every word of it. She could do whatever the fuck she wanted with me as long as Anna came back and had no part in this. I would gladly trade myself without a second thought.

"*Now.*"

She replied quickly. "That's not how this works."

In one quick stride, I was back in her face again, unable to resist the urge to stay away. "If you know what's good for you, you'll bring her back," I said through gritted teeth, my threat ever clear.

A small stream of blood trickled down from her nose as she rubbed her neck, wincing. "It's never a good idea to bring someone back from the dead."

"What the *fuck* do you mean? *You* gave me the ability. *You* did this to me!"

"No," she said, her tone was matter of fact. "I said you had the option to. You always had the choice, you just picked the wrong one."

She must've sensed my movements, because before I could grab her again, she kicked me back and hopped off the vanity. For a split second, I debated going after her again, digging my power into her until she surrendered, but I stopped when she tried to speak again.

"You think it's okay to intervene with life? With 'God's Plan'?" She used dramatic air quotes around the last two words. "People die for a reason, Thomas. They die every fucking day, whether you like it or not. It's not your decision if someone gets to live or die. And since you brought her back with the gift *I* gave you, she was *mine*."

I could feel the anger coursing through my body as I tried to control myself, my hands rolling into fists at my side.

"Do you do this to everyone? Everyone who saves someone, do you end up taking them anyway?"

"Yes."

Fucking bitch.

"Then what's the point? Why even give people the option?"

She took a step toward me, the blood from her nose seeping past her lips and into her mouth. "Ever heard of free will, Thomas?"

A groan escaped me as I rolled my head back, rubbing my hands over my face. She cannot be fucking serious right now. What is this, a Sunday morning church service?

"Free will?" I repeated, making sure this was the path she wanted to take me down. "You think this is all 'free will' when *you* were the one to kiss me on the night of my birthday? When *you* came to my apartment to take Anna's life back? How is that free will when it was destined to be that way from the beginning? I never had a say in any of it!"

She sighed. "Everything has a consequence. From saving a life, down to picking out your underwear for the day. It's all calculated. That's why you keep your fucking nose out of other people's fucking business. Let them die."

We were talking in circles. Everything we were saying was just disproving each other.

Reaching up, she used her wrist to rub the blood off her face but ended up smearing it. She turned around and faced the broken mirror, grabbed a tissue, and began to blot the blood. The wound from the back of her head was tangled and matted in her hair, and her scalp was oozing. She was lucky her hair was already the color of her own blood.

"You're a sadistic fuck, you know that?"

She ignored me as she moved to sit down, still trying to clean the blood off her face in the mirror.

Just then, the back door opened as another dancer was about to step in. She took one look at Laila, then to the mirror, then to me.

"Oh, shit. Sorry."

Laila didn't even glance in the girl's direction. "Go home, Abby. We don't need you tonight." I could feel Laila's annoyance from here. Abby was out of breath and slightly sweaty, as if she ran here. She was probably late for her shift.

Right as Abby turned and walked away, I noticed something behind her. I walked forward and extended my arm, keeping the door open. The nighttime breeze brushed against my searing hot skin, my chest sank down into my stomach, and my eyes widened at what I was seeing.

Right in front of me was a silver car.

The bumper was crooked.

The hood had a dent.

The driver's side headlight was busted.

My mind flashed back to the accident.

Anna's spine bending in half over the hood of the car.

Her bones crunching under the tires.

Her face smacking the pavement.

I turned back around and looked at Laila, who was still mindlessly wiping her face.

"Is this your car?" I asked, still holding the door open and pointing to it with my other hand. My voice was weak at the realization of it all.

She sat up straight, a tissue crumpled in the palm of her hand.

Heavy silence passed before she looked briefly at me, then back to her reflection.

"I've been meaning to get it fixed."

Stepping back into the dressing room, I let the door close behind me with a soft click. It only took me three long strides before I was back to her. I grabbed her hair, fisting it at the back of her head, and yanked her down onto the floor with a thud. She let out a yelp, and if the security didn't hear us before, they definitely heard us now.

"You think this shit is a game, Laila?"

My fist was still pulling her hair as she lay on the floor, flat on her back. I straddled her body, my knees pinning her arms down.

"Careful, Thomas. You're making me wet."

Her body wiggled underneath me as she squeezed her thighs together. She wasn't lying, she was actually turned on by this.

Reaching into my front pocket, I pulled out a folded knife that I carried with me on days I worked on-site. Thank God I was still in my work clothes. The blade itself was only about five inches long, but it will do the trick.

Flipping it open, I brought the knife up to her throat, lining it up with her jugular, my other hand still wrapped in her bloody, red hair.

"So, let's get this straight. I'm not able to save someone's life without consequences, but you're allowed to kill someone and get away with it?"

She did her best to shrug, my weight on her body making it hard to move. "I was bored. You needed a push."

Without hesitation, I flipped the knife around in my hand and sent the blade deep into her left shoulder. Blood seeped out around the blade as a hiss escaped from behind Laila's teeth.

"Now, now, Thomas, you don't want to end up like Daddy, do you? A cold-blooded killer?"

I pulled the knife out of her skin and sent it into her other shoulder. Laila pressed her lips together in a thin line and tried to hide her pain.

Pictures of Anna flashed in my mind.

Her laugh as we lay in bed together, tangled in the sheets.

Her kiss as we shower together, hot water beading on our skin.

Her hands running through my hair, her nails softly scratching my scalp.

Then I picture her decaying body on my bed, lifeless and rotting, and realize I have all the memories I'll ever have of her.

I took my knife out of Laila's shoulder and stabbed her in the bottom of her throat. The gurgling sounds happened instantly as blood pooled in her mouth. When I pulled the blade out, blood splattered all over my face, but I couldn't give a shit.

Any life left in me is gone.

She coughed and sputtered, blood showering her face with each choke.

Anger gripped my chest as I stabbed her in the stomach, right at the bottom of her sternum, the knife plunging to new depths. She tried to pick her head up, the noises she was making indistinguishable, but her body was growing weak.

Fucking good.

I stabbed her a few more times in the stomach and sides for good measure. As she laid still, a pool of blood was spreading on the carpet under her, as well as soaking into my jeans. Moving my knees off her arms, I climbed off her body and sat on the floor next to her. My breath was quick and my heartbeat was even quicker from all this adrenaline.

I tried to wipe some blood off my face, but almost every inch of me was covered in the splatter. I was just smearing it around with the back of my hand.

Looking at Laila as she lay on the floor, I tried to feel an ounce of sadness. Or pity. Or regret.

But I felt nothing.

She deserved this.

All I wanted was Anna back, and this was the closest I could come to having that.

There was a pounding on the dressing room door. A deep voice echoed, asking for Laila. It was security, and I was fucked.

I looked to the door, then back down to her. My breathing stopped as I tried to figure out what to do.

But in an instant, her eyes opened and looked at me. In a slight panic, I grabbed my knife and stabbed her again in the throat, keeping her from calling for help. Her nose wrinkled, a look of pain on her face, but she never broke eye contact with me.

With the knife sitting pretty in her throat, she reached her hand out toward the voice, and with a quick flick of her wrist, the doorknob locked.

It locked even though we were ten feet away from the door.

I could feel the blood drain from my face.

How did she do that?

And how the *fuck* was she still alive?

"I'm fine," she yelled in a garbled mess to the door. She obviously wasn't fine, but whoever it was, they took her word for it. I could hear the footsteps leaving, going back to wherever they were before.

She tried to sigh, but there was an obvious obstacle. "This is getting annoying," she said as clearly as she could, the bloody knife still sticking out of her neck, bobbing with the movement of her throat. She moved her elbows back, trying to prop herself up.

Reaching quickly, I pulled the knife out, sending more blood up onto my face, a steady stream of it pouring out of her. I grabbed her jaw, her skin slippery, and sent the knife into her ear.

"Ouch, *dammit*, Thomas."

She moved her hand up and pulled the knife out of her ear. A wave of panic ran through my body, but I pushed it out as fast as it came through.

I wasn't scared of her.

I *couldn't* be scared of her.

Any fear I had for her was pushed away the second I thought of Anna.

"I knew you were angry, but man, that last one was fucking cruel."

"Who are you?" I asked as I stood to my feet, forcing myself to talk above a whisper, holding my spine straight.

"Come on, Thomas," a playful smirk appeared as she grabbed the bottom of her shirt, wiping blood off her ear. It did no good since her clothes were already drenched in blood. "You had to have suspected it."

I stared at her big, blue eyes. She was right, I did suspect *something*. When she gave me the gift on my eighteenth birthday, part of me wasn't sure if I believed her. But the part that did, the piece of me that felt it, knew there was something superhuman at play.

Then, when the gift actually worked, everything in me knew this was real, this wasn't a human ability, and that an entire world of unknowns was beginning to show itself. But as time went on, my life slowly drifted back to normal with Anna and I pushed my thoughts to the back of my mind.

Now, I wasn't even sure as to what—or who—I was dealing with, but as everything was coming to the surface, I had an itch to know.

"Tell me who you are."

She still held my knife in her hand, but for some reason, I knew she wouldn't use it against me. Her smile widened as she stood up and faced me, her blood acting as enamel and coating all of her teeth. Red hair, bloody face, red lips, bloody teeth. If I couldn't read between the lines before, I could now.

She was not someone to be fucked with.

But that makes two of us.

With the room quiet and our sights set on each other, she spoke clearly and finally revealed herself to me.

"Lilith."

I raised an eyebrow. "The demon?"

"The one and only." She released a breathy laugh. "I'm glad you know your religious figures, babe."

The room began to spin at the admission. My first reaction was to laugh at the absurdity of it. Things like this aren't real, and even if they were, they don't happen to people like me.

But then I remembered the flick of her wrist and the way it locked the door, and I had no choice but to believe her.

Lilith.

The demon.

I don't know much about religion, but I've heard of her before. She was the first woman on Earth, even before Eve. She was the one who didn't play well with Adam and then was exiled because of it. Banned from the Garden of Eden, sent to Hell, and now apparently kissing random eighteen-year-olds in the middle of Pennsylvania, as if she has nothing better to do.

Here she was, standing in front of me, as if she was just another human.

"Lilith," I said through a dry laugh, my head tilting back in surprise. Of all ways I saw this going, Laila being the first demon in all of time was not one of them. "And your stage name was Eve? My God. How original." Disbelief rang through my words.

That got a quiet laugh out of her as she took off her blazer and set it on a chair next to her. Her white shirt was now considered red as the fabric stuck to her mutilated body.

I stared at the giant pool of blood on the carpet. "Why me?" I asked. It was the same question I asked on my eighteenth birthday. Just moments ago, I was trying to kill this woman. Now, she stood before me, not an ounce of pain in her expression.

She lifted her shirt again to wipe more blood from her face. I could see the stab marks in her stomach, still draining liquid from her body. "From the moment I saw you, I knew you were special. Different. I could feel it." She took a few steps toward me, and I held my breath deep in my lungs. Her ocean-blue eyes met mine, sending a lightning bolt into my torso. "You still are."

Silence filled the air around us as she closed the gap between us. Her vanilla scent was unwavering, even stronger than before. At this point, I wasn't sure if it was her perfume or simply the scent of her skin.

Or maybe it was the scent of her blood, since the smell has only gotten stronger as the liquid continued to pour out of her.

Her red hair was doused in blood, locks of it sticking to the sides of her head, framing her heart-shaped face.

There was a need in me, a shameful need that I couldn't fucking shake, even though my mind was screaming for me to run.

Run faster than I ever have before.

But my feet were planted hard to the ground, my shoulders square and solid. My body was stiff in *every* aspect. Laila reached her bloody hand down to my cock, grabbing it hard through my jeans. I closed my eyes, fighting an internal war in me, and bit down on my lower lip.

Laila's mouth fell open in amusement, her palm caressing me in all the right places. "Oh, you're a big boy, huh?"

Fuck, her hand felt so good. I could only imagine what it felt like *under* my jeans.

Before Anna, I always wondered what it would be like to fuck Laila, with her red hair falling over my legs as her mouth glazed over my cock, sucking everything out of me. Her pussy tight and warm as I fuck her, my body on top of hers, the sweat of our skin mixing together. All the images came flooding back as my eyes remained closed.

Laila's other hand brushed over my cheek, my knife still in her grasp, her fingertips slightly trailing over my eyelids. She let out an audible gasp and I snapped my eyes open.

"You like picturing yourself fucking me, Thomas?"

She could see everything I was imagining. Shit.

Before I had a chance to explain myself, she leaned up and planted her lips on mine. I was caught off guard, but only for a fraction of a second before my lips succumbed to hers. The blood on our faces smeared together as our lips molded into one.

This kiss wasn't like the last time. No. This wasn't a soft peck on my eighteenth birthday. This kiss was intimate. This kiss was riddled with all kinds of desire.

Our tongues slipped into each other's mouths, a copper flavor coating the inside. I pressed hard into her as she moved both hands up to my face, our kisses moving faster and growing more heated with each passing second. Grabbing her hips, I pulled her into my body, her blood still flowing out of the stab wounds I just gave her. She let out a quiet moan as our bodies connected, only the fabric of our clothes between us. Her teeth grabbed my bottom lip, biting down hard and drawing blood. I winced, but the idea of our blood mixing together in a kiss set fire in my veins.

I continued to kiss her, losing my breath in the heat of it all. Reaching lower, I slid my hands under her bloody shirt, my fingertips tracing along the cuts on her body.

But as soon as I felt the wound under her sternum, my mind flipped like a switch, falling off of Laila and turning to Anna. I could see the scar on Anna's forehead, caused by the woman, demon, kissing me.

What the *fuck* was I doing?

I pushed Laila off of me, hard enough for her to stumble backward. She regained her footing and looked at me, puzzled.

"No. No, I can't do this."

She tried to step toward me, but I put my hand up.

"Thomas, you know—"

I cut her off. "No. Stop. I'm not doing this."

Silence flowed between us before she opened her mouth to speak. "You want me," she said with confidence, tilting her head to the side.

She wasn't wrong.

Dammit, she wasn't fucking wrong.

I clenched my jaw tight, my bones ready to break with all the pressure. She took another step to me, and this time I let her. She came close enough to me to reach out and grab my cock again, still as hard as before. Probably even harder, if that was possible. I grabbed her wrist and brought it up between us, my eyes fiercely locked on hers.

"I don't."

In a flash, her eyebrows furrowed, but then she pulled herself together. She tried to press her body back onto mine, but I used my free hand to keep her off of me.

"You killed my girlfriend. Twice."

In a split second, her sexual act was gone. She no longer wanted me. Or, at least, she didn't want to show that she wanted me. All the desire that filled her eyes was lost, and now, all I could see was anger.

She looked like she wanted to kill me, and I'm sure she could. Honestly, it probably wouldn't be the worst thing for me right now.

"Go ahead. Kill me. As long as that means I'll never see your fucking face ever again."

A playful smile filled her blood-stained lips. With a quick motion, she brought the hand with my knife up to the right side of my neck and swiped down, leaving a deep, vertical line, open and gushing blood.

My knees gave out as my hand grasped my neck, trying to clamp the skin together. In a matter of seconds, I could feel blood running down my hand and arm.

"You think you're getting off that easy, Thomas?" She squatted down in front of me as I focused on my neck.

Fuck, this was bad.

"You think I'll kill you, so you don't have to face the aftermath of any of this? Or that you'll walk out of here and everything will go back to normal?"

I couldn't focus on *anything* she was saying. All I was thinking about was if she severed an artery or not. But between the smug look on her face and the fact that I had yet to feel lightheaded, I figured she knew what she was doing when she cut me. She's probably had centuries of practice.

She turned away from me and walked over to the vanity, the mirror smashed to pieces, and grabbed her blazer. While slipping it back on, she watched me watch her, waiting for an explanation.

"Nothing *ever* goes back to normal after you piss me off."

My free hand curled into a fist, a slow heat forming in my chest. I wonder what punishment she has in store for me, even though losing Anna and slicing my neck open feels like more than enough.

She stood a few feet away from me, the sight of her sending me in a spiral. She had wounds all over her body, blood-soaked from head to toe, but not a falter in her step and not a single hesitation in her stance. In fact, she stood taller than before, her posture straighter, as if she was about to conduct a business deal.

"You don't ever want to see me again? Fine. I'll make sure you don't. I've been wanting to get out of this bum-fuck town for a while anyway."

She looked around the room as she spoke, as if she was taking in the sights of the club. It was her club, and she was talking like she was leaving.

"But don't you ever think you can try to hurt me, or try to kill me, without consequence."

I looked up at her as her voice slid deeper into anger. She reached down, and with her middle finger, she swiped a sample of the blood dripping from my neck. Then she stuck out her tongue and pressed my blood on it, sucking her finger, savoring the taste.

"I have your blood, Thomas."

My eyes flared as they stayed glued to her. She threw my knife back to me, a soft thud as it hit the carpet in front of my knees.

"You will see her. You'll see her everywhere you go. Work. The grocery store. Your next girlfriend's bathtub. She'll be there, with you, always. Just like you wanted."

My breathing was heavy.

"You'll never be able to escape her."

I didn't know what to think or say. I wasn't sure if she was bluffing or not, and in that, I kept my mouth shut.

"Welcome to The Fallout." Her voice was clear as water and her eyes blazed with fire. I stayed unwavering, watching her as her face turned devious. "Now, get the fuck out of my club, before I have you escorted out."

Her heels clicked as she walked to the door to the main floor, opening it and letting herself through. The music from the stage blasted through the open space, reminding me that I was still in a public area. The door closed behind her, and I remained on the floor, frozen to the spot. I had to try my best to slip out of here unnoticed, without anyone seeing the blood on me.

The stain on the carpet remained, the mirror on the vanity still smashed, and sooner or later, another dancer was going to come in to see the mess. I'm sure Laila would have some sort of explanation, but I wasn't going to stick around and find out.

Gathering the strength and pulling myself to my feet, I quickly opened the back door and slid out undetected. The parking lot was full, and a small line was forming at the entrance. Reaching my truck, I climbed in and closed the door beside me, releasing a breath I was unknowingly holding. I checked the gash on my neck. There was still fresh blood trickling out. I needed to patch this up fast.

Now that I was alone, the quiet of my truck acting as an odd comfort, my thoughts were catching up to me.

What the hell just happened?

I leaned back, running my hands over my head, realizing I was coating my hair in blood like gel.

I needed to go home and shower.

Movement fluttered over by the entrance, catching my eye. I looked up and saw the door open, the bouncer turning to it as if someone had called his name. Laila leaned out, conveying a message to him, my eyes glued to her.

She was clean. Her shirt was white again, her blazer untouched, and her red hair balanced in perfect waves. There wasn't a single drop of blood on her clothes or body. Not a scratch, cut, wound, anything.

She was fine.

I blinked, and nothing changed.

I rubbed my eyes with the heels of my hand, making myself see stars, and looked up.

Nothing changed.

She was *fine*.

I sat back and watched her as she ducked back into the club, her conversation with the bouncer over, the door shutting behind her.

I needed to get the fuck out of here.

Turning the truck on, the engine roared to life as I drove out of the parking lot and onto the main road, heading back to my apartment.

THOMAS

Leaning in the doorway to the bedroom, my shoulders dropped as I looked to the bed. She was still there, her body sinking more into the mattress by the hour. My eyes began to water as my stomach continued to churn from the smell. I had to do something before the apartment would be permanently lined in the scent, if it wasn't already. I took one step into the bedroom and tensed up. Every part of me knew I was in over my head.

I couldn't do this by myself.

I turned around, walked to the balcony, and slid open the doors, hoping to get some of the odor out of here. I reached into my back pocket and hesitantly pulled out my phone.

I scrolled through my contacts, looking for one in particular.

Hitting the call button and pressing the phone to my ear, I pinched the bridge of my nose and squeezed my eyes shut.

A ring. Then another. And another.

Then, an answer.

"I need your help. No questions asked."

I nodded, hearing the reply on the other side of the call, gave my location along with another small request, and hung up. I had about twenty minutes to wash this blood off of me. I didn't need more questions than what I was already about to get.

After a quick shower, I looked for something to put over the gash in my neck. I didn't have anything big enough here to patch it up, so I had to get creative. I found an old towel, cut it into a thin strip, and used tape to cinch it together. It was big and ugly, but it would have to work until I could get some real bandages.

I put on the oldest clothes I could find, a bleach-stained grey t-shirt and ripped jeans. I slipped on an old pair of work boots and left the front door open as I jogged down the stairs. Forcing my hands in the front pockets of my jeans, I stood at the bottom of the steps, waiting with anticipation and dread. This was not going to be easy, and this was not going to be pleasant.

An old, dark blue Honda rolled up to the curb, only about ten feet away from me, and rolled down the passenger window. I scratched the back of my head. There were only a few seconds max where I could change my mind. To call it all off and send the car away.

I should.

Now was the time to do it.

Now was my chance.

I hesitated, uncertainty creeping up my throat like never before. All my life, I've been able to fend for myself. I've been able to adapt to anything. It's a skill I was born with. Maybe that's how I knew that now was the time to reach out and admit that I needed help.

I looked to the car, then to the top of the building, my eyes rolling with annoyance. Tensing every muscle in my body, I jerked my head toward the stairwell, a signal to follow me. I turned and began to walk up the stairs, taking two at a time, when I heard the car park and the door close.

"What's going on?" The voice quickly caught up to me, following me up the stairs.

"I thought I said, 'no questions asked'?" I said in a growl, without looking back.

We finally reached the top of the stairwell, the door to my apartment still open. I could hear a cough behind me, and I knew the smell was still potent.

We looked at each other.

There's no going back now.

"Tommy D," he began, the look in his eyes filled with questions he knew he wasn't allowed to ask. He looked better than the last time I saw him, the day he was released from jail. He had more muscle on his bones and his face looked healthier. I don't know what he's up to these days, and I don't think I care enough to ask.

"Dad," I replied, my chin held high. He wouldn't have come here if he wasn't ready to help me, to defend me, to do the unthinkable.

"I'm not going to explain to you what happened. You wouldn't believe me anyway. But all you need to know, is that none of this is my fault."

His eyes looked to mine, then flicked over to my apartment, scanning the living room. There was something hidden in his expression, something I couldn't place. It wasn't disappointment, but more like an understanding. I wasn't expecting him to believe me, but maybe he did. Maybe he's been in my shoes before, caught in the middle of a problem that wasn't his, and knows exactly how I feel.

Maybe.

I led him into the apartment, then to the bedroom, and showed him exactly what I was dealing with. He handled it surprisingly well, which puzzled me a bit, but I pushed it out of my head. I needed this level-headed mindset with me.

We divulged a plan in a matter of minutes. Before my dad turned to leave, he pulled a small white box out of his pocket and tossed it to me. It was a box of butterfly sutures, just like I requested.

"Thanks," I mumbled, with no response from him. He then headed to the parking lot, took my truck, and left.

Before I could do anything, I needed to fix the wound on my neck. I peeled the makeshift bandage off, cleaned the cut, and pulled the skin together. It took five white sutures to close the vertical line, and it probably could've used more.

Damn, she got me good. This wasn't going away anytime soon.

After I finished, with the cut still oozing but looking better, I went to the bedroom and wrapped Anna in the blankets she was lying in, giving her one last look before I covered her completely.

I could still hear her laughter ringing in my ears.

Fuck.

I wrapped her in my white comforter, holding her body in a soft cocoon. Throwing her over my shoulder, I carried her down the three flights of stairs and out the back door. My mind glitched as I walked over the back road where she was hit, the memory of her lying in the road crystal clear. I paused as I came to the spot where I kissed her, thinking I was saving her life. But all I did was ruin both of our lives.

Anna didn't deserve this. She didn't deserve any of it.

Fuck Laila.

She took an innocent life for the sake of fun. Because she was *bored*.

Because she hands out a curse, masking it as a gift.

Then you fall for it, all because she wants to test you, as if she's a teacher handing out a pop quiz.

And then she takes it all away, only a year later, because you failed her test.

Because she wants to be the one in control. She wants all the power.

Fuck. Laila.

I kept walking, past the road and onto the grass, heading for the trees. I could hear my dad pull up in my truck, parking it along the back road, a red gas can and a large metal barrel from the warehouse in the bed. He stepped out, grabbed the gas can and barrel, and carried it to the trees. With a swift but gentle motion, I placed Anna inside the barrel and set the gas can on top.

Choking back unwanted emotion, I sniffed, all of this feeling so fucking impersonal.

Once she was in, we both went back up to my apartment and hauled my mattress down to the woods. My dad was able to push the mattress behind me as I carried the barrel, leading the way with sweat beading down my forehead.

There was no path, no trail, nothing. I had to keep track of our direction every step of the way, all while fighting my thoughts of Anna, of Laila, of this entire fucking shitshow. Neither one of us said a word, whether it was from exhaustion or from our disconnect from each other, it didn't matter at this point. The only sound around us was from the cracking of branches under our feet, leaves being brushed away by our shoulders, and the barrel and mattress being pulled and dragged along the dirt.

We walked about a half-mile into the woods, finding a small clearing and setting everything down. My dad was panting, wiping sweat off his face with the sleeve of his shirt.

"I gotta get in shape."

I ignored the comment as I stared at the ground, my hands on my hips.

"You ready?" my dad asked. I gave a single nod, not looking up.

He took the gas can, opened it, and poured the liquid on the blankets and the mattress. Then, he reached into his back pocket and pulled out a matchbook. A single match flared, a small almond-shaped flame illuminating the space between us. I wanted to stop him, to tell him to put it out and go, to let me be with her one last time.

But I knew that was only prolonging the inevitable.

He dropped the match on the blankets, and in a second, the flames grew but were neatly contained by the barrel. They deepened, engulfing the blankets inch by inch, the white comforter turning black as it crumbled into ash. He lit another match and dropped it on the mattress, similar flames overtaking the bed. Even though the fire from the mattress was bigger, hotter, and looked like it would catch the whole town on fire, I couldn't take my eyes off the barrel.

My dad shifted next to me, rubbing his chin with his hand.

"I grabbed some jugs of water from the warehouse. I'll go grab 'em."

I blinked as a form of acknowledgment, still staring at the orange flames.

My dad stepped away, only getting a few feet away before turning to me again. He pointed to the fires, unspoken words in the motions of his hands, a red glow coloring the side of his face. As if doing this was a favor to me, and he was already collecting his debts.

"I'm taking the company back."

A beat passed between us as I tore my eyes away from the barrel to look at him.

He was serious.

He didn't do this for me. He did this so he could hold this over me.

Honestly, he could fucking have it. I was done fighting.

I was done.

I was *defeated.*

He turned again and walked away, his body growing dark as he moved farther into the trees. Once I heard his footsteps grow quiet, knowing he was far enough away, I crouched down, balancing on my feet. My body felt weak, my chest felt empty, and my soul felt shattered. Everything I'd come to know was gone, and everything I wanted was unattainable.

I placed my elbows on my thighs, holding my face in my hands.

And I broke.

I lost it.

The tears came in waves, my overflow at my limit.

I lost Anna, I lost the company, I lost everything.

There was a deep roar sitting in my chest, pounding in its cage, waiting to escape.

So, I let it.

I yelled, so deep in the forest and away from the town that no one could hear me.

I yelled, and yelled, and yelled until my throat bled and my sutures ripped open.

I yelled, hoping to feel something.

But instead, I felt numb.

My heart was pumping, my lungs were expanding, I was bleeding, but I wasn't here.

I don't know where I was, but I wasn't here.

The flames spread warmth on my body, blanketing my skin, and for a second, I wanted to jump in the fire. There was a desire to feel myself burn, let the fire engulf the world, and take it all down with me. I watched Anna's body blaze, the orange and red flicker swallowing her whole, and I wanted to burn with her. I wanted to *be with her.*

I could hear my dad walking back with the water, his footsteps giving him away with the crack of sticks under his shoes. I stood back to my feet, not bothering to wipe my face or the blood dripping down my neck. I took a jug of water from him. The fire from the mattress was the first to dwindle, the cold dirt on the ground below it helping to decrease the flames. My dad opened the jug and poured water on it slowly, careful not to send any hot embers flying, and soon the mattress was only a pile of ash.

Then, the fire in the barrel became smaller, the glow darkening, leaving a small, contained pile at the bottom.

I set the jug down on the ground, knowing the rest of the fire had nowhere to go, nowhere to spread to, and leaned in to look.

There she was. The woman I loved, the woman I was going to marry, the woman I thought I saved, reduced to nothing.

My dad cleared his throat next to me. "Hey, uh, I'm gonna head out."

I nodded, knowing if I were to speak, the words would come out cut and broken.

"If you have any more of her shit, burn it. Burn everything. Get your story straight, in case anyone asks."

He turned to leave, handing me the keys to my truck and taking his empty jug with him.

"See you Monday."

THOMAS

I should've told her everything. I should've told her about my night with Laila on my eighteenth birthday. I should've told her that she died the night of the accident, and my kiss brought her back. I should've told her that I wanted nothing more than to kiss her the night she came and brought me beer—and every moment after that—but I was absolutely terrified. I didn't want to reverse whatever it was that brought her back.

But then *she* kissed *me*, and nothing mattered anymore. She stayed alive, and more than that, she became every part of me. My mind, body, and soul.

And there's no reversing that.

I should've told her there was a house, even better than the one I took her to, that I wanted to buy for her.

For us.

One that I helped build. One that I carved her name into, on a foundation stud on the first floor. One that had an even better view, with seclusion and a garden and a path in the backyard that led out to the river.

I should've told her that I wanted to marry her.

But I didn't tell her. She died not knowing any of that. And now, I feel like she's gone while I'm still holding onto these secrets.

I stood at the barrel for another thirty minutes, watching the embers slowly fade from red to black. There's no way in hell that I could leave her ashes out here, alone, by herself, so I picked up the barrel and carried it back to my apartment. At this point, my muscles were screaming at me, my arms and legs were aching, and I felt like I could pass out at any moment from sheer exhaustion. The rough metal was scratching the skin off my arms as I finally made it to the edge of the woods, planting the barrel down as I inhaled deeply.

I looked up to the road in front of me, the spot where Anna was hit.

And there she was.

Anna.

Standing in the same spot, looking at me, staring at me, unblinking and emotionless.

My heart dropped to my stomach, and I was unable to look away.

No. No. *No.*

This can't be real. This is my mind fucking with me.

But then, I thought back to what Laila said.

You will see her. You'll see her everywhere you go.

I swallowed the lump in my throat, my chest suddenly weighing a thousand pounds.

She'll be there, with you, always. Just like you wanted.

I stepped around the barrel, quickly glancing down at the bottom to make sure the ashes were still there. And they were. *That* was Anna, no matter how much I hated admitting it. The woman standing in front of me wasn't, and I don't know who—or what—she is.

I walked to her slowly, uncertainty guiding each one of my footsteps, and stopped once my feet landed off the curb. Our positions matched exactly how we stood the first night she came back, wanting to see where she was hit, and my memory was instantly thrust back to that moment. The way the headlights of her car shined behind her, the way she immediately recognized me, the way she shook her head at me and smiled.

I owe you.

You don't owe me anything.

As the ghost of her stood in front of me, I couldn't help but feel myself ache for her. Her scar from the accident was still visible across her forehead. She had the splatter of freckles across her nose and the full lips I could never get enough of. She was wearing one of my shirts, a light grey t-shirt that ended right at the middle of her thigh. It was the shirt she found and wore after we had sex for the first time.

God, I always loved when she wore my clothes.

Her hair was down, locks of it brushing across her cheeks as it tumbled in the wind.

Except, there was no wind.

The air was completely still around us, the leaves on the trees behind me were motionless.

"Anna?" I barely choked out in a hushed tone.

Her lips curled up in a smile, making my legs feel even weaker. I could feel my eyes grow wet, and before I could stop it, a tear trailed out of my right eye.

"I'm so sorry."

Her lips fell out of the smile, and I could feel myself begin to tremble.

"I'm so *fucking* sorry."

The words fell out of me so fast, so quick, there was no chance of keeping them inside. A moment passed as my heart continued to ache.

"Loving you was the easiest thing I've ever done."

The hair on the back of my neck stood up, sending a shock down my spine.

It was her voice.

"Everything about you was perfect to me."

My lungs squeezed out every ounce of air in them as I struggled to catch my breath. No fucking way.

"The night I met you was the night I came alive. My life was always with you. Even as my blood poured out on this road, the beat of my heart was always in your hands."

I tried, with everything in me, to go to her, to grab her and hold her and kiss her. But I couldn't. I knew this wasn't her. At least, it wasn't a version of her that I could have.

"Goodbyes are never easy, Thomas."

I didn't think I could break any more than I already have, but hearing the word "goodbye" come out of her voice absolutely shattered me. I could feel the void in my chest crack open, ripping me to shreds, losing any chance of ever being fixed again.

"Our love for each other will never end."

Another tear slipped out as I managed to take a step toward her. She reached out her hand and brought it to my face, and my eyes closed instinctively. I could feel a light brush of wind on my cheek where her hand was, but I couldn't feel it anywhere else on my body.

"There will never be anyone else but you."

I opened my eyes, and she was gone.

THOMAS

It's been a year since Anna died. For the second time.

And I'm still empty.

Anna's ashes sit in a wooden box next to my bed. I handcrafted it myself, starting on the night I burned her body. I didn't sleep for days.

On the inside of the box, there is a small compartment in the lid. In that compartment holds something extremely special to me.

My mother's ring.

I wanted to marry Anna with that ring, and just because she's gone doesn't mean she can't have it.

Jackson Diesel is back at the company, returning to his seat as owner. Seeing him sit in the chair and at the desk that Anna bought for me heats the anger that slowly simmers inside me every day, adding to the portion that's already burning. Part of me wants to take a sledgehammer to it all, to smash it all to pieces, not letting anyone have it, including myself.

But I can't bring myself to do it.

It still feels like a piece of her, something I can still touch and hold onto, even though it's just material that can easily be replaced.

My dad acts like he never left, and the guys at work do the same. I don't blame them. They still treat me as one of their own, but I know they wouldn't put their job in jeopardy to say something in my defense. Not that I need them to, since I give my dad shit on the days I feel like speaking to him, which isn't often. He still knows how to run the place, but I know I did it better. And I'm counting on the novelty of it wearing off, or him getting too old, and I'll have my spot back.

Until then, my secret is held in the silence between us.

I haven't seen Laila since the night I tried to kill her. Stoney's shut down the week after our fight, which was odd, considering the amount of money they were always pulling in. There were rumors floating around town of bankruptcy, alcohol being served to minors, the building not being up to code, you name it. Even Officer Harper, Laila's number one customer, was named in a rumor of a drug bust at the club. Not doing the bust, but being busted.

No matter what the reason, there was no more town tradition. I'm sure the high school kids were upset about it, but I wish they knew how much of a good thing it was.

No one was one hundred percent sure why they closed, but I had a feeling it had to do with Laila leaving, if she actually did. I haven't heard from her, so I have no idea if she kept her word and left. If I had to guess, I'd say she's gone. There's no reason for her to stay, and she's too much of a coward to stick around.

But even though she was no longer here, I still saw her every day in the vertical, fleshy scar on the side of my neck. It was my only reminder of her.

As for Anna…

I see her everywhere. Every day.

Laila wasn't bluffing.

Anywhere I look, she's there. Sometimes, I have to work to find her. I'll feel her watching me, and I'll search, and she will end up being hundreds of feet away, standing completely still, eyes glued to me. Sometimes, she'll be on the other side of a parking lot, or inside a building across the street from me, barely visible. Other times, she'll be so close to me that I feel like I can grab her and pull her into me, away from whatever ties Laila has chained to her.

But I can't.

And to make things even heavier, no one else can see her. Only me.

For the first few days, I would point her out, or comment on the scent, but no one understood what I was talking about. After that, I stopped mentioning it, and no one asked about it.

Alone, but never alone.

She'll be in the office at work, on the balcony at the apartment, even standing in the corner of the bedroom while I sleep. Her hair caught in a breeze, my shirt draped over her shoulders, the scar running across her forehead. Her evergreen eyes never tore away from me, not even for a second.

The first Christmas without her, I took the tree we bought together out into the woods and set it ablaze. The plastic fumes I inhaled couldn't do nearly as much damage as what her absence already had. And the ghost of her stood there, standing across from me, watching me through the flames.

It never changes. It's always her. And wherever I go, she goes too.

To me, there are two sides to it. On one side, I absolutely loathe the fact that I can't reach out and touch her, kiss her, or hear her voice. Even though I'm not sure if she can see me, I can see her, and that's as far as it goes. I've tried talking to her, but she hasn't said anything since the night I burned her body. I've tried touching her, but my hand goes right through her with no reaction.

Everything I've tried has failed.

For a while, I was angry. I would go to bed with a hardened ache in me, watching her watch me until I fell asleep, feeling caught in a battle I could never win. I carry the weight of it on my shoulders, and I know I always will.

There will *always* be the thought in my head that I ruined her life instead of saving it.

Over time, pieces of the anger faded, the edges blurring, turning me empty. My body felt as hollow as she looked. That emptiness never went away, it only became easier to cope with.

On the other side, I find comfort in her company. I can sit out on my balcony, and I know she'll be there with me. Her presence is something I can always feel, and it's something I can always count on. The feeling she gave me the first time I ever saw her, the fire in my chest, the certainty that she and I were more than words, it never goes away. And I know that one day, maybe sooner than later, I'll be on the same side as her, and we will be together again.

But one thing's for certain.

Laila has not seen the last of me.

I will find her, even if it takes me the rest of my fucking life.

She will pay for what she did.

She will come to regret ever choosing me.

I have *nothing* to lose.

She was right about one thing. There's something different about me.

I'm going to be the one to take her down.

No matter the cost.

And I'm bringing Anna along for the ride.

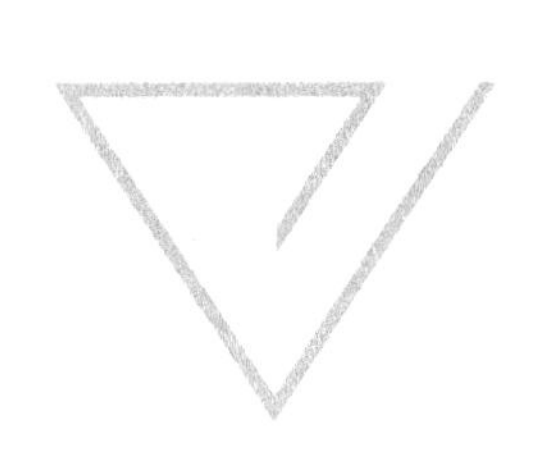

www.ingramcontent.com/pod-product-compliance
Lightning Source LLC
Chambersburg PA
CBHW020130310726
48970CB00006B/1810